Published by:
Grand Mal Press
Forestdale, MA
www.grandmalpress.com

Copyright 2012 Matthew Darst

ISBN 13 digit: 978-1-937727-15-4
ISBN 10 digit: 1-937727-15-7

Library of Congress Cataloging-in-Publication Data
Grand Mal Press/ Darst, Matthew

p. cm

Cover art by Matt Hale
www.ablerock.net

FIRST EDITION

DEAD THINGS

by
Matt Darst

GRAND MAL
PRESS

I dedicate this book, with love, to Dad.

Thanks for teaching me to wonder.

"The sun . . .
In dim eclipse, disastrous twilight sheds
On half the nations, and with fear of change
Perplexes monarchs."

—*Paradise Lost,* John Milton

Chapter One:
Of Nightmares and Neckties

THEY stream like army ants, climbing and clawing through the jagged mouth of the shattered bay window, ripping their forearms and torsos into ribbons.

Something competes with his fear, stealing his breath. Something sickly sweet, pungent like decay, tumbles over him like a churning wave. Fetid, it suffocates him, makes him choke.

A man's hands, trembling but strong, shield him and his mother from the encroaching horror. The man rushes them into the closet, the heavy down coats cushioning their impact. The door slams behind them, locks. A key slides under the half-inch gap beneath the door.

The shrieking begins.

SHRILL shrieks. Blasts from the alarm.

Ian spastically searches for the clock, his hand pitching about the nightstand, a pale perch out of water. His fingers find his wallet, then his keys. One last convulsion, and he locates the snooze bar. Just ten more minutes—

"Ian!"

—or not. His mother bursts into the bedroom. Rise and shine, she sings, and give God His glory. She tears the curtains open wide, and his room explodes in sunlight.

Ian winces. The sheets do not offer him sanctuary. He is caught like an escaped prisoner, pinned against a wall, encircled by the guard tower's spotlight.

She says something in her southern lilt about not being late for church. Again. Today is special. Today people will want to say their goodbyes.

Oh, and one more thing: he should wear a tie, perhaps his father's. It makes him look . . . distinguished.

She emphasizes her impatience with one word: Seriously.

Ian feels his mom standing at the foot of his bed. The color behind his eyelids turns from orange to cool purple as her long shadow passes over him. She is not leaving, so he submits, flipping his sheets and sitting upright in a fluid motion. "Happy?" he blurts, huffily.

He sees her nod through eyes that are little more than slits. He thinks he spies a smile spreading across her apple face. Her hazy outline glides from his room.

Ian stretches and yawns, groaning like a bear waking from a long winter of hibernation. He clutches at his Stranglers tee, wrestling it over his head. He wads it up and hooks it, Doctor J style, toward the hamper in the corner.

The shirt sails through the air in a high arc, the final seconds of an imaginary shot clock ticking away. This is still Kentucky, after all, and basketball, like life, finds a way. The shirt dances on the hamper's edge and falls to the floor, taking up residency with a drift of socks and jeans. Shit, he mutters, a goat once more.

His mother raps on his brother's door. "Josh, rise and shine . . . "

❖ ❖ ❖

THE tinted window of the butcher shop is his mirror.

Ian watches his dark twin attempt the Windsor knot for a third time. The beige and navy stripes bulge and wrinkle as he pulls the knot tight. He hopes like Goldilocks that this time it's just right.

His stepfather never taught Ian how to wear a tie. Bobby Joe does not own one. Fashion is as foreign (and, technically, as dead) to him as Paris, Milan, New York, and all of those other far off places associated with haute couture.

Bobby Joe calls neckties "nooses."

The front of the tie hangs just above Ian's navel, the rear falling like the tail of a kite below his waist. He sighs, starts to untie the knot.

From his perch on top of their horse-drawn cart, Ian's brother regards him with a mixture of fascination and derision. To Josh, Ian's fixation is alien and too . . . *adult.*

Josh says to forget it. Let's go. Mom's going to get pissed.

The horses secured, Ian's mother and stepfather are already walking. They are several paces ahead.

As if on cue, she calls for him to stop fussing. He looks fine. He is beautiful, just as God intended. So *puleease* get a move on.

Ian grimaces. Yes, the Lord intended many things, but he is fairly certain He never intended "please" to have three syllables.

Josh snorts. "Yes, let's go, *Beautiful.*"

Ian abandons his mission, and jogs sluggishly past their twin horses toward his parents. He delivers a light elbow to Josh's shoulder as he passes.

Josh hops to Ian's side. "What's his name?" Josh asks in a whisper. Ian looks confused.

"You know," Josh caws. "The guy you're getting pretty for!"

Josh is crude, but clever. Ian knows and loves his half-brother for it. But, there are limits to publicly recognizing Josh's wit. Paying his brother such respect would be viewed as weakness.

Like canines, siblings smell fear, and there can be only one Alpha Dog. If Ian subverts this universal dogma, he's certain the space-time continuum will fold in upon itself. So Ian never acknowledges Josh's teasing. He does what any brother does. He escalates, just as the canons of diplomacy and flexible response require.

Ian knuckles Josh in the shoulder—something his buddies call a "frog." It's immature. It belies his twenty-two years, but he can't help regress as all brothers do when a sibling pushes a button. And Josh knows all of Ian's buttons. Josh may as well be tapping out A-C-T-space bar-J-U-V-E-N-I-L-E on the keys of Ian's mental typewriter.

They laugh.

Bobby Joe is annoyed by these boys, by their commotion and by their lack of respect. They pass the empty stockade, the wood of its frame, and the gravel in its shadow, dark with dried blood. It is a constant reminder of the law of God as prosecuted, applied, and adjudicated by men. It should be a reminder to these boys that they must behave . . . or else.

Bobby Joe hisses at them to control themselves. They are just steps away from the weathered brick façade of the cathedral.

❖ ❖ ❖

THE Third Church of the Tribulation and Second Coming of Christ, Established During the 3rd Year of the New Order, is not a church. For Ian, it is a prison sentence meted out in two-hour increments, fifty-two times a year, more if including Christmas and Easter.

It is also a compound comprised of a rectory, a school, a community center, and a small cemetery. The cemetery is a remnant from a time before the New Order. The church is built on an "L," an allowance for the twenty or so worn headstones that remain.

Church elders govern day-to-day matters, spiritual nurturing, gospels, sacraments, and infrastructure. Ian knows most of the elders by sight, if not by name.

It is what Ian doesn't know that concerns Bobby Joe. The power of the elders is illusory, for supporting them is a dark network of buttresses, shoring, and struts known commonly as the church court. The church court, or synod, convenes in the compound as well. It is the law of the land, judging all matters brought to them for resolution, including matters of discipline. Disputes are resolved privately just as Matthew 18:15-16 dictates. That is, unless, someone wants to "tell it unto the church." Then the questions start, and all hell breaks loose.

The synod hides behind Deuteronomy and the Quaestores, inquisitors acting with the church's full authority. If a denouncer accuses another of sin, the inquisitors can call secret hearings. But they rarely bother. They have other methods. Their methods are shadowy . . . but effective. Acquittals are rare.

The guilty are paraded before the parishioners. The lucky ones are penanced, tortured or locked in the galleys only after publicly renouncing their sin. Or, they are reconciled, whipped, imprisoned, and stripped of property. Relaxation is reserved to the worst offenders, witches and heretics, like scientists and teachers who make the mistake of giving voice to Darwin's ghost.

"Relaxation" is, of course, a misnomer. Sinners rarely find being burned alive "relaxing."

❖❖❖

IN the church, Ian's mother rejoices. There is an open pew.

An hour later, the wooden bench has cut off Ian's circulation. He cannot feel his lower extremities. His right leg from just below his buttock is asleep, buzzing like a hive of honeybees. The choir sings, "Christ My Very Peace Is." *At least my ass is at peace*, Ian thinks.

But there is no peace for Pastor Statten. Statten is agitated this Sunday, as he is every Sunday. He wrings his hands, like a mad scientist contemplating the end of the world, and paces furiously before a great oak dais. Then he freezes as if becoming aware of the congregation for the first time, as if they have surprised him. It is an oft-repeated dramatic gesture, but Statten is a gifted thespian, and he sells it every time.

He tells his "friends" that they are in their final days.

Ian can almost mouth the words of the lecture in unison. He's heard it all before. The spiel has been a staple of Statten's for more than a decade. By now the concept has lost much of its imminence.

Statten drifts from the anchor of the dais, his small frame moving to the foot of a vast, stained-glass window. He is silhouetted by shards of ruby, cobalt, emerald, and violet.

Images of angels . . .

The vibrant colors look as radiant today as when Ian first beheld them as a child. The colors of hard candies, he is lured by their brilliance, if not by their subject matter.

. . . Angels descending upon the Earth . . .

Statten's tone is brimming with tension. He tells his friends that they stand at precipice of time. They stand at the end of—

The end of the world, Ian finishes. *If so,* Ian begs, *please let it happen now.* He cannot take any more of this sermon.

Statten says they are at the threshold of Christ Almighty's triumphant return. Soon those reborn in His light will go home. His arms are outstretched. He is bathed in the glow of the windowpane.

. . . Angels, their great wings spread wide, eclipsing the sun . . .

Statten drifts back to the podium and recites from a massive Bible. He quotes Saint Paul, Thessalonians 4:13 through 17. "For the Lord Himself shall descend from heaven with a shout, with the voice of the archangel, and with the trump of God: and the dead in Christ shall rise first. Then we which are alive and remain shall be caught up together with them in the clouds . . . and so shall we be ever with the Lord."

Simply taken, it is the story of the second coming of Christ. That is, should these wretches dare take the word of God *simply*. Like a horse to water, St. Paul is leading them to salvation. But they must drink and drink deep. Only those who drink shall survive the tribulation. Only those who drink shall meet those who *peacefully* sleep. They will meet them in the sky and be saved, leaving the walking dead to their damnation.

Here it comes, Ian reflects. *Here comes the fear. Served to us like colorful plates of Chinese food.*

Week

after week

after week.

But the course is hollow and empty, and it will always leave our bellies aching for more.

Armageddon is here, Statten declares, as if on cue. For those who have already felt Satan's steely grip, it is too late. They will never pass through heaven's gates.

Ian's cheeks flush with growing anger.

It is too late for the people of New York. It is too late for the heathen of Chicago. Eternal damnation, a living death, awaits those who dare to allow Sodom and Gomorrah to be built in their backyards.

 . . . Angels armed with great, flaming swords . . .

Statten tells a story of a time before the New Order. Just eighteen years before, the heretics used labels to describe themselves, labels like civilization, nation, and society. All worthless. All meaningless.

Statten brings a single boney finger to his chin. He acts as though a new thought, planted by God Himself, is germinating in his skull.

Even as a child, this homily poked at Ian. Like the prodding of a rotting tooth, it grows more painful . . .

Week

after week

after week.

Sometimes it takes everything Ian can muster not to jump from his seat. He wants to denounce them all as liars, scream down at those who purport to know.

Civilization? Statten spits the word as a query, an indictment, for no civilization can exist if the civil teachings of God are forbidden in public schools.

Nation? No nation can be great if it pays homage to God in word only. "In God We Trust?" Eighteen years past, just an empty promise, just an advertisement on the green face of shreds of paper once called currency.

Statten's hand strikes heavily on the pedestal, more heavily than it should be able, his strident voice starting to crack.

Society? How can there be a society if the social tenants of the church are subjugated to the demands of a purely secular electorate?

Nothing but words devoid of all sense when the influence of the church is absent.

 . . . Angels, expressions serene and heads bathed by the glow of halos, battling the throngs below them . . .

Choices and evil intent set the plague upon the world, but the parishioners are survivors, and they have one last opportunity. They must pray. Pray to be kept safe to the glorious rapture. Pray to stay in the minority that will meet the Spirit in the sky. . . . Or else walk the Earth damned like hundreds of millions of souls lost before them.

 . . . Angels destroying a world of ghouls . . .

Ian's head spins with thoughts of his father—not Bobby Joe, but his birth father. He grits his teeth. The homily is nearly over.

❖ ❖ ❖

YELLOW, Ian considers. The Fellowship Hall is bright yellow. The deacons painted its cinderblock walls with stock salvaged from a crumbling Home Depot.

Some once might have called the color maize, or goldenrod, or even sunflower. But those designations lost their usefulness in this world, a world without quarterly catalogs, global shipping, or a demand to supply. So, despite what the dead and buried buyers for J. Crew, Restoration Hardware, or Ralph Lauren may have once thought, the Hall is, simply, yellow.

Ian is sweating. But for the rainbows, stars, crescents, and other scrawled likenesses of second-rate Lucky Charms added by youth groups through the years, Ian swears he's standing on the surface of the sun.

Churchgoers mill about, a disorganized colony of bees. Instead of curious antennae, they greet each other with firm handshakes, wide smiles. They bite into homemade donuts and muffins, not scones or paninis, and slurp coffee, plain coffee, not frappes or dopios, from bland ceramic mugs.

Ian and Josh observe the hive of activity before Ian puts a hand on Josh's shoulder. He's ready to face the gauntlet. "You first," Josh challenges. Ian takes just two strides before Pastor Statten impedes his path, and Josh quickly disappears into the veil of parishioners.

Statten says Ian's name and extends a tiny hand. Ian clumsily takes it, offering compliments for a great sermon. Statten does not hear the lie in Ian's hushed words. He says something about "onward Christian soldier."

Yes, Ian ships to the northern front in less than a month. The pastor invites Ian to pray with him next Sunday. Ian respectfully declines. No, he has other plans.

Statten greets this revelation with silence. He glowers at Ian.

The seconds seem like an eon, the quiet deafening. Ian grows increasingly uncomfortable. He fills the void: Vacation. On Padre Island. Near Corpus Christi. In Texas. For two weeks. With Van Gerome.

It is the last bit that stuns Statten. "Roger Gerome's son?" he asks.

Ian nods, cranes his neck, looking for Josh to toss him a lifeline.

Statten ponders this. His lips purse, and the sides of his mouth go

white. Roger Gerome does not come to church. His work—"mission-
ary work," or so the elders call it—takes him outside the realm of the
church's influence and into the wilderness. It is work deemed as too
important to require his attendance at one of Statten's masses.

This reality tweaks Statten. Statten wants to curse Gerome. Unconsciously he starts to sneer, his face becoming the mask of a demon.
Ian watches the transformation, his eyebrows twisting in surprise. Statten realizes this and catches himself. His face softens. A predatory smile
crosses his lips as he offers Ian some advice.

"Wherever you go, God goes with you. He is everywhere, everything. Take him in your heart, and you need not avert your eyes from
his gaze." Statten says more; he will pray for Ian, pray for God to clothe
him in His armor of Righteousness.

And then Statten offers something else: an invitation. "Tell Van to
stop by the church before he leaves. I haven't seen him since Easter . . .
two years past."

Chapter Two:
Baggage, Emotional and Other

VAN is incredulous. "Statten wants me to do what?" He pauses, draws from a joint, and sinks deeper into the leather recliner. Drugs are illegal, but Van worries little about reprisals sitting in his father's study listening to Journey's "Only the Young." Roger Gerome apparently has a thing for Journey.

They are surrounded by a collection of artifacts, things found and rescued from oblivion by Roger Gerome during his explorations. Wall-to-wall displays of novels, compact discs, DVDs, albums, artwork, and other relics compete for Ian's attention, pulling it to and fro.

The titles are odd, unfamiliar. Most have been purged from the libraries, titles like *Catch-22*, *Fahrenheit 451*, *The Catcher in the Rye*, *A Clockwork Orange*, *Of Mice and Men*, *East of Eden*, *The Grapes of Wrath*, *The Martian Chronicles*, *Slaughterhouse- Five*, *One Flew Over the Cuckoo's Nest*, *Where the Sidewalk Ends*, *The Adventures of Huckleberry Finn*, *To Kill a Mockingbird*, *For Whom the Bell Tolls*, *Carrie*, *Cujo*, *Firestarter*, *The Shining*, *Frankenstein*, *American Psycho*, *Lord of the Flies* . . . .there are hundreds. Ian itches to read them.

Ian assumes *Superfudge* is a cookbook, *1984* an almanac, and *Brave New World* an atlas. Except for the *Star Wars* trilogies and some "Star Trek" films, Van rarely invites Ian to watch these movies or read these books. Ian suspects they are something to keep Van occupied during his father's expeditions. He doesn't suspect Van has been instructed to keep them privileged.

But there is one item that Van can't hide: an aging American flag, ragged and faded, hanging on the wall behind Roger Gerome's immense desk. It screams for Ian's attention, and his eyes can't help but heed the call and settle on the tattered stars and stripes.

"Still," Van wheezes, a little smoke escaping from his lungs. "I got to give old man Statten props. He's keeping hope alive."

Keeping hope alive? Ian doubts that. More likely, Statten's just thinking of a new way to fuck with Van. Van has not been to church since . . . since a lock-in when they were just twelve or thirteen.

Ian remembers that night. Van got caught feeling up Maxine Brooks. Maxine was penanced. Ian never saw her again—they shared a defensive tactics class—but he hears there are scars on her back to prove it. Van, however, escaped punishment. Anyone can be an escape artist, anyone can be Houdini, when they have a father like Van's.

Nevertheless, Statten and Van have an implied agreement. Essentially this: if Van doesn't come back, then the Church won't have to ask him to leave...or worse.

Statten's invitation is provocative. It is a dare.

The Church hasn't held a lock-in since. "I'd love to take credit for that," Van snickers, "but the teen pregnancy rate spoke for itself." He's right. Allowing virgins to get nailed in the Fellowship Hall is definitely not good governance. Plus, you can only go to the till with the whole Immaculate Conception pretext once every couple millennia or so.

Van offers the remains of his bud to Ian, but Ian waives him off. He doesn't do that shit. "You sure?" Van asks. "You're not going to get another chance for, like, another four years." But Van doesn't wait for a response. He is already taking another drag from the roach, finishing it.

"You know," Ian says, "you shouldn't do that shit either." After all, Van's shipping out in a few weeks, too. He'll get busted.

But Van has a plan. "Yes," he replies with zeal. "I'm counting on getting busted." He flicks the joint away with a quick snap of his fingers, discarding it as easily as he discards Ian's criticism.

This begs a question from Ian: how is getting caught a good thing?

"Don't you see? Drug addiction, man."

Ian doesn't get it, but he's seen Van like this a thousand times. Van's road is meandering, but at some point, he'll arrive at his destination . . . even if he's forgotten why he left for it in the first place.

Van scolds, as always. "Try to follow me here, man. This isn't adult swim." Van reasons: "Drug use equals inability to serve. Inability to serve equals automatic discharge. Discharge equals, well, anywhere but the front line." He leans back, awaiting accolades. They never come.

Instead, Ian guffaws. It is, by far, the most stupid thing he has ever heard. And that says something, because Van says a lot of stupid shit. Van says only stupid shit. And Van talks a lot. Did Van ever happen to consider while he was hatching this brilliant scheme, when he had this epiphany, no doubt fueled by the very cannabis in question, that any resulting discharge would be *dis*honorable?

"So?" is all Van can muster.

So? Ian will gladly explain. Dishonorable discharge is distinctly different. Honorable discharge equates to citizenship. Dishonorable discharge amounts to a hard life. A very hard life.

Like living and working in squatter rows lining the crumbling country roads of Corbin and Middlesboro in the shadow of poisonous dust clouds spewed forth by iron and coal mining operations.

But Van disagrees with Ian's assessment. "No, man, it's an addiction, a disease. They can't dishonorably discharge you for a disease."

There are just two problems with Van's line of thought, and Ian is eager to point them out: first, Van's argument that pot is not addictive, used so many times on Ian and other innocents, goes out the window. Second, the Church would keep Van hospitalized or in a stockade until he's clean. Then it's right back to the front.

"Shit." Van looks momentarily dejected. He rubs his tightly cropped hair, then he brightens. "I better switch to beer here on out. Want one?"

Ian shakes his head and excuses himself. He's got to pack for the flight. He tells Van to drink some cranberry juice, start cleaning those toxins from his system.

Van laughs. "Yeah, fuck you, too, straight edge."

❖❖❖

"ARE you packed, Honey?" Stella Mayberry asks from the shadows of the hall. She stands just outside her daughter's bedroom door.

"Yes," Anne replies flatly. She is stoic. She shows none of the zest a teenager should, especially one traveling alone to Padre Island to allegedly spend time with a grandmother she has never met.

Mayberry steps toward the door. She places a scarred and mangled hand against the frame and leans in slightly so that she can see Anne with her good eye. She reads Anne's face easily, like reading an astrological birth chart. "You're worried, aren't you?"

"Yes." Anne's eyes are downcast. She looks up. "And no."

Why yes? And why no?

"Mom, I saw the meteor last night. Right on schedule." Anne sighs. She knows what it portends, and that answers both questions.

Mayberry smiles behind the remnants of lips. She soaks in this moment with her daughter, realizing this is the instant her child makes the jump from being a girl to being a woman.

Stella Mayberry has pinched pennies for five years so Anne can take this trip. She started saving when Roger Gerome's discovery of Padre Island was announced by the Church, and she learned of her own mother's survival.

The island fared well like many other islands, the inhabitants largely

protected by a natural moat. The survivors on Padre Island were especially enterprising, blowing the lone bridge and filling the bay with
offal—human and marine—to attract a host of hammerheads and bull
sharks, even some great whites, to keep the ghouls at bay.

But Mayberry has taken terrible risks to pay for Anne's flight, earn-
ing money clandestinely, in ways the church deems profane. And she
should know better. She wears the church's rebuke permanently on her
skin, something like a scarlet letter, but more horrifying. Should the inquisitors ever learn of her return to the old ways—ways practiced by the
ancients, the Babylonians, the Greeks, and the Mayans, ways taught by
Pythagoras, Plato, Aristotle, Ptolemy, Copernicus, Galileo, and Jung—
they will take more than just her skin.

"So, despite what you know, you still want to go?"

"Come on, Mom," Anne responds. "Of course I do. As above, so
below, right?"

Stella Mayberry nods approvingly.

Anne smiles. "Hey, let's make some ice cream."

❖ ❖ ❖

IAN hears the final boarding announcement for Flight 183 to
Brownsville. Then the air marshal says, "Time to go."

She has observed Ian for an hour, watching him glance at his watch
every few minutes as if he might be able to stop time with his mind.
Then the pacing started. He could take just ten strides in the modest
gate before he had to spin and repeat his steps. At each turn, he paused
and looked for . . . someone.

The air marshal wonders if it is a girl. She sees it every year, young
lovers, their marriages newly minted, escaping their families and friends
to steal precious and final moments together before leaving for the
front.

It is not unusual for an air marshal to accompany a flight. In fact,
they travel on most, especially those making passes over, or even approaching, the forbidden zone. Air marshals provide safety instruction
and security. But in the forbidden zone, or "the wilderness," as some call
it, they provide something else: insurance.

She takes a surprised Ian by the elbow and ushers him across the
tarmac toward the twin-prop Eagle designated as Flight 183.

Ian dissents. "Look, Ms.—" he locates her name on her chest, "—
Wright. I'm just waiting for my friend." He tells her that he should be

here in just . . . a bit.

She can't help but be intrigued by the "he" part. No girlfriend? She guessed that wrong. But otherwise Wright doesn't care. Her grip is firm as she escorts him across Stanford Field.

"A bit." It's a relative concept, Wright tells Ian. Twenty passengers on this flight alone, air traffic controllers, who might need to modify flight vectors because of constantly changing weather patterns; flight 353 from Chattanooga, hanging in the air right now, directly above, burning fuel, unable to land until 183 has departed; and dozens of schedules in disarray, all impacted by "a bit" of delay, some kid's selfishness, and a need to vacation with his friend.

Ian cannot argue with her logic, but "kid?" He is at the age of majority, and she is only a handful of years older. . . .

Wright tells him to have a seat in 5A, and to enjoy his flight.

Confounded, Ian does as he is told. He shambles to his seat, accidentally making eye contact with a man four or five rows back. The man is in his forties. He sports a *Phantom Menace* baseball cap and grins at Ian through a thin red beard.

The Phantom Menace? Ian hates the film, and "film" stretches suitable use of the term. First, *Menace* wasn't even printed on celluloid. It was digital, technically not a film at all. Second, only good movies should be called films. *Menace* is an aberration, the bastard child of George Lucas' incestuous rape of his first three installments . . . or episodes four, five, and six . . . or whatever. Ian couldn't watch any of Van's other *Star Wars* movies after viewing that pile.

So Ian can't smile back at the ginger man. He just sighs, shakes his head, and aims his attention toward less demanding tasks. He stows his luggage, spreads the creases from his faded jeans, picks a piece of lint from the sleeve of his "Punk's not Dead" T-shirt. Accomplishing these monumental chores, Ian focuses on the forward door and tries to will Van's arrival.

THE plane is an Eagle J-150, a miniature of the metallic dragons that used to traverse the globe in leaps and bounds. It is an antique, just a single row of ten seats running along each side of the cabin. There aren't many planes left, just a handful of puddle jumpers maintained with cannibalized parts. Ian's ticket was expensive, paid for by two summers of mowing lawns, his last hurrah before conscription.

He watches the air marshal ready the cabin. She moves like a panther, lean and confident. The cockpit door opens, the captain smiles, says a few words. Wright nods politely, but Ian detects something else, like annoyance, before she secures the hatch.

Damn Van. Probably got caught sneaking weed on the plane.

Ian ponders sleeping on a cold, damp beach for two weeks. He thinks about how, for months to come, he'll find sand in areas of his body he doesn't yet know exist.

The air marshal begins talking about flight safety. She's interrupted by a yelp from the tarmac.

She peers through a saucer-sized port, shakes her head in disgust and smirks. There's a passenger down there.

Wright leans into the cockpit, tells them to halt preparations for takeoff. Ian clearly reads the curse that crosses her lips.

Another cry, this time louder.

She pops the door, shouts: "Let's go, Molasses. Move it."

Van bounds aboard, frantic, like a cat that's bitten into an electrical cord and found the marrow. He bounces about, looking wildly from side to side.

Wright tells Van to take his seat. Now.

A Cheshire grin flashes across Van's face when he spots Ian. He stomps to his seat, his giant army green duffle slapping the faces of passengers he passes. A heavyset man rubs his temple and stares at Van icily.

Ian tries to become invisible, but avoiding embarrassment is a difficult task considering Van is talking to him right . . . now.

"That was close," Van starts. "Hey, this container's pretty small, huh?" He palms the walls of the plane on either side of him.

Wright shakes her head. Does this kid have ADD? She has to tell him to take his seat again. The captain cannot start the engines until he complies.

Van swings halfway around, nearly decapitating Ian with the duffle. "Oh, yeah, sure." He spins back, this time catching Ian square in the shoulder and pressing him hard against his seat.

"Sit down," Ian urges under his breath, shoving the bag from his chest.

Van drives the pack into the storage compartment under the seat before him. It does not take a geometrician to compute the volume of the bag exceeds that available under the chair, but Van is resolute. He grunts and kicks it like some mad punter, and the flurry has the intended consequence. Inch by inch the duffle squeezes into the storage bin, the woman in the seat before Van bouncing with every jolt.

"Here," he says, handing Ian a small backpack. "Stick this under your seat."

"Fine," Ian huffs.

A baby wakes, somewhere aft, and launches into a howl, eliciting a communal moan from the passengers.

"Dude," Van calls, prodding Ian from across the aisle. He shows Ian some old *Playboy*s. They're from Roger Gerome's personal collection, published sometime in the 1990s, maybe something he owned prior to Van's mother dying, but probably something he picked up since. Men have needs, after all. "Do you want Miss March or Miss August?"

Ian ignores him, ignores the danger the mere possession of these magazines would pose to most, by feigning sleep. He prays for actual sleep to take hold, and soon.

THEY are clawing at the door, the wood splintering. It is always the same.

Pounding.

Pounding.

Pounding.

Ian awakes to a thunderclap. It takes a moment for him to get his bearings, to understand that he is here in the air in the present and not a kid in a closet eighteen years before.

Lightning. Glowing veins of rain pulse across his window.

One-one-thousand.

Two-one-thousand.

He counts off the seconds, each equating to a mile, as he has done since childhood.

Three-one-thousand.

He swivels to find Van staring at him. Four—

Boom.

"Punk's not dead?" Van asks suddenly, lightning alternately illuminating and silhouetting his face.

Ian is still groggy. What is Van talking about?

Boom.

"Punk's not dead," he repeats. He points to Ian's chest. "Your shirt says, 'Punk's not dead.'

So?

A tinny voice over the intercom warns them: keep your seatbelts fastened. The captain is going to try to get above the weather.

Flash.

One-one-thousand.

"So," Van asks, "what the hell does your T-shirt mean?"

Two-one-thousand.

Ian grumbles, "It means what it says."

Flash.

Boom.

Boom. Boom.

The thunder rolls in bursts, like heavy jungle drumming. The natives are not just restless, they want blood.

Van's not satisfied. "No—what does it mean to you?"

Flash.

Ian elucidates: "While the godfathers of punk—the Ramones, Sex Pistols, Panic Attack, Stooges—have died—"

Boom.

"—the roots of their disaffection live on."

Van winces upon hearing Ian's theory. "That's a prepared statement if I've ever heard one." Van has a different theory. Of course, he'll share it. If punk's not dead, it may as well be. If punk's not dead, then it's in a coma and on life support, hidden away in some forgotten hospital.

Flash.

Ian takes the bait. "Punk's about questioning authority. It's about not taking things at face value . . . not accepting the status quo."

Boom.

Van scoffs. "That shit is totally Christian now. It must be really hard for the disenfranchised youth of today, their mommies styling their pink Mohawks before their daddies drive them to the church parking lot for the sound check. Face it, bro. The punk message is dead, and the so-called punk aesthetic has been co-opted by a bunch of snot-nosed, Jesus-hugging brats."

Flash.

Ian's defensive. He calls Van a hippie.

Boom. The thunder's like an exclamation point.

Everyone has a hang-up about an extremely personal matter, his or her "thing." The lucky ones are driven by ideology, like politics, charities, religion, or ethnicity. The less fortunate are guided by trivial concerns. Did you hear about that pig Altha Phelps entered in the fair? I can't believe it was corn fed . . . Clint Cooper brought down two bucks with one shot. One of them had an image of the Virgin Mary in its hide, so you know it was a miracle! Aren't we lucky that Elder Sarah Palin was campaigning in Frankfort when the plague hit . . . and where did she get those amazing boots?

Ian's thing, trivial or not, is punk. Save for an old striped tie, all Ian has left to fill a vacuum are a few of his father's old compact discs found under the seat in his mother's defunct car. They speak to Ian, revealing to him something about his father that others, even his mom, could never know or understand. He imagines his father playing the Clash maybe for the first time, reading while singing along to the lyrics. This is Ian's only connection to his past, this and his nightmares. His mother decided long ago to let the memory of his father slip away . . . all but the tie and the music. Ian's face contorts into a grimace.

Van sees that he has driven the shovel too deep, unearthed too much, and he beats a hasty retreat. "Punk's not dead? It doesn't even matter, anyway. 'Dead' doesn't even have the same meaning. Not anymore."

Flash.

Ian silently sulks.

Van is contrite. "And when has my opinion meant anything, anyway?"

True enough. Ian's mood improves slightly.

Van reads this, calls Ian a hardcore "punk rocker," an "original gangster." He makes quotation marks with his fingers.

Boom.

Ian scowls. "Shut up."

Van's not done. No, straight up. Ian's Iggy Pop, Sid Vicious, Paul Weller, and Willie Nelson all rolled into one.

Ian shakes his head. "Willie Nelson is a country singer."

"Exactly," says Van. "Nonconformity with expected punk norms. Nothing's more punk than that."

Ian laughs.

Flash/Boom.

The cabin goes bright white. The passengers go deaf. The airplane shakes violently, battering them.

Ian's body seizes, lurches about like a doll broken at its waist. His belt strains but stays him, cutting across his thighs. His surroundings are shapeless, shaken to a blur by massive turbulence.

The hulking propellers go silent. Their steady hum is replaced by howling current, air that snakes about the hull. Blue and orange flames lap from the fuselage.

They pitch forward, on this insane fun-park ride, this rollercoaster diving from its apex. They are falling from the sky. And, as if on cue, they scream like children.

Chapter Three:
Plane in Vain (or, the Clash)

IAN'S head is held firm against the seat. The compartment is dark. He strains to find Van through a dark cloud of smoke and ozone. He calls to Van. Through the haze, he discerns an outline, Van's limp arm hanging over the armrest. He is unconscious. He did not buckle his belt. He has hit his head.

Things go from bad to worse. A resounding pop, and the cabin loses pressure.

A shopping list of items, papers, pens, bottles, jackets, hats, nuts—swims upstream, hurtling toward the rear of the plane, toward Ian. He covers his face with a forearm.

His lungs feel constricted. He fights for oxygen. A mask connected to a clear bag drops. It slaps Ian about the face, toying with him as he tries in vain to grab it. He throttles the tubing high up and works his hand down, taming the serpent. He wraps the elastic bands about his head, feels the air flow freely.

He remembers something. *Make sure your mask is securely in place before assisting children.*

Van.

The smoke exhausts rapidly from the plane. Van is slumped forward, blood streaking from a gash on his forehead and flying from his hair in droplets. Ian lunges at the mask dangling above Van. His seatbelt labors to hold him in place. The belt stretches hard, nearing its limits. Ian's back throbs, G-forces trying to fold him like a poolside chair. He works feverishly to secure Van's mask, but the elastic straps are slick with blood and make slow work of it. Over one ear, then the other, he finishes and tries to return to his seat.

A first aid kit tears through the air. It looms larger and larger until it strikes Ian between the eyes. The irony is almost lost on him, his consciousness threatened.

He feels himself going limp, his spine bending, his arms fluttering like streamers over his head. His oxygen line pulls taut, threatens to break. Blackness visits Ian from the edges of sight. He's facing the rear of the plane now, and a sickening revelation shocks him to life.

A ragged hole, two to three feet across, occupies the space where a passenger once sat five rows back. Ian watches the sky pluck another, screaming and still strapped to his chair, into the abyss, as effortlessly as a child ripping the head from a dandelion.

His seatbelt is slipping. He claws for a hold, laboring to pull to a seated position. His biceps and shoulders burn. His abdominals tense and knot. He leans forward, preparing for the imminent crash. Dear God, not like this.

The plane screams, muscles toward a more gradual descent. Ian feels the gravity slam him again. It is still much too quick, much too steep, yet the cabin pressure is closing in on that of the air howling about the plane's shell. The aircraft pierces the clouds, plunging through them, a diver with no thought of ever surfacing.

From the jump seat, Wright shouts at the top of her lungs. She orders them to assume crash positions. But no one can hear her over the maddening drone of the plane slicing through the black sky. The noise is terrifying, but Ian dreads the coming silence more.

There isn't a young adult who hasn't at some point or another considered his or her legacy in the wake of a premature death. Ian has. Like others his age, he kind of dwells on the thought. Understand, Ian is not suicidal or depressive. He likes dark and mysterious things, but the thought of taking his own life never enters his head. Too many people have sacrificed themselves, sacrificed for him, to end it all because of some selfish caprice. In Ian's dreams of death he finds martyrdom. Or, better, justification for his existence as a tragic epic hero:

Ian the Selfless.

Ian the Courageous.

Ian the Defender of the Helpless.

In truth, he believes he is something less, something akin to Ian the Frightened, something akin to Joseph Conrad's Lord Jim.

Ian's assessment is a little unfair. Fate has never found an opportunity to present Ian a significant risk. Unlike Lord Jim, Ian has never confronted a ship flailing in a storm or an army of pirates. Sure, there had been schoolyard fights, and his defense mechanism kicked in. But those shoving matches never really amounted to much beyond juvenile posturing.

There are greater things to be scared of than middle-school bullies. Things like this. This is different. Neither fight nor flight is an option. Even if they were, Ian doubts he could make a decision between the two, conscious or not.

Ian's fear supplants all else. His breath comes in desperate pants.

Panic engulfs every fiber of his being. An insane scream builds deep in his chest.

There's heavy tapping against the plane's undercarriage, the heads of trees snapping. Ian braces as the plane bounces, then drops heavily into the foliage. Cedar elms and spruce pines flog the aluminum body. Their limbs lacerate the wings, like whips against swollen flesh, pulling away metal and exposing the frame. The airplane's husk pops and bubbles, a cauldron. Firework displays of glass explode, raining upon Ian's neck and shoulders.

The thumping intensifies. Swampbays now slap the plane back and forth, delivering crushing blows. The cabin threatens to split, until—

A convulsive lurch. The plane comes to an immediate, screeching stop. The nose cone digs deep into soft soil, hundreds of pounds of thick clay, roots, and mulch jetting from the impact crater. The plane's tail heaves upward, revealing the rough break in the underbelly and threatening to spin the craft on its tip like some giant top. Its line rises, perhaps forty degrees, before groaning to a halt. The slain dragon expels a final breath before its belly crashes hard against the forest floor.

❖❖❖

IAN is on the floor, spilling into the aisle, his seatbelt finally giving way. He hears Van from somewhere above him. He is griping about the oxygen mask on his face. The bastard was unconscious, basically sleeping through the entire ordeal.

The air marshal orders everyone to stay calm. She offers Ian a hand, asks if he is all right. Her fingers are thin, almost delicate, but she lifts him with one swift jerk. "Are you okay?" she asks again. Ian thinks so.

Van is a different story. "Holy shit! I'm bleeding!" He stammers something about needing medical marijuana.

Wright asks Ian if Van is all right.

"Seems normal to me," Ian responds.

She surveys the cabin. One of the passengers is a doctor. His name is Heston. He's traveling to Mustang Island, just north of Padre, first to fix a child's cleft palate then to fix his relationship with his wife. Wright enlists his services and asks Ian to assist the doctor with the passengers.

Ian feels her warm breath dance on his neck as she whispers, "Work quickly and quietly. Keep them calm. I'll be back in a minute." She needs to check on the crew.

Before Ian can question whether the pilots' survival is even possible, she is gone. His query dies on his lips.

❖ ❖ ❖

THE cockpit door is difficult to open, its frame twisted. Wright gives the door her shoulder, and it pops open, but just a foot or so. There are inches of soil on the floor, preventing further access. She doesn't hesitate, sliding in with purpose, closing the door behind her with her back. She leans against it momentarily, panting lightly.

It is pitch, the nose is buried, and she smells something like the scent of cut lawn. She steeled herself for the destruction, but she's not sure she's ready for the complete truth.

An emergency beacon blinks weakly, painting the room in blood red. Earth pours in from the shattered windshield, burying the dead instrument panel and...the captain. He lurched forward upon impact; his upper body is entombed.

The co-pilot was no luckier. His head was punched from his shoulders by the fist of a splintered tree trunk. His corpse remains seated, his skull dangling behind the back of his chair. Bits of spine, muscle, and sinew just barely lay claim. She need not worry about him.

Wright moves to the captain's chair. Straddling him, she plunges her hands deep into the soil. She doesn't have much time. She feels along the pilot's shoulder and upward toward the nape of his neck. She uncovers his collar and tugs the body free. The soil breaks and crumbles to the floor as he emerges. She grunts, bares her teeth, leverages a foot against the console. With one last mighty heave, she frees him from his filthy shroud. The pilot sails backward, his barreled torso resting stiffly in the seat. His mouth is agape, full of mud. His chest looks compressed, punched by the steering column.

Her hands work quickly, moving across the Captain's face, delicately but swiftly pushing dirt from his cheeks and eye sockets. Her eyes begin to well. She looks for a pulse, finds none. "Oh, Richard."

There's no time for this. She dives into the dirt, furiously clearing away mounds of soil. She's looking for something, but earth seeps in, frustrating her. She needs the coordinates of the plane. How funny, she thinks, she can't even make time for him in death. *Sorry, baby. You were right again. I'm just a selfish bitch.*

She pins down the location of the dials, finds the red glow of the longitude and latitude. *But today, at least, I've got a reason to ignore you . . . at least one other than hating you.*

She draws her face in close to the dim red glow. She hangs her head low, shaking it from side to side. "Damn it." They are off course. They did not follow the flight plan. And then, to the Captain's reclined corpse, she spits, "Richard, you fucking bastard."

She hurriedly digs for the radio, tossing dirt between her legs like a Jack Russell terrier hot on the heels of a burrowing chipmunk. Soon, her knuckles scrape metal, and she feels its rectangular face. She fingers the power switch, toggling it up and down.

Nothing. No power.

The device is ancient. Despite this, she keys in frequencies frantically hoping against all hopes for something. Before long, she realizes it is pointless. This unit will not broadcast.

There is no time to sulk. She has to move. She unbuttons the top of her blouse, clasps a key on a chain from around her neck, yanks hard, pulling it free. She pounces to the wall behind the helm in one feline bound. Deep red courier on the panel says, "Emergency Use Only." She locates the dimpled keyhole and pops the lock.

Inside are her tools.

In a heartbeat all of her training comes back to her.

❖❖❖

DOCTOR Heston asks if Ian knows basic first aid. Ian thinks so, and Heston sends him to the front of the plane.

He administers first aid as best a former cub scout barely attaining the rank of Webelos can. What if someone has had a concussion? Let them sleep? Don't let them sleep? He knows how to start a fire with sticks, how to lift ten times his weight using pulleys, but he cannot remember the basics of first aid. So he treats everyone for shock, mumbling repeatedly under his breath, "If the face is pale, raise the tail; if the face is red, raise the head." Just scrapes and contusions, no one (no one left on board, anyway) looks too—

"—Ian," Van shouts from three rows ahead. "This lady looks hurt."

The doctor's at the back of the plane attending to the woman with the baby. *Shit*, Ian thinks. "What color is her face?"

❖❖❖

WRIGHT'S holster needs no adjustment. It fits snugly, tight around her waist and chest. She handles the pistol, feeling for errant dirt. The clip slides in, and she thrusts a bullet into the chamber. Then she removes the machete.

They don't always come back from death. No, as often as not, slumber is eternal. But sometimes the proverbial dirt nap is just that: a nap.

Before the Church, before the concept of earthbound souls, doctors put a more clinical spin on death, declaring it nothing more, yet nothing less, than a process. Death is something beyond a single temporal event, something beyond a sheer moment in time.

The heart stops, and with it, blood flow. Deprived of oxygen, brain cells die. The body cools, blood settles, then other cells, like muscles and skin cells, die, disintegrate, and decompose at varying rates.

Unless something hijacks the process.

For the lucky ones and their friends and families, death runs its course. For them, peace is everlasting and a place in heaven is secured. For the unlucky, those damned in the eyes of the church, death is suspended. Not reversed, but *suspended.* The dead can rise again in a day, an hour, or in the mere stutter of a faltering heartbeat.

The problem?

One can never know. So assume the worst.

Wright stands above the Captain's torn face. The machete feels heavy at her side. *Be a good soldier. Remember your years of preparation, your training. Remember that he's no longer your lover. He's not even the man you grew to hate. He's dead. Or something else . . .*

She raises the blade above her head; her gaze locks on his neck, just below his Adam's apple. Her will goes with her knees, and she nearly loses her balance.

"Damn it!" she cries, tears now running down her cheeks, a hand at her brow.

But then a noise, a soft crackling, like dry leaves . . .

She is taking too long. She gathers her composure lest she be interrupted or lose her resolve altogether. She wipes her face, leaving dark, raccoon-like streaks about her eyes. With a final and hearty sniff, she brings the weapon above her head once more. She steadies herself, switching her weight from foot to foot. Her countenance goes cold, her strength returns.

She thinks she sees a twitch, maybe a slight change in the reflection off the whites of his eyes.

Now.

She severs his head at the line of his jaw, through his brain stem, the part of his brain housing his motor cortex, connecting his forebrain and cerebrum. His head spins away like a demented dreidel. She wipes the blade on his chest, and her hands on her shirt. The machete slips into the sheath at her hip. She gathers her gear. "Rest in peace."

❖ ❖ ❖

"FUCKING badass," Van exclaims. He's staring toward the nose of the plane.

"What?" And then Ian sees.

Wright stands before them, her face lined with mud, blood splattered on her chest. A pistol sits on her hip, a machete on her thigh.

Ian feels something in his chest, an unfamiliar flutter. Fucking badass? He gulps. Eyes wide, all Ian can do is nod in agreement.

❖ ❖ ❖

THEY are out, eight of them anyway, scurrying single file, little ants under cover of night. They stay low to the ground amid the brush, halting abruptly when Wright raises a hand. They clamor noisily behind her, wind chimes in a storm. She makes them drop to their bellies, hiding whenever lightning strikes threaten to give up their positions.

Minutes tick by, their chins and waists deep in the mud. Eventually the little ants start their march again, the larger world oblivious to them, the only evidence of their existence a ruined plane and the passengers who chose it as their tomb miles behind. Blind and dripping in the moonless darkness, Ian replays the events of the last hour in his head. The pandemonium reveals itself in fragments like grainy and shaken pieces of a looping Zapruter film.

Wright pulled Heston and Ian aside. "Is anyone hurt?" Wright asked. "It's hard to say," the Doctor replied, "but it doesn't look like it."

"Good. So these people can travel?"

Heston nodded, "I think so. But there's a woman with a baby. They're sleeping now, but she may be suffering from minor shock."

"Her face was pale," Ian chimed in. "I raised her feet."

Wright addressed the other passengers. She asked for their attention, her voice barely cutting through the din. Already they were complaining, bickering amongst themselves. But, soon, whispered hushes spread row by row throughout the cabin, touching each like lice spreading amongst third-graders. Wright finally had their focus. Save for the drumming rain, the cabin was silent.

"My name is Kari Wright," she began. "I am Flight 183's Air Marshall." Protocols required that she inform the passengers that the flight had "landed prematurely." But Wright was more direct: "Flight 183 has crashed." The passengers stared, a few openly and deeply sobbing. This displeased Wright. "I am going to need your full cooperation. First and foremost, I need you to remain quiet. Please hold all discussions. I will provide further instructions shortly."

That wasn't good enough for one of the passengers, the heavyset man in the third row. He stood and bellowed for the pilot. He said he was owed an explanation.

Wright remained poised. "I'm afraid that's impossible, sir. Please cooperate and have a seat."

But the fat man would have none of it. She was full of shit. He demanded the pilot's presence now. A woman, possibly his wife, put a hand on the man's waist, a weak effort to calm him. He shook her off.

The rest of their exchange was choppy, bouncing back and forth like a screenplay for a movie.

Wright: Sir, please.

Fat Man: I want to see him, now!

Wright (to the entire cabin): Again, that is impossible. (More subdued) The captain did not survive the landing.

The passengers gasp.

Fat Man: Let me talk to the co-pilot, then.

Wright (sternly): You are now speaking to the ranking officer, Sir.

Fat Man: What, the co-pilot, too?

Wright: The first officer did not survive the landing either. I am now in command of this vessel and flight. We will be disembarking immediately, so I ask that you quickly and quietly change...jeans and trainers, hiking boots if you have them . . . anything water repellent.

Mr. Phantom Menace: My name is Burt. Burt Feldman. Is there any danger of an explosion?

Wright: No. The captain dumped the fuel before landing, but we remain in danger and must move quickly.

Burt (nodding): Okay, good. By the way, has anyone seen a Spiderman comic about? Numbered 129?

And that's when the mutiny started.

The Fat Man cajoled the passengers. How could they expect a woman with child to leave the comfort and safety of the plane? Why should any of them, really, be expected to go anywhere? He, for one, was not going. He was going to stay right there, stay right there and wait for help.

Wright hissed at the Fat Man to keep his voice down, but he defied her.

He screamed that none of them would leave at least not until they had received answers.

Wright tried to explain. He didn't understand the urgency of the situation.

"Then why don't you tell me?" he countered. "Enlighten us all!"

Wright looked past him, realized the whole cabin was staring at her, even the kid in the punk rock shirt.

She resolved to tell them of their predicament. She told them the truth, or as close to the truth as she could muster. She recapped: things are bad.

One. The plane is down.

Two. The captain and first officer are dead (she allowed the passengers to assume they died upon impact and said nothing to counter that assumption).

Three. The radio is non-responsive.

Four. Supplies are limited.

Five. They had gone down in the wilderness. Down outside of the republic's territory, outside the protection of human armaments and fortified walls.

They were in the forbidden zone. The wilderness. The dead zone.

Wright's statement begged the question that a young blonde woman asked: "Are you saying that those *things* are out there?"

Yes. There were gasps.

The blonde wondered how far they were from the border.

Dozens of miles. Maybe many more. Wright said it was impossible to be sure.

She did not give voice to her true suspicions, however. They were in southern Louisiana—or what was once southern Louisiana—hundreds of miles from both their destination and home.

Then a brunette said what everyone else was thinking: "I'm not going out there with those monsters!"

The Fat Man found his entry. "You can't expect us to trek that distance, not with those dead things out there, not with a baby in tow. It will draw them right to us!"

Now it was the mother's turn: "I am not going to risk my child out there!"

The Fat Man was now up, giving Wright his back, addressing the cabin: "Look, I was a scout, and when you're lost, the number one rule is to stay in place. Let help come to you. She's telling us to do the exact opposite."

"When you were a scout," Wright muttered, "the only worry you had was wetting your sleeping bag. No one was exactly handing out merit badges for surviving an assault by the walking dead."

Another man, bookish and bald, had a question: "Is this plane equipped with a homing beacon?"

Wright stammered. "Yes, but—"

"Was it activated?"

"Yes, but—"

The Fat Man jumped in again: "Well, there you go. We sit back—"

The bald man agreed: "—and wait for the cavalry."

Wright rested on her military training and flight protocols. No one is going to strike out to rescue them. It's just not standard operating procedure.

But the passengers felt they knew differently. They felt their leaders were righteous. As righteous men, they would come for them, SOPs be damned. And they trusted them much more than this . . . woman.

They put the issue to a hand vote. Should we stay or should we go? Ten voted to stay, eleven including the infant, even after being reminded that the crash would draw attention, and that the cabin was breached and wasn't secure. Eight, mostly kids, voted to go. Ian had to help raise Van's hand for him. And that was that.

Wright's shock was momentary. Her jaw resets, strong and square. These ten had chosen their eleven fates, choosing their undoing over the possibility of life. Granted, it was a slim possibility for the eight, but it was a damn shade better than what awaited those left behind. "Let's go," Wright spat.

Chapter Four:
Knock, Knock . . .

THE plane is dark, silent, save for the steady patter of rain and the slight sucking sounds of an infant at her mother's breast. Now and then lightning strikes, illuminating the grim faces of the passengers who stayed back. The cabin goes dark again, leaving them to their thoughts and the foreboding rumble of thunder.

Hours pass like this, their hopes falling like the sheets of rain outside. The Fat Man suggests campfire songs.

As morning approaches, their spirits momentarily brighten when they hear a fateful rapping on the hull.

Chapter Five:
Vintage Van

IAN is roused in the early morning hours, nudged by the muddy toe of a combat boot. Wright stares down at him. The skies are starting to clear. Shards of light pierce the gray cloak of clouds above her. "Time to move," she says, her voice a gust amongst the reeds.

Ian rises from his bed of pine needles. His cohorts are busy piling an odd assortment of belongings—perfumes, candies, skirts, shoes, shaving cream, moisturizer, bug repellant—into a stack in the middle of a white bed sheet.

Van approaches the pile with a look of disgust. In his hands is a bottle of cologne and a pair of red Converse. He looks at the shoes, shakes his head from side to side, and tosses just the cologne on the pile. He strokes the canvas of the trainers like a pet cat, then catches Ian's gaze. He walks over.

"What's going on?" Ian asks in a hush.

Van sighs. "She's making me throw away my cologne. And my All-Stars."

Why?

Van says something about traveling light—"lean and mean or some shit"—and that scents attract them. Only non-scented deodorant or antiperspirant and a few changes of clothes. One pair of shoes. Everything else stays.

Ian shrugs. It makes sense to him, despite Van's accusations of fascism. Then Ian examines Van's feet. "But you're already wearing a good pair of trainers."

Van explains his conundrum: "Yeah, but these don't go with my red polo. I've got to have the vintage Converse when I rock the red polo."

Ian has a solution. Leave the polo, too.

Van pleads. He doesn't have room to hide them in his backpack.

Ian concedes. He might have room in his bag. He takes the shoes.

Van perks up, thanks Ian, but then warns: "Try not to scuff them, though."

Ian tears through his pack. He settles on a spare pair of jeans, a hoodie, T-shirts, socks, underwear, and toiletries. The rest he discards.

Everything, that is, but his father's necktie. He stands at the edge of the heap, clutching the tie before him.

"Toss it," Wright commands.

Ian did not see her approach. He shares his reservations: "It was my dad's."

"Is he alive?" Wright asks.

"No, he died when I was just a few years old."

But Wright is preoccupied by a thought. The tie has jogged a memory, a lone moment among thousands during the height of the outbreak. She was twelve. Hundreds of motorists were stuck in traffic on I-65, her family among them, waiting in vain to drive to God-knows-where. Or, God's nowhere. Because no place was safe, not even your car.

Wright saw one of them, freshly turned and still strong, reach through the driver's side window of some guy's car—maybe an attorney or a salesman or something—and grab hold of his necktie. The attorney/salesman hadn't seen it in the rear view, hadn't seen it slither from the back of an idling ambulance parked directly behind him. He had been too busy honking and shouting at the cars ahead of him.

Now he was tethered, and he couldn't escape. The thing pulled itself into the car through the open window, climbing the tie like a rope. They struggled, the guy nearly choking to death before he emerged, bloody, from the passenger side. He sprinted full out down the median, screaming.

He would have been better off being strangled to death by that tie.

"Toss the necktie," she repeats. "They don't call those things 'nooses' for nothing."

Ian miserably complies.

❖❖❖

VAN rests against a tree, watching the seven other castaways scamper about. They are a motley group, bound together by their confusion, discomfort, and anonymity.

He spies Ian talking to the air marshal, a bearded guy sneaking off for a piss behind a pine, a middle-aged couple bickering in whispers. They are the oldest here, the doctor and his wife. Though it's obvious she's had some work, she is still a MILF.

More importantly, there are a couple of chicks. Sisters, maybe? Van guesses one is a year or two younger than him. And, man, is she on point. She bends over her duffle. *Dibs*, he thinks.

The other is a few years older. Maybe she's already served if she hasn't received a deferral. She's cute, too, just a little heavier, with glasses, but nice still.

The girls introduce themselves to each other. They smile at each other, shaking hands. No, not sisters after all. Van looks forward to getting to know them.

It's like a modern day *Canterbury Tales*. Traveling with them will be a character study, with one significant difference: Chaucer's troop wasn't in danger of being devoured, at least not by the undead.

Van resolves to get to know these girls sooner rather than later.

❖❖❖

WRIGHT orders them all to fall in.

"Fall in what?" the younger girl asks. She's already braiding the other's hair, like this is summer camp.

The couple is squabbling over whose decision it was to put their car—they are obviously wealthy—in short-term parking. The bearded guy named Burt pays attention to Wright, but not to his surroundings. He is knee-deep in a patch of poison oak.

Wright's going to have to start at the top.

"Lean" they are. "Mean?" Unlikely. And a "fighting machine?" Never. Regardless, they will take and obey commands just like any military operation. They cannot afford to be sloppy. Carelessness will not be tolerated. Be vigilant, she instructs, or be prepared for death . . . or worse. She is not about to become an entrée because someone can't hold his or her shit together.

They are scared. Good. Fear keeps soldiers on their toes. Fear motivates and guards against complacency. But fear, eventually, paralyzes, and that outcome is always lethal. She will need to be careful with this group, walking the tightrope and hoping for the best.

This and every morning before they move out, they will secure the campsite. Leave no traces. Today it is Van's turn to discard the debris. Wright instructs him to tie their belongings in the bed sheet, and scale a nearby tree. They hand the bundle up to him, and he secures it in a cradle created by a fork in the branches, approximately 20 feet or so off the ground. They must also bury their waste.

They will follow her in groups of twos, each pair ten paces behind the preceding pair. No more, no less. Wright is first. In time, they will each learn to "take point." For now, they will watch her and follow her every move. If she halts, they halt. If she hides, they hide. And if she runs . . .

One person takes up the rear. Today it is Ian. If the person manning the rear notices anything, *anything*, strange or out of the ordinary, he or she must sprint to the front to alert the point.

Conversation and noise will be kept to a minimum, or, if Wright dictates, prohibited entirely. "They" do not lose their ability to hear upon death—at least not immediately—and, although no official study has been released, Wright believes their faculties to be as acute, perhaps better, as when they lived. At any rate, now is not the time to play the part of the control in an experiment. As she did with Captain Richard King, once her lover, she will continue to assume the worst.

She stops them just an hour past noon. A quick head count, and she distributes packets of freeze-dried meat and vegetables. They are hungry and eagerly tear into their rations.

Van gags. "What is this? It tastes like shoe leather."

Wright sits on the roots of an upended tree, about six feet in the air, where she has a view in all directions, and where she considers that Van probably isn't far off. She hops down from her roost. "This . . . would be beef," she says, taking the morsel from Van. She tosses it back. "The chicken is more of an orange color."

"That explains what *I'm* eating, then," Ian offers, holding up a pumpkin-colored stick of chalk.

Burt is sitting at the base of a tree. He raises his hand for acknowledgement, as if he's in grade school. Wright nods. "How much of this do we have?" he asks.

Unfortunately, they don't have much. Most of it was left to those remaining on the plane. They will be happy to know, though, that Wright left them most of liver-flavored rations.

Their laughter is nervous and stunted, but it is also a sign that a shared identity may be forming amongst this band of strangers.

And what will they do after that? This is the question from the young brunette.

"Jessica, is it?" Wright asks, and Jessica nods. Things get considerably harder after that. For what they lack in taste, the rations make up for in vitamins, minerals, and carbs.

The rations are basically the same stuff the U.N. airdropped to starving countries in the early 2000s. They haven't been improved upon too much. They are freeze-dried, so there's very little scent. The wrapper is biodegradable, but no longer reflective. Once the rations are gone, safely feeding the passengers becomes much more difficult. But there are ways, and Wright will show them.

With that, Wright stands up, checks her compass. She looks over her shoulder, toward a cluster of trees that, apparently, represent "north." She turns to the passengers. "Mr. Feldman—"

"Please, call me Burt," he responds.

"Okay, Burt, please collect all of the wrappers. They need to be buried. Cover the area with dead leaves and debris to blend with the surroundings. Anne?"

"Yes?" replies the younger girl, a blonde who Van watches intently.

"Please distribute the canteens, one per group of two, and then the rear." Wright declines a canteen for herself. "They'll need to be filled at the next stream. Everyone else: be ready to move out in fifteen minutes."

❖❖❖

THEY arrange themselves in a circle that evening, head-to-head in a small clearing, Van making sure he's near the blonde. They are beat. Wright has marched like this countless times before, but even she feels the fatigue tugging at her, as if the Earth's gravitational pull has been magnified.

There is an amazing light show in the works for those who can stave off sleep and watch the sky for a few minutes more. Streaks of fire, meteors, move west across a chandelier canvas.

Van introduces himself to Anne. He tells her he's Roger Gerome's son. That always reels them in.

But this one is different. She's not interested in his status. She asks Van in a whisper if he ever watches the sky.

"No, not really," he replies. They continue to whisper as the others slumber.

Anne tells him of comets and meteors, of the Leonids, of the fall of nations, and the birth of kings. She tells him how their destiny is foretold by the sky. She tells him of a saying her mother taught her: "As above, so below."

Wright hears every blasphemous word.

❖❖❖

THE next morning, Ian's left foot is sore. He has a blister, and it encompasses both his big and secondary toes. It is pink and full, bubbling even across the ball of his foot.

"Yuck!" Van cries, gagging. "Does it hurt?"

Ian shrugs. "Not so much. It is more uncomfortable than anything."

"Hey, Anne," Van mockingly calls. "You've got to see this."

Ian is surprised. He's already on a first-name basis with her? "Van!" he objects.

"Take it easy, man," Van says. "She's out of earshot." He's right. Anne did not hear him. She's busy talking to Jessica. "Go ahead and pop it," Van urges.

Ian shakes his head. He's going to wait it out.

Van is unconvinced. "Come on, man, you got to pop that thing."

Ian glowers. "I'm not popping it. All I need is an infection. Shit, I'll lose my leg to gangrene or something out here."

But Van has a first aid kit. "I'll lend you some antibiotic ointment," he says.

It is Ian's turn to be incredulous. "You have a first aid kit? And I'm carrying your shoes? What are *you* doing with a first aid kit?"

Van smirks. "Apparently saving your leg. It's your lucky day."

Ian shrugs. "Well, I don't have a needle, anyway."

"I've got a sewing kit, too." Van replies. "We'll sterilize the needle with my lighter."

Ian's eyes are wide. "You have a sewing kit, too?"

Van sighs. "Let's not go through this again. Better pop it now. Look, you're my friend and all, but don't expect me to carry your ass, literally or figuratively."

The needle's hot. It pierces Ian's skin effortlessly with a slight hiss. Pus flows easily from the ingress. The volume of fluid that erupts from the wound amazes him. It streams down his elevated foot. He begs Van, "Do you have something I can wipe this with?"

"I don't know," Van replies, rummaging through the first aid kit.

"How about that red shirt?" Ian asks, smiling.

"Funny." Van finds gauze and tosses it Ian's way. "That polo is worth more than your life."

Ian wipes the area clean with some gauze. He digs a small hole, then buries it. He applies Neosporin, and finishes up with a bandage. The polo lives to see another day.

Van and Anne are walking side by side. He dresses nice, she thinks. Of course, his father is Roger Gerome.

She wants to talk about things that girls like. Not dolls, dresses, or the stuff of kids. She wants to talk about him.

But Van wants Anne to tell him more about her. The quickest way to bed a girl is to be a good listener. "Tell me more about comets and meteors and stuff."

She shouldn't have said a word to him yesterday, but she senses he is someone she can trust, even if he is a little vain. She's makes him promise to never repeat a word.

She starts with a quote. Shakespeare. "'When beggars die, there are no comets seen; the heavens themselves blaze forth the death of princes.' Isn't that pretty? Doesn't it just make your heart melt?"

What does it mean?

It's a reference to astrology, using the position of stars and planets to understand people and predict events.

Van laughs. Right. "You don't really believe that stuff, do you?"

Anne is taken aback. Van wasn't so damning of her views last night. He wasn't so cavalier as he held her hand furtively under the cloak of night.

No, he admits, because he was on the verge of sleep. Her voice was a lullaby to him, but her words held no meaning.

She's hurt. Hurt because of his insensitivity, but hurt more because she does believe. She believes in what her mother taught her. Her mother wouldn't have sacrificed so much for just an astrological whim or caprice. And sacrifice, Stella Mayberry did...

❖❖❖

THE inquisition came early one spring morning, nearly fifteen years past. They took Stella Mayberry prisoner in shackles, hecklers decrying her as a witch as they rode away.

Anne was taken to be cared for by the church.

It was one piece of a greater power play, a complex attempt by the fledgling church to consolidate power and eliminate competition for the souls—if not the hearts and minds—of the people.

The ends, if not the means, were defensible.

One of every three Americans polled prior to the New Order believed in the power of astrology. In the years following the plague, that number exploded to nearly one of every two survivors.

The church was losing ground. It needed parishioners, it needed donations, it needed missions. It needed to prey upon public fear to fill the empty pews and the coffers.

The inquisitors publicized their capture of Mayberry and hastily tried her for heresy. Statten prosecuted her himself, accusing her of providing readings of horoscopes and natal charts. Mayberry never denied this fact.

They made the case that her philosophy was sacrilegious. Stella Mayberry practiced divination, predicting the future for a list of clients whose names she never supplied, even as her fingers were broken.

She pled her case, relying on history, and the movement of planets and stars, as well as comets and meteors, to support her beliefs.

She could not work from notes. She could not hold a pen. It didn't matter. She wouldn't have been able to turn a page anyway.

She did her best.

The ancient Greeks and Chinese trusted astrology to divine their fates. They used celestial bodies, especially comets, to portend disasters.

Disaster: the word itself means "ill-starred."

Shooting stars are malefic messengers, cosmic wildcards that prophesize paradigm shifts. Consensus exists from Ptolemy to Bonatti. The train of a comet predicts war and desolation: the fall of Jerusalem, the eruption of Vesuvius, the deaths of the Emperor of Rome and of King Ibrahim ben Ahmet, the Black Plague, the signing of the Declaration of Independence (a blow to England's colonial intentions) the spread of influenza (a term used to describe illnesses "influenced by the planets"), the Civil War, the fall of the Alamo, the United States' loss of influence in Southeast Asia, the failure of the U.S. automobile industry, fuel shortages, and the rise of the oil cartel in 1973, the end of the Cold War, countless coups and assassinations, extreme weather conditions, earthquakes, and on . . .

And on . . .

And on.

Mayberry cited event after event, each meteor falling like a locust leaving desolation in its wake.

Statten and the inquisitors never objected to her lengthy discourse. No, it pleased the court to have every last word on the record. She was doing their job for them. With every breath, Stella Mayberry further sealed her fate.

She explained how astrology was once almost indistinguishable from astronomy. Astronomy, a hard science, has its roots in prediction and divination.

This did not help. The only thing the church hates more than other religions is science.

She was adjudicated a pagan. "Only God can influence life on Earth," the synod ruled, not planets or other interstellar movements.

Even after they tied her to a stake, stoned her with rocks, and burned her arms, torso, and face, she did not recant or provide the names of her customers.

Only after the stomachs of the spectators collectively turned at the sight of this beautiful woman literally melting before them, did the synod grant a reprieve. She was spared, the first to lose her citizenship in this new church-state.

Citizenship. Obtaining that stature doesn't necessarily convey benefits, but it does ensure one's privileges are not limited. Non-citizens—so-called conscientious objectors (for how can someone object to the destruction of a ghoul?), draft dodgers, and others like Stella Mayberry whose citizenship was revoked by the church—are fated to a lesser life. If they are able to work, they are doomed to the worst and most dangerous of jobs, like working the coalmines or maintaining the radio and phone towers in the forbidden zone. The towers are the only link to places like Padre Island, Captiva, and the Keys. Without them, communication to the colonies would be lost.

Anne still remembers when she was returned to her mother six months later. How could she forget? Her mother was half wrapped in rags, like some creature from Egypt in a creature feature. How she cried when her mother pulled her hard against her despite the immense pain it must have caused.

❖❖❖

SO, does Anne really believe this stuff?

Anne can't muster a reply. She starts to weep silently.

"Anne, I was just joking around," Van says. "I didn't mean anything by it. I'm sorry. I can be a real idiot sometimes. Just ask Ian. He'll tell you. But I never really mean anything by it. Honest!"

She sniffles and nods.

Van smiles and gropes clumsily for her hand.

She has to smile back, not so much as a response to Van, but in recognition of her convictions. She knows something deep in her heart that the doubt of others cannot shake: she is here, now, for some greater, yet unknown, purpose.

She knows this. She's read it in the stars.

❖ ❖ ❖

THEY move north along a deer path, Ian noting the sun's passing through foliage above. A patchwork of light and dark shadows passes across his left cheek as evening approaches, mimicking camouflage.

As dusk sets in, the terrain abruptly changes. The bogs and marshes that they battled most of this day and the last give way to sturdier trees and rockier earth. It reminds Ian of parts of eastern Kentucky, places he and Josh hunted with his uncle over long weekends.

For Kari Wright, the change of scenery carries more weight. Her face remains impassive, concealing her private delight. Although the hills will provide challenges, they also provide cover. The marshes and their murky waters are better suited to hunters than their quarry. The castaways have been lucky, so far, to have not come under attack by predators, natural or otherwise.

And if Wright is correct, the deciduous forest means that the plane went down much farther north than she originally calculated. While there are likely wetlands ahead, the party is far abreast of New Orleans and Baton Rouge. Those cities are surely teeming . . .

They are graced with a full moon and cloudless sky. The blue glow allows them to drive several more miles into the night before setting up a camp upon a projecting crag.

Fortunate, for it puts distance between them and the shadows that doggedly stalk them.

Chapter Six:
Walk Like an Egyptian

DAY three, and Ian is alone in line again, trailing the gang at the rear, no partner with whom to share whispered confidences.

Van is two pairs, perhaps twenty paces, ahead, and Ian occasionally catches him leaning in to murmur into Anne's slight ear.

She covers her mouth, attempting to stifle laughter, and Van flashes the patented Gerome smile.

Anne rises on her toes and utters mysteries into his ear. Her balance slightly off, her chest presses against Van's arm and stomach.

Van is a womanizer. Granted, he's no Casanova, but he's a "player," as they used to say. Van's life is measured by conquests. He counts the skirts he chases and tallies the skirts he catches.

Ian wonders if Van would be this way, so willing to break young hearts, if he hadn't lost his mother at such a young age. He winces as he watches Van slide a hand around Anne's waist.

Literally and figuratively, Ian is last in line.

He cannot dwell on it now, though. Wright has just signaled them to seek cover.

❖❖❖

U.S. 167 bifurcates Louisiana, running north and south. Wright happens upon it much like most archaeological discoveries: accidentally. Surprisingly, its lanes remain relatively smooth and unbroken. She takes out her compass. Follow the road north, and they would likely be on their way home.

"Let's go!" Van urges. He and Anne are next in line behind Wright. He begins to rise from his belly, but he feels a hand firm on his back, Wright pressing him to the ground.

"Stay in the reeds," she says quietly. "We don't know what's out there yet." She knows the ghouls are territorial. It is safer, here, at the edge of trees, thirty or so yards from the highway itself.

She looks up the interstate. The woods runs along the roadway, rising and falling with man-made embankments carved from the limestone decades ago. Here and there it gives way to open prairie. There, in the grassland, they will be the most vulnerable. Wright will need to steer them to the hem of the woods, avoiding whenever possible the open plain.

In the rear, Ian is becoming a master of the army crawl, clawing his way forward on elbows and knees, ass close to the ground. His reptilian crawl is accentuated by his color; he is stained green and yellow from his chin to his shins. Ian is so adept, he often threatens to overtake the pair before him.

Averaging their years, the Hestons would be considered middle-aged. Mr. Heston is the older of the two. Despite being a doctor, he carries too much mass about his mid-section. Heart attack potential, Ian thinks.

Ms. Heston is, well, a doctor's wife. She is ten years his junior and overly tan with a practiced smile full of large, luminescent teeth. Once, she was probably striking, but repeated augmentation has left her with a constant look of surprise, a weathered version of Munch's "the Scream."

Worse, the Hestons are painfully slow crawlers. Ian is forced to move at a snail's pace, sometimes stopping entirely, before budging. These lulls, alone and defenseless in the dense grass, are unnerving. Ian feels vulnerable, like a turtle forced to lie on its back in the sun. He waits anxiously for the pair to noisily progress.

Mr. Heston carries his ass too high—a beacon in the mid-day sun, a neon sign that screams, "Fresh Meat." His body thrashes about, causing waves of grass to crash about him like ocean swells.

Ms. Heston is no better. She yelps and chirps every time a bramble catches her hair or her elbows strike a pebble.

Together they are sure to draw a horde of the dead. Never would a meal come more easily.

The Hestons halt yet again, this time near the top of a slight slope, barely concealed. The prairie grass is much thinner here than in the valleys. Ian is annoyed, but, as the minutes pass, his anger gives way to alarm. Just what is happening up there? Are we separated from the group? Panic creeps up his spine.

And then he sees movement. Just to the right of the couple and slightly farther up the hill, something is stirring, shifting through the grass, advancing on them.

The couple is oblivious of the danger along their shoulder. Ian wants to warn them, but the lump in his throat conspires with his better judgment to stay his call. Perhaps the creature will pass and leave them undetected. No, it moves forward still.

Frantically Ian searches about for something, *any*thing to use as a weapon. Dead grass. A twig. A large clod of dried dirt plowed decades ago. It will have to do. Ian grabs it, prepares to engage . . . or flee.

The grass before him undulates in little bursts. It creeps past the Hestons, moving with intention towards Ian. He sees something taking shape through the blades now six or so feet away.

Ian's heart races, beating hard in his chest, drumming against his rib cage. It will surely hear him. He starts to inch forward, to take this monster on before it is upon him. Maybe the Hestons will alarm the others once he is engaged.

It is just an arm's length away.

Then . . . it speaks.

"What are you doing?" it whispers.

It is a hushed voice. A woman's voice. Wright's voice.

"Christ!" he growls, dropping his wedge of mud. "You scared the shit out of me."

Wright edges forward, revealing herself in inches. She stares at him, raises a critical eyebrow. "You were going to kill me with . . . a dirt clod?" She can't help but smirk.

But Ian is distressed. "What the hell do you expect me to do? Play dead?"

"Okay, okay," Wright raises a palm, gesturing Ian to calm down. "Come up front with me."

He asks, "What about the rear?"

She is less concerned about that, and more worried about what stands before them.

❖ ❖ ❖

VAN is given the duty of point and asked to stay back while Wright and Ian crawl fifty yards farther up the road before halting in a deep patch of grass.

"Is it safe to be here?" Ian asks, flat on his back.

"We're fine," Wright replies, "barring a sudden change of wind direction."

Ian rolls his eyes. "Great."

"Okay, here," she says. She passes him binoculars. "Take a look. But, take care not to move about too much. Any reflection from the lenses might attract it."

Ian shakes uncontrollably, kind of like a wet dog. He takes the binoculars in both hands in an effort to steady his hold and mask his fear.

Wright notices. "Easy, Ian. Just take a deep breath."

He gawks at her in disbelief. Then, slowly, he rolls to his chest and scratches his way to the verge of the knoll. Rising on his elbows, Ian peeks.

Emerald and gold dance before him, a twisting kaleidoscope. He stabilizes himself and takes a deep breath. The viewfinder settles upon a swath of gray. Adjusting the focus, the asphalt of U.S. 167 crystallizes in front of him. There are two lanes in each direction, separated by a median. At the top of the frame there's an off-ramp.

"A little more to your right," Wright whispers.

Ian pans. The scenery blurs and bounces until he sets his eye on the red roof of a Stucky's. He lets his focal point drop to the entrance. He sucks air in a quick burst.

Ian grew up conscious of his attempts to limit his exposure to the creatures, just books and TV, nothing direct. He once had a chance to see them up close on a field trip to the Cincinnati zoo. Rather, he opted to linger in the primate house. He was more comfortable with the monkeys—these unbeknownst ancestors—than the monsters that plagued his dreams.

Kari Wright watches Ian with interest. She notices his initial gasp, the fright taking hold. She watches for signs of nervousness, twitching around the corners of his mouth or tremors in the furrow of his brow.

But Ian seizes control. His jaw clenches and juts forward in a determined fashion. He readjusts his grip on the binoculars.

A minute passes, and Ian lowers them. Wright moves to relieve him of their weight, but before she can take them, Ian deftly adjusts the magnification. Oblivious to her, he raises them back to his eyes and leans farther into the landscape hundreds of feet before him.

It is hidden in the shadows of the overhang near the diesel pumps.

Its face is gaunt, almost skeletal, but not without features of the living. Dry, dark skin stretches taught across the creature's cheeks and forehead, the bones underneath threatening to pierce their thin veil. Vestiges of cartilage remain, the thing's blackened ears and nose shrunken and shriveled. Shadowed by the sharp ridge of its brow, two alert eyes survey the lot before it. Bright white with dead pupils, they dart back and forth, scanning.

Ian is struck that it remains ambulatory, despite extreme decay.

"Robby," as indicated by the name tag clinging to its shredded gas station attendant uniform, shuffles slowly in the shade between the pumps and the broken lobby entrance. It has worn a path through shattered glass that blankets the sidewalk and parking lot. Ian looks more closely. It has also worn the shoes and much of the skin from its feet. Strips of leather and tissue trail its skeletal ankles.

Ian drops his focus. "How can there be anything left of them? Shouldn't they have decomposed by now?"

"I don't know," she lies. She has barely begun to gauge how much she should tell Ian, when suddenly she finds herself blurting out a word: "Mummification." She says it like fact, not a guess.

Ian's eyebrow arches. Wright is privy to information unavailable to him and the populace in general. His lips part—

She anticipates a question and cuts him off. "Ian, you must keep what you've seen to yourself, at least for a little while." She explains that she's only showing him this—this ghoul—because he has been manning the rear. He should be aware of the dangers surrounding them.

And, she contemplates, *this kid may just end up leading this group should something happen to me.*

Ian agrees to keep the proverbial skeleton hidden.

❖ ❖ ❖

THEY drive deeper into the woods, Wright choosing to forego both the guidance, and menace, provided by the road. The trees are safer for now. She pushes them hard, forcing them to cover nearly a dozen more miles before nightfall.

Quiet and hungry, they devour their rations and welcome sleep in turn.

All except for Wright and Ian, who sneak away to meet in the pitch in the shadow of a dark oak.

"Mummies?" Ian asks.

"No, not 'mummies.' Mummification," Wright rejoins impatiently. There is a world of difference. Mummification is a process. Mummies are the result. Not mummies in the conventional sense, wrapped in gauze and stumbling about, victims of some ancient curse spelled out in hieroglyphics. Rather, preserved human remains.

Wright's face is different. Illuminated by traces of moonlight, she looks soft, almost serene, maybe even angelic. Ian tells her he wants to hear more.

"Mummification is the preservation of dead bodies." She goes into detail: tissue decomposes at varying rates, with skin and organs rotting more quickly, and connective tissue and bone taking longer. But a mummy is unlike a fossil or a skeleton; it retains soft tissue. Skin, hair, sinew . . . all can remain intact for years, especially if the conditions are right.

"Hold on," Ian interjects. "The Egyptians created mummies. These things can't be mummies."

True, Wright allows. These ghouls weren't created by people. They are not anthropogenic mummies, or mummies made by purpose. These are natural, spontaneous mummies.

The human body needs precious little to be preserved. The Egyptians knew this. They dried out the body using salts, reducing moisture in the body, eliminating decay. Sodium increased acidity, creating an unfriendly environment for bacteria. She weighs whether this information is useful. "Stop me if you've heard all this before."

Ian shakes his head. "Not a word of it. I mean, I know about King Tut, but that's about it."

Wright sighs. She's not surprised. The practice predated Christ. Mummification was critical to ensuring a king's rebirth in the afterlife under the watchful eye of Anubis, the god of embalming. That history is heretic today.

These creatures, though, are different. She calls them creatures instead of mummies for good reason: unlike mummies, they are not dead, at least not in the conventional sense. These creatures are preserved naturally...in theory, anyway (she stresses that this is just a theory). But there may be things about their "condition" (another term of art) that lend themselves, perhaps, to the natural preservation of the human body.

"For instance?" Ian's curiosity is a fresh breath, blowing away cobwebs from the corners of her memory. Wright finds herself fully engaged. It reminds her of a spark she once had and lost long before.

Drying the corpse, for one. Egyptian mummification rituals took only two months or so. Before the New Order, a group of scientists recreated the process using medical cadavers in about half that time. The Egyptians, like the Peruvians, positioned bodies on an incline or totally upright to use gravity to drain away fluids. Perhaps something similar happens with these creatures. They remain standing, so bodily moisture must leak away.

"Through their feet," Ian concluded. "Holy shit. I mean, 'amazing.'"

Wright half smiles. "No, you were right the first time. 'Holy shit.'" But she digresses. There's more. It's conjecture . . . just speculation. She hasn't any evidence to support it.

Ian's mouth is dry. He nods for her to continue.

She resumes. Bacteria. Fungi. Neither can grow without moisture. Both are responsible for decomposition. But the condition may retard the growth of microorganisms. Although rapid drying is common in man-made mummies, preservation can really occur anytime decay is stunted.

Example: most microorganisms can't live in freezing temperatures, so extreme cold in conjunction with dehydrating winds can produce a mummy.

"Freeze-dried mummies?" Ian jokes.

"Don't be smart," Wright demurs. Some have been discovered dating back more than 5000 years. But Wright suspects something different.

Example Two: mummies were uncovered in northwest Europe in peat bogs. Microorganisms need air, and the peat seals off oxygen while the acidity of the bog preserves their tissue, giving "bog mummies" a dark brown, leather-like appearance.

Ian's mouth puckers. He's confused.

She advances her arguments, hopeful he will connect the dots. The condition may exacerbate drying and stave off decay. Whatever it is— a virus, bacteria, or other pathogen—may be out-competing bacteria and fungi for water and other natural resources. Survival of the fittest. "Ever hear of Darwin?" she asks.

"Was he a saint?" Ian wonders.

She almost forgets the schools don't teach evolution anymore. She chuckles. "No, he wasn't a saint." She takes another tack.

"Or, the pathogen creates an inhospitable environment through elevated pH levels, for example." She continues, almost to herself. "That could explain the darkening of the skin."

Ian wants to take a step back. He asks a question. "You said mummies have been around for hundreds, even thousands of years?"

Wright nods. Yes, they are incredibly resilient.

He asks another question: "Do you think that these creatures are capable of that . . . resiliency?"

"Lasting hundreds or thousands of years?" Wright chooses her words carefully. "According to the church, no. They'll be swept away in the Rapture."

"Fine, but what do you think?"

She ponders. The truth, after eighteen years? We know about as much now as we did back then. We haven't even scratched the surface of understanding the mechanisms behind their existence. Short answer: "Anything's possible."

Ian thinks on this a moment. "What are these things?"

Wright dodges his question. "Like I said, they're mummified corpses."

Ian senses her evasion. "No, I mean, what are they, really? Why are they here?"

It's a question Wright has asked herself a thousand times in some form or another. She recollects early radio reports of resurrected cadavers. The first accounts came out of southeastern Texas. Conservatives immediately seized on the issue, seeking political advantage by blaming the incidents on an illness spread by illegal aliens from Matamoros, Mexico. Within days, however, outbreaks of mob violence were inundating the eastern third of the United States, places like Pittsburgh, Charleston, and Hoboken, places with little or no connection to the third world. On TV, a scientist speculated that an explorer satellite returning to Earth after orbiting Venus was to blame. The U.S. military in an attempt to prevent some hitchhiking organism from reaching earth, he contended, had detonated the satellite in the atmosphere. NASA denied it.

Wright sums things up for Ian: "Honestly, I don't know."

Ian sighs. Whole new worlds are opening to him, but he wants to make sure he'll be around to explore them. "Kari?"

She doesn't remember a time when she was called by her first name. Even Richard called her by her surname. She doesn't know quite how to feel about it.

Ian continues. "Would you mind talking to the Hestons for me? For us?"

Wright agrees. "About what?"

"About not getting us killed."

He's right. She's noticed it, too. That talk is long overdue.

Chapter Seven:
Look Who's Coming to Dinner

PALE, ravenous hands tear at the soil. Although it contains limestone, it has recently been stirred, and their frenzied fingers dig easily. They push against each other, bellowing as they clamor about the widening hole.

But a set of fat fingers finds the remnants of the gauze first. Aroused by the scent of blood and pus, the others moan balefully and grope at the larger ghoul in their midst. They struggle in vain to seize the morsel, one tossing aside the small corpse of an infant in her zeal. Their mad swings, however, are futile. The fiend's obese mitts are somehow more nimble, and they snatch the prize from the hungry claws all around.

For tonight, this meager meal will not be shared. It is his alone.

He swallows the gauze.

And he wants more.

Chapter Eight:
The Reluctant Doctor

IAN stirs early the next morning, or, at least, he thinks it's early, as he somewhat doubts he slept at all. He was preoccupied with a world of new ideas, and they danced about his head like a jam jar full of fireflies. He's confused, almost overwhelmed to be privy to such information, but, at the same time, he finds it invigorating.

The ritual begins again. First, he starts down to the lavatory—a hole three-feet deep fifty paces downwind carved out by Burt the night before. Then, he brushes his teeth with a scentless baking powder mixture. This he follows with a weak, non-scented deodorant.

Soon, however, he will need a proper bath, as will they all.

He glimpses Wright across the campsite. He stares, maybe a tad too long, and she catches him. She blinks, then turns to business again. She stoops down to wake the Hestons.

Ian walks the perimeter of the camp quietly avoiding waking Jessica. She's curled in the fetal position, and she whimpers slightly as Ian passes. Nightmares, too? Perhaps Ian will talk to her today.

He approaches Van. Van is slumbering front to back with the blonde, spooning (although he's sure Van would rather fork), arms about her to keep off the chill, a puddle of dirty drool pooled about his cheek. Ian considers "accidentally" tripping over the couple, but instead angles toward the camp's makeshift latrine. He is in better spirits today, and he will not allow his jealousy to further eat away at him.

TODAY Wright decides to change the pairings. She decides Ian will be point. She instructs him to stay to the edge, to be overly cautious. He is overjoyed to be anywhere, even if alone, other than behind the Hestons.

Wright is pleased that he is pleased, but she has other reasons, personal reasons, for this modification. Her discussion with Ian stirred a scrap of something buried, some remnant of who she used to be, a person who probed rather than accepted the status quo. *What are they, really? Why are they here?* Early on it didn't matter. Everyone was just trying to survive. But it's eighteen years out, and it is time for people to start caring, regardless of the church's position. Wright wants answers, and she decides to create her own opportunity to test some ideas and do a little recognizance.

Wright teams with Dr. Heston for the day. They exchange formalities for an hour before Wright surreptitiously digs into his past . . .

❖❖❖

HESTON wasn't always a doctor.

No, his first love is animals. Not people.

He completed veterinary school at the University of Illinois twenty years before. Two years later, when the epidemic hit, he was working in an emergency animal clinic in southern Illinois. Just months later, the event was pandemic, infecting with 100% communicability, and killing—so to speak—with 100% certainty.

The medical community was hit hard. Safety protocols could not reduce the likelihood of transmission. The disease spread too quickly, replicating and taking over the host in mere hours or less.

It decimated staff, filled emergency rooms, and overwhelmed those brave souls who remained at their posts. There weren't resources or grant funding to study the pathology or infectivity—ingress to the host, survival in the host, and spread.

And spread it did. Crossing the globe in just one spin on its axis.

So containment, rather than treatment, became the operative word. And veterinarians, like Heston, were pressed into service to fill the void left by the early responders, like EMTs, nurses, and physicians.

❖❖❖

DOES Dr. Heston mind questions about his work?

"Not at all," Heston replies with a wink, "And please, call me Neil." He's happy for a respite from his wife and their bickering.

Wright obliges. "Neil, do you have a hypothesis about the origins of the walking dead?"

Heston chokes. He can't believe she's asked *that* question. To speculate is heresy, but he finds himself compelled to answer. "Of course, it must be off the record."

"Of course," Wright grants.

The subject matter is taboo, so Heston chooses his words carefully to protect himself. "*Some* in the medical community speculated that a pathogen might be involved. *They* suspected a virus."

But his response begs additional questions, and Wright sees her opportunity to push the envelope just a little further. She needs to give him an out, though. "Tell me more about what *those* practitioners said."

Heston sighs. He's wanted to tell his story—confess his sins—for years.

❖❖❖

HESTON and a team of local veterinarians accompanied the Illinois National Guard into Kentucky. Guard units were dispatched across borders upon orders of the President himself to the nearest urban centers. Heston volunteered to assist in Louisville.

He could never have known the horror that awaited him at Baptist Hospital East.

He could never have known that he would never see home again.

Utter chaos greeted their unit at the hospital's doors. The sick and dying all over Louisville were being deposited there. The administrators, though, had largely abandoned the hospital. Staff failed to report to their shifts. Those who did bore witness to the bedlam and soon decided to flee for their homes. Only a handful of nurses, and maybe a doctor or a resident, remained at their posts.

The National Guard unit was led by a young lieutenant, a man maybe just nineteen years of age, who had just finished officer training two weeks earlier in North Carolina. He was a nice kid. Heston can't remember his name—Clayton or something—but he was green. Real green. Everyone with any experience was off fighting Al Qa'eda in Husaybeh, insurgents in Mosul, Taliban in Kabul, and pirates off the coast of Baraawe and Haradheere. No one with any real experience stayed home.

The driveway to the emergency room was already full of prospective patients, crying and rocking and holding open wounds. The waiting room—a fitting name, as everyone was waiting and no one was being attended to—was worse.

The lieutenant took one look at the emergency room, and he ordered the troops to establish a triage center. These people needed attention. Fast.

It was a noble thought. But the officer didn't think properly about containment. He didn't follow the protocols for dealing with a biohazard. He didn't secure the facility.

Heston had dealt with contagion before, albeit with dogs and cats. The reality is the methods for dealing with people are very similar to dealing with animals: assess the risk, establish a quarantine, observe the infected, and, if necessary . . .

Heston chose not to think of the last step, at least not yet.

Assess the risk.

Three-quarters of the patients waiting for aide were victims of massive bites, human bites. They told stories of friends, family members, and neighbors complaining of bites days or hours earlier. Then they recounted how those same friends, same family members, and same neighbors in turn bit them. Some were ill with fevers and intense migraines. Others lapsed into unconsciousness. Some seemed to be in the early stages of kidney and renal failure.

There are generally three vectors for transmission of a communicable disease: intermediary organisms, like fleas or mosquitoes, contaminated food or water, or close proximity.

Close proximity, like bites.

Biting can be a form of host manipulation, the modification of behavior by a parasite or pathogen. Biting is an assured way to spread contagion.

None of the military or medical personnel had ever witnessed rabies, but Heston had. He saw rabies first hand, usually farm hounds coming into contact with a rabid bat or raccoon. Rabies is a virus. It finds a home in the salivary glands of its victims. The host can't swallow, its mouth froths with contagious saliva.

But that's not the trick. This is: the virus needs to spread, and it has evolved to ensure this. Rabies infects the brain, inducing tension and, ultimately, violent behavior, including biting. With each bite, the microbe proliferates.

Oddly enough, rabies even may have given birth to the werewolf myth.

Unfortunately, rabies is 100% fatal unless treated within 24 hours by a vaccine, a series of painful shots. It can only be detected if the host is caught and its head removed so the brain can be tested.

Establish a quarantine.

Heston approached the lieutenant as he supervised his work from the top of an armored personnel carrier. The officer nodded with self-satisfaction as his soldiers ushered the wounded into tidy little groups. "Lieutenant, I need to have a word."

The lieutenant looked peeved, but he jumped from the carrier in two bounds and ushered Heston to the rear of the vehicle. "Shouldn't you be in there, assisting the wounded?"

Yes, Heston should, and he would, if this kid took the right precautions. "We need to set up a quarantine. We need to secure this facility."

The lieutenant frowned. He wasn't the smartest cadet, but he was smart enough to realize that fact. He set aside his pride. "What do you need, Doctor?"

Doctor. The title stuck with Heston at that point. He would never be known as anything but a doctor. He would never again care for animals. He would never again do the work he truly loved.

Heston ordered another level of triage, isolating those bitten from the rest, starting in the waiting area where patients waited . . . impatiently. "Separate anyone with a bite," he directed a sergeant. "Anyone with a scratch. Make sure no one leaves. No one infected can leave. Detain anyone who resists."

Infected. He said it. It had been just an assumption . . . until he gave it voice.

Observe the infected.

Heston moved quickly through the emergency room, the lieutenant and a dozen guardsmen in tow. It was empty, not an anesthesiologist, nurse practitioner, intern, or doctor to be found.

They entered the elevator, Heston pushing the button marked "two." The second floor, the intensive care unit. The entrance to Hell.

Before the elevator doors opened, they could already smell the death. The stench made them cover their mouths; it made them gag.

The doors opened.

The lieutenant had never witnessed—not in all of his manuals and textbooks, not in all of his war games—anarchy and torment of this magnitude.

The ICU was completely full, its hallway cluttered and clogged with gurneys and by people . . . .dead people. Dead people, patients and medical staff, shambling about, gnawing and tearing at other people who were already dead or would be dead soon.

One of the soldiers retched.

One of the monsters heard him.

It went for the lieutenant, sinking its teeth into his left hand between the forefinger and the thumb before being beaten off him by the Guardsmen. It reeled five or six feet and found its balance, and it came at them again.

Heston furiously pressed buttons. The first floor button. The button to close the doors, the button with the arrows pointing to each other.

The thing gasped as it approached, eyes wide and eager. The soldiers laid down suppressing fire to no avail. The bullets tore into the creature's chest and gut, but still it drew nearer. Its odor choked Heston. It groped for them.

And the elevator doors closed.

When the doors opened again, Heston half expected to see the creature waiting for them. But the elevator had successfully descended to the first floor. Heston punched the elevator alarm to hold it in place. The creatures would have to take the stairs.

They went to work immediately, closing off the wings, chaining the stairwells. Patients worsening in the waiting area were escorted to the emergency room. They were given beds. That's all Heston and his team could do.

When patients started to die and come back to life in the ER, when the screaming started as the creatures attacked those who were dying, Heston came to a conclusion: The bites were fatal. No, worse than fatal.

Assess the risk, establish a quarantine, observe the infected, and, if necessary . . .

Euthanize.

Anyone suspected of an infection was permitted to enter the hospital. All others were escorted out. Then the doors were locked.

The lieutenant had one question for Heston: "Am I going to become one of those things?"

Probably.

The lieutenant shook his head. He razed the building. Then he raised his pistol. It was in his mouth in a flash. His brains were on the pavement in another.

❖ ❖ ❖

WHY is Heston telling Wright all this? He doesn't know. Maybe he needs to talk to someone about science. Hard science.

The church doesn't just frown upon science, it vigorously dissuades it and anything approaching it. The practice of medicine isn't allowed to move beyond traditional treatments. The church doesn't believe in R&D. Electron microscopes, and other tools with the potential to unlock the secrets of life, are illegal, and those who wield them or seek to find alternative answers are criminals.

Or maybe he thinks it just doesn't matter. They will likely die out here. Why not share what he knows? And if he dies and Wright lives, maybe he's left a trace of himself—or what was his living self—for posterity's sake.

Or maybe Heston feels guilty. On that fateful day eighteen years ago, he provided dozens with a release from death, but he stole the life from dozens more. Maybe it's an opportunity to confess his sins to someone who might actually care, someone other than the pastor in the church who pinned a medal on his chest and printed an M.D. on his letterhead.

Because in hindsight, there was no need to execute the few who suffered from the rakes of monster fingernails but showed no signs of mauling. Of course, Heston didn't know that scratches weren't a vector.

He didn't learn more about transmission until his future wife was attacked later that year.

Ms. Heston (nee Brodie) was assaulted at a retreat on the banks of the Ohio River. A ghoul dragged itself from the depths and scored her arm deep with a swiping paw. She was brought to the ER, where Heston was the attending physician. He took one look into her beautiful, frightened eyes and made the decision right then and there to break protocols.

He secreted her away in the empty oncology wing, strapped her to a gurney and sedated her. He hooked her to an IV and pumped her full of antibiotics. He watched over her for hours, biding his time stroking her face, whispering to her, "Everything will be okay."

The hours became days and still the wound did not fester nor did her vitals change.

Three days later, he released her with strict orders to visit him daily for the next seven days. She stopped by unannounced on day eight. Again on days nine and ten. They made a date and the rest fell into place.

It's no matter. His lack of data then is hard to square with the deaths of so many innocents at Baptist East, many of them children.

❖ ❖ ❖

WRIGHT is not jarred by Heston's story. Everyone has a story, and she expected a microbe. She expected it to exploit the host. She even expected transmission through a bite.

But it can't be that simple. If it was that simple, the story would be over.

There are too many unanswered questions.

Which microbe?

How does it exploit the host?

And, most important, how does transmission through a bite explain the potential reanimation of those who died naturally?

Wright starts asking. Which microbe? "Are we dealing with a parasitic virus, a protozoa, or a bacterium?"

Heston shakes his head. Possibly one of the above. Possibly more than one. Possibly something else altogether.

He thinks back to his veterinary practice, remembers CTVT—canine transmissible venereal tumors—a sexually transmitted disease in dogs. It is a tumor not spread by a virus like HPV, but by transmission of the cancerous cells *themselves*. It is a parasitic cancer caused by the mutated cells of a single dog that died 2,500 years ago. It is the longest living mammalian cell line known. The condition could be caused by something similar or very different, but equally unusual. Who knows?

Heston has not reduced the options. He's increased them. *Strike one*, Wright thinks. "Well, then, how does it exploit the host?"

Diseases have unique methods of taking advantage of their hosts. Heston cites various examples of host manipulation.

Malaria incapacitates so completely the infected are powerless to swat the mosquitoes that feed on them and propagate the disease.

Guinea worm larvae ingested in stagnant water reproduce in the small intestine and then burrow toward the host's lower extremities, erupting in painful blisters. The infected seek to sooth the pain finding relief by soaking in water and allowing the worms to begin their life cycle anew.

Cholera causes diarrhea, both a symptom and a mode of transmission when fecal matter infects water supplies. Wright is all too aware of the impact. Most of the survivors are.

But Heston thinks that this microbe takes host manipulation to an elevated, but not unprecedented, plane.

"Not unprecedented?" Wright asks.

"Correct," Heston says. "Zombification occurs every day in nature."

There it was. Heston said it. The "Z" word, banned by the church-state.

❖❖❖

GOVERNMENTS ban words all the time. George Carlin skewered the FCC and the Supreme Court for illegalizing seven "dirty words."

But this prohibition is different. It is collective, pervading everything from the media to water cooler conversation. It is broad, going beyond the mere word to the concept. Much like China's bans on discussions of the Falun Gong and of Tibetan Independence, the ban is enforced and enforced strictly. Persons convicted of violations are dealt with ruthlessly.

But, in truth, Heston knew of zombies in nature long before the human outbreak.

He knows of grasshoppers forced to drown themselves in ponds by parasitic hairworms that devour their hosts and control their brains with proteins. The hairworms eat everything but the head, legs, and exoskeleton. After successfully coercing suicide, the worms eject and spread their seed.

He recalls a wasp that lays its eggs in spiders. The larva feed off the spiders and control their brains, like the hairworms do the grasshoppers. Here, though, the invader enslaves the spider, compelling it to abandon its daily web-making and to construct a cradle. There, the surrogate mother sits, allowing itself to be consumed as the larva begin their transformation into wasps.

And the protozoa toxoplasmosis targets cats using mice as the delivery system. The protozoon manipulates mice, making them take risks, risks that ensure they'll be devoured. Infected mice don't fear cat urine. Infected mice don't hide along the edge of a wall. They cross rooms in plain sight.

Heston has some vague ideas about this microbe, but nothing proven, nothing firm.

She senses Heston's hesitation. *Strike two.* For now.

A frustrated Wright asks her third question. "So, how is the plague transmitted?" She assumes there are two vectors. One must allow transmission through a bite, while the other must reanimate those who died naturally. "What do you think?"

Heston sighs. "There are plenty of ways to explain transmission. Too many ways, really. But here's your mistake, I think: the theories of transmission need not be mutually exclusive."

Wright cocks her head.

"Necroanthrophagism"—a term coined by Heston before the rise of the church, meaning, literally, the dead eating their own species—"might be triggered by intimate contact with a revenant, through direct passage of the microbe, superinfection, or the transmission of a deadly bacterial infection. Or it may be initiated by the natural death process of a previously infected host—something lying dormant, possibly even incorporated into the human genome."

In those bitten, direct infection of a pathogen seems the obvious answer, and the obvious answer is usually the right one. Heston subscribes to this theory, but there are other possibilities that have yet to be ruled out.

Superinfection, or reinfection, is well documented. A terrible disease called auto immune disease syndrome, or AIDS (or God's Revenge, depending on who one asks), as historical now as the Black Death, the Plague of Galen, and the Spanish Flu, was triggered by a virus called HIV. The Centers for Disease Control confirmed that re-infection with a second strain of HIV after a primary infection could exacerbate the initial infection. Higher viral loads and viral escape result from re-infection, a possible explanation for why someone dies so quickly following a bite.

Wright understands. "So most of us may already be infected with one strain, the strain that causes us to return from the brink of a natural death, but a second strain passed through a bite might bring about that death more quickly."

Heston nods. But he has another theory, something he calls the "Komodo Dragon Theory." Here, the infection is again innate, but there is no proximal transmission. The Komodo dragon—the largest of the reptiles and a true dragon—kills its prey effectively, if not expeditiously. It bites its victims, but the bite itself is rarely immediately fatal. The dragon is not venomous, but it is extremely toxic. Its mouth is so full of bacteria a single bite will lead to infection. Untreated, the slightest nibble is fatal. Always. The dragon needs eat only once per month, so it has the luxury of patiently tracking goats or the occasional human through the jungle over days or weeks and eating the carrion.

Imagine a revenant, deep in the throes of decomposition, bacteria running rampant in its mouth. Imagine those bacteria are poisonous and drug-resistant, and they've been introduced into a human's bloodstream through a ragged bite. Sepsis and death aren't just likely, they're assured. Imagine the inherent pathogen taking hold. Imagine the dead walking.

The relationship, the dance between bacterium and pathogen, may be even more complex. It may be symbiotic. The bacterium living in the host's mouth and the pathogen may gain mutual advantage. If the pathogen causing necroanthrophagism is somehow intrinsic, perhaps it uses the bacteria as a trigger. Bacteria are passed to others via a bite, causing death (or something like death) and unleashing virulence.

"It is not so crazy," says the former veterinarian. He remembers the aquarium in the wood-paneled waiting room of the animal hospital. It was designed to calm the frayed nerves of anguished pet owners. It was the home of a little orange clownfish. Safeguarded by a layer of mucus, it would hide among the tentacles of a poisonous anemone. In the wild, they protect each other from predators. The clown guards the anemone, chasing off hungry scavengers, and the anemone's stingers shelter the clown from larger fish. Mutual advantage.

"And what benefit would the bacterium derive?" Wright wonders.

Heston has an idea. "Maybe behavioral changes caused by the pathogen, like masticating and biting, help transmit the bacteria. Maybe the pathogen keeps non-symbiotic bacteria in check by inhibiting their proliferation through competition. Or, maybe it attacks them outright." But he is quick to point out, "There are lots of maybes."

"So, if we're already infected, how did we get it?"

"Again, I don't know," Heston says. "For instance, the disease could be airborne, infecting most people and hiding in the hypothalamus or in the nervous system like chicken pox or herpes."

"So," Wright concludes, "the disease might be biding its time, waiting for our immune system to grow weak, waiting for the early stages of death, to present itself."

"It could, in theory. The process of reanimation might allow it to avoid competition from other pathogens, too. When a host dies, so do the pathogens within it. Maybe it is hardy enough to outlast them. This, too, might allow it to enter the brain, nullifying the barrier effect." Heston nods to himself. This is an option he had not thought about before. "Again, a number of maybes. Unfortunately, there's no way to prove or disprove any of these theories."

"Strike three," Wright mumbles.

But Heston is still talking. He's frustrated. "There's no known culture. So there's no way to isolate the pathogen, no way to test blood or tissue. So we can't even begin to treat or cure. And we never will as long as the church has its way."

Oops. Heston realizes he's said too much. He shouldn't have said that last bit. He shouldn't have criticized the church. The inquisitors use moles to ferret out independent thought. He should really be questioning Wright's motives.

"But maybe we are simply witnessing God's will," Heston says, backing off. "I need not remind you God hasn't been adverse to using the occasional plague to get His point across."

Wright thinks Heston's covering his ass. She's right.

Heston doesn't think it's God's will. But he also doesn't believe the plague's manifestation strictly supports Darwin's theory of survival of the fittest. Evolution is more than that, especially on a cellular level. Evolution can be driven by cooperation, interaction, and shared benefit, too. To paraphrase Carl Sagan, life populated the globe less through combat and more through networking. But he says nothing of this to Wright.

"You know," Heston says, "the Church concluded this is not a medical event—"

Wright interrupts. "Please don't play coy, Doctor. I'm not a spy. If I was, I would have stopped talking to you an hour ago."

"Okay, I'll accept that you're not a spy," Heston says. "But did you stop to wonder if I am?"

Chapter Nine:
Shopping Mall or Shopping Maul?

AFTER lunch, Wright takes point. She thinks about Dr. Heston and their talk. She knows moles. Hell, Captain Richard King was probably a mole. Heston, however, is not an operative. But she gets his point.

Being a little cautious, being safe, isn't necessarily a negative. She needs to be a little less eager and show some patience. *Be smart*, she thinks. *Be safe.*

Despite her desire to trust Ian and Heston, the truth is the only person here she can truly trust is herself. She needs to remember that, especially with the others.

Be safe.

Their conversation was anything but that. It didn't just dance on the line of treason. It hurdled past it with all the grace and speed of a comet.

Still, be safe.

But if she is so committed to safety, why has she led the group out of the woods? She hadn't even noticed that she had steered the party back, back toward the highway. The signs warn that the mall is just an exit away.

Their lives are in her hands. They head back into the woods.

❖❖❖

AS the billboard states, the Kecksburg Mall has everything—food courts, sporting goods, lingerie, watches, leather purses, luggage, high-heeled shoes, jewelry, DVDs, cell phones, televisions, memorabilia, comics—yes, everything . . .

And nothing. Nothing necessary. Nothing justifying the risk.

Wright hopes none of her troupe saw the sign. Otherwise, she'll get questions. Why don't we go there? Won't there be food? Might there be survivors?

She doesn't have to rehearse her responses. They would come in rapid fire succession. No. No. Hell, no.

The mall will be crawling with them if, as Wright suspects, the creatures are driven by memory and habit. In her experience, there is something more than instinct that drives these monsters. Her experiences were horrifying . . .

Within a week of the plague, a fledgling militia, locals armed to the teeth, rescued her and her family. They blasted their way out of Oldham County, burning everything in their wake. They moved quickly toward Louisville, picking up other random survivors like ticks on a deer.

The Macaroni Grill sat a mile outside of the city. That's where she saw the state troopers. Twenty or more of them, along with a few former customers, all "turned sour," as one of the rednecks said, like bad milk. All of them victims of the contagion, all trying to tear their way into the restaurant.

The Macaroni Grill wasn't exactly Zagat rated, but one rule exists in life and death: cops always know where to get good food. And they had returned to their favorite restaurant, obsessed with filling their bloating bellies, not with pasta or filet mignon, but with the employees and patrons who had locked themselves inside.

The fighting was short but brutal. The militia rescued ten people that afternoon. They lost four. A net gain of six, plus some revolvers, shotguns, and ammo.

There are no survivors to save in the mall. There can't be. There are likely hundreds, if not thousands, of revenants in and around the shopping center. So they will stick to the trees, safe in the knowledge that they will never truly know.

JOLENE Heston yearns for a spa day.

Her husband wants to pet his dogs again, a Blue Tick named Oscar and a Golden Retriever named Brooke.

Anne pines for her mother's homemade ice cream.

Now Anne prods Jessica. It's her turn to tell those gathered around the campfire what she misses the most.

Jessica's answer is easy: toilet paper.

"Me, too! Me, too!" Ms. Heston chimes. She holds her hand above her head and gives Jessica an awkward high-five. They laugh.

Dr. Heston stokes the fire. He says he remembers a time in his life, a time when he was a bachelor prior to meeting his wife, when a roll of toilet paper would last more than a day, more than an hour.

Ms. Heston rolls her eyes. She says that if he doesn't watch it, she'll see to it he has all the toilet paper he could ever need. They continue laughing.

Dr. Heston wants to change the subject. He looks to Burt for help. "What about you? What do you long for?"

Burt doesn't hesitate. He grieves for his Spiderman 129, wherein the web-slinger fights the Punisher. If it hadn't been blown from the plane, he would have traded it to a clandestine dealer on Padre Island, known only by the uninspired moniker "The Dealer," for DC Comic's Superman number 10. Superman 10 is a real prize. Only 200 copies were printed back in 1939. The Dealer has two.

Van yawns. They are all tired of hearing Burt carp about Spiderman 129. "Anything else?" Van asks.

Yes. Burt also misses his collection of graphic novels.

"Graphic novels?" Van asks dubiously. "Don't you mean comics? Albeit, really long comics?"

Burt cracks a smile. "I guess I do."

"Why comics?" asks Anne.

For Burt, comics, as well as science fiction and fantasy, are an escape. "They let me transport myself to a place where there's something better, more freedom . . . " Burt hesitates. That sounded critical. He shifts gears. "They're also an inspiration. There are still good people willing to do good things in the world."

Jessica asks, "Who is your favorite superhero?"

"Easy," says Burt, "Superman. He's the best."

"What?" Van demands. "The Man of Steel?" His voice drips with sarcasm. "I mean, the tights are bad enough. But the whole Superman premise is pretty cheesy. Batman, at least, was more realistic."

"They *are* called superheroes, after all," Burt defends. "Comics aren't meant to be entirely realistic."

"Sure," Van accepts, "but you can only suspend disbelief for so long. There should at least be some basic recognition of the laws of physics."

"Plus, Superman's kind of gay," Dr. Heston chides.

"Neil!" Ms. Heston lectures, sternly.

"Well, he is," Heston grumbles to himself.

Burt ignores Heston. "What do you mean?"

"I mean, he likes men," Heston replies.

There's snickering about the fire.

"No," Burt groans. "I was talking to Van."

Van clarifies. "Well, for instance, Superman is incredibly ripped. In all the cartoons—"

"Comics," Burt corrects.

"Yeah, right, comics," Van continues. "In all of the comics, Superman is huge, a mountain of muscle."

A confused Burt says, "A lot of superheroes are muscular."

Van says, "Right, but they're muscular because they work out. Superman was born with superhuman strength, so answer this: how does he get that big? Nothing could provide enough resistance. Really, he shouldn't be any bigger than, say . . . Ian."

Ian shakes his head. Van is such an ass.

But he's not done. "What's that planet he's from again? Klingon?"

"Krypton," Burt replies, flatly.

"Yeah, right, Krypton. And the gravity's, like, what? Ten times our own?"

Burt thinks it's seventeen. Seventeen-point-eight, to be exact.

"Okay," Van allows, "seventeen. That means he's got to be doing three hours of curls twice a day using freight trains as weight just to put on muscle, right? Wrong. He's not, because that's too conspicuous. Plus, his schedule's not going to allow for it. The guy's fighting bad guys all over the world—"

"And some off-world," Ian adds.

"Right!" Van persists, "outer space baddies, too. And then he's got this job reporting on stocks and restaurant closings and crap at least a couple hours a day, assuming he's not a shitty reporter."

"But this guy's not winning any Pulitzer," Ian inserts.

"No way," Van maintains. "Not with all that gallivanting around. Let's be honest, he can play the 'exclusive interview with Superman' angle only so long before it gets tired, or people figure out Peter Parker is actually Superman."

"It's Clark Kent," Burt amends, peevishly. "Clark Kent is Superman's alter ego."

But Ian is talking over him. "It would be better if he worked for a television station." To Van he says, "What if he had an interview show?"

Van agrees. "With cousins dating their pets and that stuff. That's perfect. You know, I bet women would gobble that eye candy up, especially the 24- to 35-year-old bracket."

"So would the gay demographic," Dr. Heston quips.

"He's not gay," Burt sniffs to himself. He is outside the conversation. It has taken on a life of its own, and it carries on around him.

"Oh," Ian exclaims, "here's a story they should cover: Ghost Payroller on Staff at Daily Bugle."

Burt shakes his head. It's the Daily Planet. Spiderman worked for the Daily Bugle.

Ian is still talking. "Think of it. He clocks in and then disappears for hours to take care of his private affairs."

"Since when is saving Earth a private affair?" a frustrated Burt inquires.

"It's a private affair if he's doing it on the company's dime," Ian scoffs. "Anyway, half the time he's saving his chick from some danger of her own making."

"Oh, yeah," Dr. Heston says, "Barbara is always getting into trouble."

Burt's jaw clenches. Lois Lane. Not Barbara.

"At best," Ian argues, "Superman is unethical. At worst, his behavior borders on the illegal. Think of the advertisers and readers he's defrauding. How much of every paper sold is going to fund that?"

Van nods. "Talk about giving a whole new meaning to 'Man of Steal!' At least Batman does it with his own money."

Burt leans back, dejected.

Wright realizes the sharks are circling and that this morale-building exercise has gone awry. She needs to put a stop to it.

More importantly, Wright realizes she, too, may soon find herself in an uncomfortable position. Soon the question will be posed to her: just what do you miss?

Family? A popular restaurant? A guilty pleasure? Shopping? What?

Wright would have to lie. How could she answer, "Nothing," even if it's the truth, even if she doesn't miss a thing?

Or so she thinks.

Yet there is a tug at her subconscious. It says that "nothing" is not entirely accurate. She does miss something. She recognizes the void. But returning home will not fill it. It is a hole that can't be filled with food, sex, alcohol, or money—although she has tried them in countless combinations. Her loss is something greater, intangible, but precious still.

Burt looks exhausted. So is Wright. "Okay, everyone, lights out. Time to extinguish the fire."

Van protests. He didn't get a turn to talk about what he misses. "Too bad. Lights out," Wright repeats stiffly.

Good, Ian thinks. Ian misses something deeper too, but it's something he's been missing since he was little. Tonight he will dream about his father again as he does nearly every night.

Chapter Ten:
History Derailed

IT is a brisk November morning, eighteen years earlier. Peter Sumner blows into his hands. His breath lingers before him, specter-like, dancing about his fingers. He stamps his feet, looks toward the end of the Addison elevated platform. No train yet.

His morning routine: shower, kiss his wife and young son goodbye, and board the train. The Chicago Transit Authority picks him up less than a block from Wrigley Field. From there it submerges underground, and deposits him in the Jackson subway station, steps from his office.

The CTA is universally maligned. Riders complain that it is dirty, inconvenient, and, as a rule, late. But, with gas prices and parking taxes soaring, there is little choice for thousands but to take it.

The CTA is a monopoly. It has no competition. As such, commuters aren't really customers. They are hostages, and their relationship with their captors is love/hate. It's textbook Stockholm Syndrome.

Peter can relate to the CTA, though. He has been an attorney for the city for ten years, the Department of Revenue, no less. The only thing people can stomach less than a lawyer is a lawyer enforcing parking and tax codes. In terms of public sentiment, hatred towards Peter's department easily surpasses the CTA, Hillary Clinton, and French émigrés combined.

There are stereotypes that befall most professions. Usually, those stereotypes can be summarized by a single question. For cops: "Have you ever shot anyone?" The question is as loaded as a cop's revolver. It assumes not only that the use of force may be required, but also that there is a propensity toward it. For Peter, the question he is asked dozens of times from people as disparate as drunken Cubs fans to dignitaries: "Can you get me out of my parking tickets?"

The question offends Peter because it supposes that there is still corruption in Chicago, and that, as a public employee, he is inclined to partake in it. Also, it just plain lacks originality.

Peter does not believe Chicago government is a broken system managed by dysfunctional people. He works with too many bright people with innovative ideas and a genuine love for the city to ever think that. But he cannot deny that there are rotten apples. Even if they have not spoiled the bunch, the rotten apples seem to be the ones that residents consistently eat with distaste.

Peter wants to change perceptions, so he lobbies to do so and gets carte blanche. It isn't hard. With scandal after scandal tracking across the covers of the papers like a sports ticker each day, the Mayor needs a win.

A bureaucratic monster stands ugly and glaring before him. He meets with various personnel, and is pummeled by excuses.

"We don't make widgets."

"We don't have customers."

"This is how we've always done it." This last offered by Tommy Rails, a procurement manager. Rails is a rotten apple, lacking the skills to properly supervise and the intelligence to realize those skills are non-existent.

But Peter is up for the challenge. Ninety-six percent of all problems result from breakdowns in processes. Peter studies processes like a boy with a magnifying glass, transforming them, filling in gaps, removing redundancies, and establishing best practices.

But four percent of problems are people, people like Rails. More and more, Peter's magnifying glass sweeps over Rails and his cronies. It draws them into relief. Soon it will bring light, and with that, heat. Peter will fry them like the bugs they are.

But not today. Rails staged a protest, calling in sick. It is a coordinated strike. Nearly twenty percent of the staff called in as well. The absences trouble Peter. Several supervisors participate in Rails' blue flu, including a few of Peter's acolytes.

Besides, Rails' story isn't even plausible. After all, who stays home because of a bite, especially one from his teenage daughter?

Right there, Peter decides on his next crusade: combating chronic absenteeism.

Peter's peers like to say Peter is "in the zone." The reality: Peter is never outside the metaphoric zone. His mind is a constant hive of activity, and he lives with a constant, pulsating buzz that, despite its deafening silence, drowns out interpersonal stimuli.

Peter is trapped in the zone.

There is an otherness, an apartness that prohibits him from really engaging his fellow man. He lacks the ability to empathize.

That's not to say Peter doesn't have feelings. He can feel anger, happiness, and the full range of emotions. He just doesn't feel them toward *people*.

But he's a good faker. He's faked it for nearly thirty years. He's done everything people would expect, basically everything his father had done before him. He went to college, courted and married his wife, got a job, got a car, got a house. He goes to neighbor's barbecues, holds Super Bowl parties, laughs at his boss' horrible jokes. He takes up smoking with his co-workers even though he hates it. Years ago he even considered having an affair. Not because he was attracted to the woman, but because he thought it was the normal thing to do.

In short, Peter Sumner goes through the motions.

At least he used to.

Almost four years ago something changed. His son was born. As soon as Peter held Ian in his arms, looking upon his helpless face, he felt his icy heart break and warmth pass through him in waves. Peter learned what it was to love unconditionally.

The train approaches, gliding on three rails, the electrified third supplying power to the locomotive. Touch the third rail, and you cook. Signs warn of this in English and Spanish, alerting travelers and vagrants alike.

The train pulls into the stop, an automated yet polite voice alerting commuters who may have been confused, that this stop is, indeed, Addison. "This is a Red Line train to the Loop."

One by one, the passenger cars noisily pass Peter, the rising sun reflecting off the windows. Despite the glare, he can tell that this morning, like most, the train is nearly full.

The train halts, and Peter makes his way to the door of the lead car. Before entering, he notices four or five people lying across seats, forcing fellow passengers to stand. Peter approaches the door, but stops in his tracks. He's assaulted by a horrible smell clearly emanating from the car.

The homeless, he thinks, wincing.

He threads his way back through the throng, his briefcase angled to open a path before him. He makes his way back to the centerline of the platform, and jogs to the car directly aft. He squeezes on just as the doors slide shut.

"Excuse me," he says, moving past the passengers blocking the doors. This is Peter's pet peeve: ignorant passengers who fail to clear the car's entrance, prohibiting others from coming and going, especially when there's plenty of room in the center.

Peter starts towards the car's front. "Pardon me," he begs again, slipping between businessmen and students. He is awkward with his bag and his heavy jacket, and he breaks a sweat as he approaches the emergency door. Fortunately, the area is clear. Peter leans thankfully against the door, his lower back resting against the horizontal handle.

True to routine, he drops his briefcase to his feet and sinks both into his copy of the Tribune and anonymity.

"Next stop, Belmont," a disembodied recording announces. "Doors open on the right in the direction of travel."

Peter loosens his tie, the brown and gray stripes wrinkling. He runs his sleeve across his forehead. Since work began to repair the tracks and replace the train stations on the line, the commute has become even more unbearable.

At Belmont, passengers impede each other's progress off and on the train.

An elderly woman presses against Peter apologetically, and he looks with disdain at a seated teen who fails to offer his chair. The teen does not make eye contact with her or Peter. He's withdrawn into the world of his gaming system.

The future of America, Peter thinks gloomily. The train proceeds.

"I love that I can just, you know, veg out with him, you know?" a young woman brays into a cell phone. "It's just so nice to not have to say anything. We can just be quiet and not have to think, you know? We don't even have to talk. Hello? Can you hear me?"

Peter considers telling this twenty-something to use her "inside voice." But his way is to avoid public attention. So he keeps to himself, knowing that the tunnel, the subway, will soon silence her phone. But not soon enough.

"Hello?" she bellows. "Oh my God, I thought I had lost you!"

"Fullerton," the mechanized voice announces. "Change for the purple and brown line trains at Fullerton. Doors closing."

Peter turns to page five, an article about a prison riot in Mississippi orchestrated by some nut job named Ira Ridge. The prisoners have control of a cell block. It's day three, and negotiations have broken down. The warden and several guards are feared dead . . .

Then he hears it: something like a muffled scream over the clickity-clack din of the wheels grinding against ancient rails. He surveys the cabin.

No one returns his gaze. They are all like him, eyes down, their heads plugged with ear buds, totally ignorant of each other's existence. No one stirs.

Perhaps, Peter thinks, *a squeaky brake-pad*. He starts to read his newspaper again.

A muted male voice cries again. "Help." It's unmistakable.

Peter snaps to attention, dropping the Trib to his side. Still the other passengers do not move.

Then the pounding starts . . .

. . . from behind him.

Peter whips about and stares out the rectangular window of the emergency exit. About two feet separate his car from the lead. A narrow catwalk guarded by ropes of thick chain forms a causeway. During a crisis, passengers should use the emergency doors to move forward from car to car until able to safely disembark.

The sun's shimmer on the window bounces his image back. He looks intently for several seconds, trying to identify the source of the noise. A flicker of a shadow skips across the window as the train passes a tree, briefly allowing Peter to peer into the illuminated cabin.

There is movement.

Lots of movement.

Peter's face moves in, closer to the window. He cups a hand over his brow, almost presses his nose against the glass.

Again, just his mirror image, perhaps a shadow on the other side of the reflective pane.

Then, another flicker, silhouettes of a number of people, bodies all seemingly crowding into the rear of the passenger car. They are trying to push past each other toward the exit, toward Peter.

The scene is wiped away by the sun again. The effect is like a strobe light, the view outside Peter's window rapidly alternating between a stark reflection and a panorama of commuters. They seem to move in slow motion as they struggle.

Peter feels G-forces press him against the door. The train starts a gradual dive, a twenty-degree descent that takes it into the subway's mouth.

The stifled screaming of one voice becomes several, the pounding of fists more intense.

As the train dips into the darkness, the light of day disappears.

"What the . . ." Peter mouths as he peers into the forward car.

The forward cabin is fully illuminated, but his view is obscured by hands and faces pushed against the window.

They're trying to get out, Peter realizes.

He sees their desperation. They can't escape because they are pressed against the door and the door opens in. Is there a fire? They are either going to die under their own weight or burn to death!

And then the blood.

Not a trickle.

Not a smatter.

A shower . . . a fountain.

The window goes red, opaque, except for the streaks of fists pounding on the glass.

He thinks he sees someone—one of the homeless?—biting . . .

Peter gulps hard.

...biting into the face of a middle-aged man. The man flails his arms and screams, his hands striking the window casing. The homeless man pulls him down to the floor.

Peter's mouth goes agape, his eyes wide. There's no fire. This is something worse.

He spins, finds his fellow passengers sedate. They don't know, so he tells them, "There's a problem in the next car!"

Seated and standing alike, the passengers stare at him with contempt. How dare this lunatic interrupt the isolation of their morning commute?

The intercom breaks in. It is not the pleasant sounding recording. It is the voice of the conductor, full of desperation. "Passengers, there's trouble in the front car!" He breathes heavily over the intercom as if he's winded.

Now the passengers in Peter's car start to look worried, and they all try to look past him trying to determine just what he knows.

A man with dark, slicked-back hair removes an ear bud. "What did he say?"

Peter does not have time to answer. The conductor's plaintive shriek cracks over the intercom, and the train lurches forward. The passengers yelp as they're tossed backwards. Peter bounces like popcorn, goes to his hands and knees. He's lucky. The man with the slick hair catapults deep into the car. He lands somewhere twenty feet or more back, legs kicking in the air. Others are knocked out of their seats or into the laps of fellow passengers. They are a jar of shaken beetles, appendages tangled, wrestling with one another to get free.

The train whirs. It is speeding up, building momentum. As it races forward, it rocks to and fro violently. The lights flash, the train losing and then gaining contact with the electrified third rail.

Train stations fly past. North Avenue. Clark and Division.

We are going to crash, Peter thinks.

He crawls back toward the front of the car and pulls himself halfway under a seat. He wraps his arm at the elbow around the supports.

Grand Street Station. "This is Grand," the automated voice coos. Really?

And a moment later, the locomotive does just what Peter predicted. It strikes the caboose of the train just leaving Grand Street Station.

The collision lasts less than a full second. But to those there, it happens in slow motion, edited like an action sequence in a Will Smith movie. The events could be dissected, specifically:

The front of the train implodes, aluminum flowering at the impact site.

In a chain reaction, the second car, Peter's car, collides with the first, the former popping off the rails to the left and striking a subterranean wall, windows exploding;

The rear of the second car spins to the right, angling upward, the third car slamming it, pushing it over the platform's edge, throwing sparks, and scattering commuters like dandelion seeds in a strong wind;

The third car burrows beneath the second, driving the latter into the ceiling, mortar and rebar raining down; and

The fourth, fifth, and sixth cars pancake, bending and twisting like molten toothpaste, sealing off the northern portion of the tube.

❖❖❖

PETER slowly comes to. He sits up against the end of the car, shards of glass rolling down the front of his shirt. His ears ring, just as they had done when he was a teen shooting his twenty-gauge on his grandfather's farm in Kentucky. He smells the ozone of an electrical fire, and he struggles to see through the midst of smoke that quickly fills the car.

The car sits on a 35-degree angle. No one moves. Despite some distant crying and weak groans for help, no one really makes a sound. A small fire erupts in the rear.

Peter tries to stand, falters, catches himself. He winces and raises a hand to his crown. It feels wet, stings at his touch. *Subdural hematoma,* he thinks.

He reaches forward for a handgrip, white-hot pain shooting up the inside of his left arm. His teeth clench. Muscle tear, he reasons. He squeezes his arm at his elbow, pulling it to his waist.

He hobbles toward the center of the cabin, the main entry, until—

He remembers the face of a man . . . before it was ripped from his skull.

Peter stops dead in his tracks and glances over his shoulder toward the emergency exit.

There's a fire inside that car, too, yet larger, and growing out of control. Dark shadows bounce in the red and orange light, lurching across a canvas of sprayed blood and fractured glass. Their heads move in violent nodding motions, their hands jerking wildly about their faces.

Peter freezes.

My God. They are eating, tugging, and pulling at . . . each other.

He takes a step back, bile rising in his throat.

That's when one of them hesitates. He diverts his attention to Peter, focusing on him, turning his head slightly like a dog in thought. Then he growls and rushes the emergency exit.

"Fuck!" Peter exclaims, the crazed man banging on the exit.

The man hits the door with force, pressing his face against the window and twisting from side to side for a better view of Peter. The man snarls, blood flowing from his lips, and he charges the glass of the exit with his shoulder.

Spider web cracks appear, expanding as the man hurtles at it again and again. That psycho is going to break his skull wide open!

Peter sets off towards the main exit again and hesitates. There are more of them, more of them feeding on the commuters. If he runs from the car, they'll be on the platform—and him—in seconds.

So he races the other direction, quickly diving to his left and out a broken window.

Chapter Eleven:
A Bottled Message

THE page runs up the stairs, tripping over his billowing robe as he goes. He slips down three stairs and bangs his shin. He cringes as the pain shoots up his leg. He crumbles the paper in his hand and finds the strength to lift himself. Then he's running again. He has news, and his news has too much weight for him to give in to the throbbing.

He knows, too, that this pain is nothing compared to the hurt Statten will inflict if he fails to deliver this message in a timely manner.

He takes the stairs two at a time.

When he gets to the top of the flight, he's nearly out of breath. He knocks on the large oak doors, holds his knees, and waits for an invitation.

"Come in," an annoyed voice moans.

The door creaks as the page enters, echoing Statten's groan. The page breathes hard. He can't yet bring himself to speak.

Statten doesn't look up. He is signing documents, passing them left to right. He adjusts his glasses as he reads another parchment. He blows, annoyed. "What? Out with it already."

"We've lost a plane," the page says. "Flight 183 to Padre Island."

Statten holds his petite hand out. "Let me see the manifest," he snaps. "Now!"

The page watches Statten read the creased sheet. Statten glowers as he draws a finger down the registry. Mostly nobodies. Except there, Richard King. Richard King will be missed. He was good at providing information about the comings and goings of the flock.

And there, Doctor Heston. His mouth twists. The people, more than Statten, will miss Heston. There was just something about him, though, that Statten didn't trust. Perhaps too much free will.

He continues through the manifest until . . . his finger stops on a name.

Statten's eyes thin, then widen, a glow rising in them slowly like a newly lit candle. His cheeks plump as the edges of his mouth turn up, revealing a ravenous-looking set of teeth.

The page thinks Statten looks like some villain from an old black and white film. All Statten needs to do is twist an imaginary mustache or ring his hands maniacally to complete the picture.

But this film isn't so silent. Statten laughs. No, he actually cackles as he jabs the sheet with a single gaunt finger. His finger punches one name again and again and again.

Van Gerome. Van Gerome. Van Gerome.

"Should we contact his father?" the page asks.

Statten looks up, startled. He realizes with horror he's been saying Van's name aloud. Over and over and over. All he can muster is a stunned, "What?"

"Should I contact the bishop in Cincinnati? Should we send a team out to locate Roger Gerome?"

"No, no, no, no, no . . . " Statten tut-tuts. The bishop is too busy blessing the new recruits. He's likely on the front. And there's definitely no reason to bother Roger Gerome. He's in the field doing God's work. What could be more important? Nothing.

Not even Roger Gerome's son. Especially not his son.

❖❖❖

ROGER Gerome's team moves north quietly. They do not drive tanks, or troop carriers or humvees. They use none of the heavy equipment from Fort Knox. Those machines are best suited to the front.

Instead, they bike.

Bicycles give Gerome the element of surprise. They cover miles in near silence. Plus, there are no guarantees of fuel, let alone tools and parts, should a truck break down on the road. Vehicles would require drivers and mechanics, and Gerome wants to drag as few personnel as possible into the wilderness.

The same rules don't apply once they've completed their mission and are ready to return home. Then, fully loaded with their booty, they hotwire an old UPS or Fed Ex truck, hightailing it back.

They spend nine months of the year on the move like this. The other three months they spend training. It is arduous work. It is unrewarding work. But it is work beyond the prying eyes of the church. That's good enough for Gerome.

North.

They find mostly death on the road north.

Death and cornfields.

They shoot up I65, stopping short of Indianapolis.

Gerome has learned to stay out of the cities. From there it is straight east toward the setting sun, towards Champaign-Urbana, the home of the University of Illinois and what was once the Fighting Illini.

One day, Gerome thinks, he will head further still, to the real West. He wants to see the Pacific again before he dies. Maybe in just a few years, once Van has served and is able to accompany him. He dreams of camping on the Utah plains, in Yellowstone National Park, and on the beaches of California.

He fantasizes about a father and son finally sharing quality time together.

This is Gerome's first time venturing north beyond Evansville, Indiana, in all the years he's been leading excursions, twelve in all.

Twelve years? Has it been that long? He's almost forgotten who he is, and how it all began . . .

MEDIEVAL.

That's the only way to explain conditions in the first years of the New Order. Gerome and his family lived in a hamlet southwest of Louisville, a farm on the banks of the Ohio River.

With the collapse of, basically, everything, people drew together by the need to share resources. Settlements arose near mills, mines, and farms.

Farming. It's a far cry from what Gerome does now. It's a far cry from what he used to do twenty years ago: information technology at Humana, specifically WAN and LAN support.

The transition from geek to farmhand was difficult. He wasn't used to physical labor. He was soft in the middle . . . too many Krispy Kremes. "Cuddle pudge," his wife, Bethany (nee Allen), used to say on those nights before the plague as they snuggled before a Star Trek movie on the flat screen, their son Van fast asleep in his crib.

Thank God for Bethany and her family. Without the Allens and their farm, he and Van would have been lost at the beginning.

Conditions for farming were less than opportune. Where they could, the Allens and others relied on existing infrastructure. But the worsening winters—a legacy of global warming (and the politicians called it a myth)—took their toll, hastening the disintegration of roads and bridges. The expansion and contraction of water turning to and from ice excavated giant potholes, some large enough to swallow a compact, and splintered wooden planks.

Summers were no better. The intense heat and droughts withered crops and left the fields barren. The survivors borrowed a page from the Aztecs, building vast systems of canals linked to the river. For two years Gerome wielded a shovel instead of a laptop.

Little by little the canals brought water to the fields. Little by little the crops recovered as the river's fingers stroked areas where rain would not. Little by little Gerome's body became lean, shedding flab as his nearly atrophied muscles flexed.

Better times, full of light, seemed ahead, but portents of hard luck lurked in the shadows.

As food became abundant, so did disease.

It started innocently enough.

Settlers used the canals for unintended purposes, like bathing or washing their clothes. Eventually the canals became a reservoir for trash, waste of all types: vegetable, animal, and human.

The river was the lifeblood of the struggling church-state . . . at least, that is, at the beginning of the New Order. But in year six, the Ohio River quietly went bad like some frozen dinner that's lived past its expiration date. There was no outward sign that the river had turned poisonous. The river didn't froth and boil like some witch's brew. It didn't smoke or catch fire. There were no outward signs at all . . . until the people started dying.

First came malaria, literally "bad air" in Latin, a term coined from the smell of stagnant water that accompanied the disease and the swarms of mosquitoes upon which it rode. It decimated but was contained. Defeating malaria proved fairly simple: avoid going out at dusk, keep windows closed, sleep under netting, etc. Worse than malaria was what came next: vibrio cholerae.

Cholera is difficult to hold at bay without water filtration or treatment systems. Because everyone has to drink water, and the river, the main source, the only source for most, was infected with the cholera bacterium.

Vibrio cholerae causes exhaustive diarrhea. It's like the stomach flu . . . times 1,000. Untreated, cholera leads to death more quickly than any other illness known. Bethany Gerome bore witness to this.

Roger Gerome would usually leave to work the fields early while it was still dark, especially in the summer months. Bethany would follow, Van in tow. She liked seeing Roger off. He would always kiss her and pat Van's head as they approached the bridge that served as the gateway to the farm. Then Bethany and Van would drink deeply from the channel while the water was still cool. She would then return to their home and work the farm with her mother until Roger came home.

One morning, her routine changed slightly. She kissed her husband and saw him off and drank from the channel. That morning, she could not convince Van to drink, too. He just wasn't thirsty.

Sixty minutes later Bethany was bent over with horrible cramps. She soiled herself as she fled to the bathroom. Her stool was liquid, changing from brown to pale, something doctors call "rice water." Her blood pressure dropped to hypotensive levels, and she passed out on the bathroom floor.

When she failed to show to feed the hogs, Bethany's mother went searching for her. Instead, she found a crying Van, rocking himself, alone in the family room.

"Mommy's sick," he bawled.

Calls for Bethany went unanswered, as did knocks on the bathroom door. Bethany's father knocked the door in. They found Bethany unresponsive, in shock, her pulse rapid and her nose bleeding. They instantly sent for Roger.

There was no time to call for Doctor Bosco. He was two counties away. It wouldn't have mattered. He would have diagnosed her illness, but he couldn't have treated her. He didn't have Tetracycline or Erythromycin to prescribe. All he could have done is care for her symptoms.

Bethany never woke. She succumbed to the illness the next day. Gerome could not bear to complete the preparations. The settlers took it upon themselves to remove her head for him.

Within a week, half the settlers were suffering. The waterways and the fish were loaded with bacteria. Although few germs survive the acid of the stomach, it doesn't take many to kill the host by attaching to the wall of the small intestine where they start to produce their toxins.

Rains finally broke the draught, washing the disease down stream, and saving the fledgling theocracy. But the church recognized the risks disease posed to their control. So it created an academy, taught by people like Heston, for the purpose of training medical personnel. Their job was not to research or develop new medicines or practices, but to exercise those already known, and approved, by the church.

The church took another step. It asked for emissaries—missionaries and explorers—for the express purpose of locating essentials, like medicines and fuel, in the wilderness. There were just eight volunteers. Each was given a team and allowed to pick twenty persons from a pool of prisoners, conscripts, and non-citizens. Roger was one of the eight.

All eight had different reasons for volunteering. Some volunteered because they had nothing left. Some volunteered for the power. But not Roger. He volunteered out of love.

Roger Gerome vowed never to let another epidemic infect a loved one. He left to find medicine. He left to secure Van's future.

But he stays in the wilds for another reason. He stays because he misses the world he once knew. He stays because he can't stand the regime. Staying in the forbidden zone is the only way for him to maintain some form of freedom.

Gerome knew the wilderness was his destiny the very day he returned from his first mission. From a hundred miles out, he saw the smoke, great pillars of it, turning the sky charcoal grey. As his team approached Louisville and the iron viaduct on I65 spanning the Ohio River, once a welcoming gateway turned into a drawbridge, ash fell on his face.

Oh my God, he thought in horror, *the town is burning.*

He was wrong. The town was not burning. Books were burning. Hundreds of thousands of books collected from every corner of the church state. Pastor Statten was burning books, eradicating knowledge, and eliminating individual thought.

Gerome felt for the hollow of his back where he kept a copy of *Jurassic Park* by Michael Crichton, a faithful companion during the last days of his journey. He pushed it deep into his waistband, hiding it from sight.

No, the town was not burning. The home he knew was burning.

At the start, there were eight volunteers selected to lead. They met their ends through mutiny, insanity, and the walking dead; inner and outer monsters took them all.

All but one.

Today, Roger Gerome is the last of their rank.

Gerome finds it odd that his work, the very work that frees him, actually strengthens the church's stranglehold. It is a incongruity that he has yet to work out.

Chapter Twelve:
Escape

PETER falls fifteen feet and lands on the service walk, just inches from the electrified third rail. He rolls away from it, and certain death, in a panic. Above him, dark figures enter the car. Riders stop moaning and begin to shriek.

He tries to blink the pain away and starts to inch forward on his elbows and knees, squeezing underneath the wreckage of the engineer's car. He feels the heat of the flames lapping at his back. The fire illuminates the walls of the subterranean tunnel, but he focuses beyond that, into the darkness where he will escape.

Then he feels the grip on his shoe, strong like an eagle's talon, catching him just as he clears the hulking knot of burning metal.

The creature approached silently. Shambling and scuttling, it made little more noise than the raking of dry leaves, its advance masked by the crackle and snap of the blaze.

At first Peter thinks he's snagged on a bit of debris. But when he shakes he realizes in horror that his foot will not loose. He flips on his back and sees this monster—and it is a monster, an aberration, for God would surely have mercy on a someone so wickedly torn, so treacherously scarred—and unleashes a furious kick directly into its face.

The ghoul's nose goes with a crunch, its eyes crossing, but just momentarily. It does not retreat. Instead, it speeds its pursuit.

Peter panics, pushes away from the thing, walking crablike. But it is quicker, unaware of the risk and pain, and it grabs hold again, this time of Peter's pants leg, its teeth grating.

Peter lashes out again, dislodging the monster's hold. He looks about for a weapon, anything he can use to attack, to fight. He looks to the right, then above, then to the left . . .

The third rail. It is just below him, below the service way, on the tracks.

He whirls to his belly, using all his strength to jettison from the causeway to the tracks beneath. The thing chases, sensing its prey is cornered in the depths of the pit. It plunges after him.

But the monster is not cognizant of the third rail. It falls upon it.

Blue energy courses through its body, making it shudder

grotesquely. *It's just like the movies*, Peter thinks, *just like in the Lost Boys when a vampire is electrocuted by a sound system.* "Death by stereo," one of the Frogs had said. But then the episode steers away from script, and Peter notices details absent from film. An electric arc shoots from the creature's head, feeling its way spasmodically, searching for a ground. The creature's hair catches fire.

Peter scoots away, starts to run, into the darkness. He does not see—and cares not see—the monster's eyes explode.

He sprints, his breath laboring hard, as he moves south. He considers trying a maintenance stairwell, deciding not to. He wants to get as far as he can from the Hell behind him. He makes his way deeper into the system, passing under the Chicago River, the Chicago Theater, and Macy's—until he sees the light of the Randolph Street station.

He reaches the platform, shocked to find it abandoned. There isn't a soul around. They've evacuated the tube.

Peter knows the pedway like the wrinkles and veins on the back of his hand. But the pedway, a system of tunnels connecting restaurants, shops, businesses, and government offices, is empty.

It is dead.

The fluorescent lights cast a yellow-green glow. It makes him that much more nauseous. Still, he chooses to stay below ground, and he strikes out for City Hall.

Soon he is underneath the Daley Plaza, the Starbuck's and the court information desks vacant. He can hear his own footsteps falling thunderously on the linoleum, echoing throughout the emptiness. He slows, quieting his progress. He almost cries out, almost calls, "Hello? Is there anyone here? Can anyone hear me?"

Then a rattle, somewhere in front of him to the right.

Peter considers stopping. Should he turn back, head toward street level? He reasons it will cost him valuable seconds. Instead he moves quickly to the information booth, where long lines used to form and questions were asked about speeding violations and small claims, and divorce proceedings, and things that will never matter again.

He gently unhooks a red velvet rope from a stanchion. He picks up the copper post. It is heavy at the base. He flips it, holds it with both hands like a club, and goes forward.

The rattle again, but closer. He's nearing it. Then he sees movement.

A bank of phone booths is built into the wall. One of the doors, hinged in the middle, bounces slightly, creating the clatter. Someone is shifting inside it, perhaps someone needing help.

Peter moves quickly to the door. He places the stanchion in his left hand, moving his right to pull the door open. He jerks his hand back suddenly, disgusted, at the realization of what's before him.

There are two people in the booth. One is dead. The other is dead, yet alive, too. She's a ghoul, kneeling before the former, her back to Peter, chewing.

Peter drops the stanchion as he shifts to run. It hits the floor with a piercing clang.

The ghoul twists forcefully, sees Peter, and tries to push its way out of the booth.

To Peter's horror, the door starts to slide open.

It opens an inch . . . then another.

Peter gropes for the post, panicked.

But then . . . a break: the decedent's leg slides, foot and knee now buttressing the doors. The thing cannot open the door further, and it shakes the frame furiously. It gropes at Peter through the gap.

Yes, a very lucky break.

Peter darts toward City Hall.

❖❖❖

ALMOST a thousand miles away, Warden Wayne Shepherd's skull fractures bit by bit. As his braincase bounces off the cement floor of Cell Block B, his mind struggles to come to grips with the events leading to the moment of his impending death.

Shepherd had dealt with prison riots before, and they were as noisy and predictable as the comings and goings of July cicadas.

Uprisings always start the same, the dirty bugs working their way out of the filth of their behavioral sink. The jailhouse lawyers emerge first, preaching about the food, the beatings, the rapes. Buttressed by the insects below them, they shed their fear of the guards like an old skin. They make a lot of noise, beating their tymbals and demanding the attention of the warden or the state board of corrections.

Ignore it as you may, some days the racket gets pretty bad. Some days the noise is loud enough that a good man can barely pray for patience. And some days, it's bad enough that God can't hear that prayer.

Those are the days when Shepherd would lose his cool, crushing exoskeletons under his jackboot. He'd add shifts, bringing on guards from the neighboring county. Then he'd order body bags. His guards would make a few examples of the troublemakers, sending one or two to the hospital, or maybe the morgue. Then the bugs would go silent like some great, stinking die-off. Peace would be his again, at least until the next cycle.

Yes, the raucous lifecycle of these insects was always the same . . . except this time. This time things were different.

THERE were no requests for reform, no complaints. There were no acts of disobedience. There was just a level of escalating panic and violence, starting with some of the Bloods being attacked, bitten, specifically, in the showers. Shepherd blew it off, true to plan, reasoning it was just some kinky fad.

Within a day, though, all out warfare had broken out in the yard. The instigators were obviously hopped up on something, chewing on and tearing at the other inmates. It took the guards several rounds to bring some these crackheads down. Messy fucking business, too, guts and brains and paperwork everywhere.

But the locusts didn't crawl back into their holes. Even Creedy and Chili One Nut, generally smart jailbirds who kept to themselves, raised a ruckus, screaming wide-eyed about the devil and demanding release.

Events went from bad to worse. The guards got jittery. Some of them stopped showing for their shifts. The county couldn't lend him staff. Neither could the National Guard. They were faced with shortages of their own. Everyone was calling in sick.

Shepherd was forced to operate with a skeleton crew. Short-staffed, he ended visiting hours and began sleeping nights in his office. Frustrated friends and family members congregated outside the prison walls.

The prison break came at dawn just three days before. The guards, waiting to be spelled by a morning shift that was long overdue, were exhausted. They were easily overrun. The lucky ones had their throats cut straightaway. Some weren't so lucky. They were carried off into the bowels of the beast, turned into human pin cushions. The prisoners took their keys and the guns and used them to get more keys and guns. They passed through the checkpoints unabated. Not a single alarm sounded.

When Shepherd woke that morning, he immediately knew something was wrong. He checked the video monitors and stared in disbelief. The prisoners were running rampant. They were destroying the facility, fighting each other, beating the guards.

Monitor one: Cell Block A was on fire.

Monitor two: Snow instead of a pan on Cell Block B.

Then Shepherd looked at monitor three. What he saw shocked him to his core: the visitors outside the gates had grown from fifteen to fifty. What's more, they looked like they were...eating each other.

He called for help on the intercom. There was no response. He tried again.

With no food, no water, little sleep, and just a revolver for defense, it's amazing that Shepherd was able to fend off the rioters. Day in and day out, they beat on his metal office door. Finally, though, it came off its hinges, and the prisoners swarmed in.

They seized Shepherd and pulled him screaming down the passage. He clamored weakly for a hold at the passing doorframes. No use. They carried him through the labyrinth to Cell Block B, murderers' row.

They kept him bound and gagged for the better part of a day. That night they delivered Shepherd to Ira Ridge.

Ira Ridge smiled wide. Shepherd despaired. He knew something of Ridge's story. Diminutive, but as dangerous as a scorpion sting, Ridge had killed his wife and her lover. But Ridge's wasn't a crime of passion. It was ruthless, premeditated evil.

Ridge had kept his wife and her lover, a local salesman, gagged and bound in an empty cistern behind an abandoned farmhouse. He had prepared the kill zone with plastic tarps and duct tape, the floors and walls lined.

Ridge then gave his wife's Toyota and her credit cards to his nephew Kenny. The kid had outstanding warrants, and Ridge told him that the police had stopped by, looking for him. "Hightail it to Mexico," Ridge said. And Kenny had.

Ridge had gone to the police 24 hours later, a forged Dear John letter in hand. She was leaving him, it said, going to Acapulco to be with the love of her life. The police assumed the lovers had run off, and they verified their steady progress to Mexico using his wife's credit card trail. While the cops hunted in vain for the couple, Ridge began the ugly business of punishing them, as the court records later indicated, "for violating an oath to God."

Ira Ridge had butchered them, filleting them piece-by-piece. A pile of flesh—fingers, toes, and ears—had grown in the corner. Ridge took his pound, then another, then more. All the while he was sure to leave their eyes intact so that they could watch each other slowly disappear.

Eventually, though, the mound of decay had drawn a pack a feral dogs. Officials from Animal Control discovered the grizzly remains of Ms. Ridge and her unfortunate lover a full three months after they went missing.

Shepherd may have mumbled something to Ridge, cried for his life in vain, as the inmates held him down. He can't remember. Bits of his memory fragmented and melted away like shards of a broken ice.

Ridge sauntered forward, reptilian, beaming. He said nothing as he straddled Shepherd's chest, the warden's arms still held taut. Ridge took the warden's skull in his hands, almost gingerly, at first. "Praise be to God. Hallelujah." With that, he slammed Shepherd's head against the concrete. Hallelujah. Bang. Hallelujah. Bang. Hallelujah! Bang! HALLELUJAH! BANG!

TEN minutes of praise later, Shepherd's brain is soup. Images and sounds are a blur. He thinks he sees another prisoner, a farmer named Connor, tackling a grimacing Ridge just as everything eternally and mercifully goes dark.

Chapter Thirteen:

Footprints and the Prince of Darkness

MORNING comes. Burt is sullen. He shambles about, eyes downcast. He knows he's never going to find Spiderman 129. He's never going to trade it for the Superman 10. He wonders how he would have fared if he had stayed back at the plane.

Ian feels like young adults his age do: somewhat remorseful, but mostly absolute in his position that they really did nothing wrong the night before. Ian has yet to learn to value of diplomacy, and his nonchalance is the result of a still-developing ego more likely to burn bridges than to build them. Saving face is a kid's game, but it is one he will continue to play until he learns better.

Besides, Ian has other concerns. He's taking lead again.

He's a bit surprised. He thinks Wright overheard him complaining to Van, "It's an exercise in futility." Hour upon hour of staring at trees, brush, and other flora. Hour upon hour trying to perceive something beyond the foliage, trying to penetrate their veil, to no avail.

But Wright wants to talk to Dr. Heston. She'll work on breaking down his defenses just a little more today.

❖ ❖ ❖

THE revenants can be found anywhere. They can be found at anytime. But they generally stay hidden in the shadows or under the cloak of night. This has been Wright's experience and that of others as well. Perhaps they are nocturnal. Has Heston ever heard of anything like that?

He has. Parasites not only influence the "how" of transmission, but the "when."

There's a fluke that is not satisfied with leaving reproduction to chance, so it makes its own luck. It lays eggs in the intestine of a cow, and the eggs are expelled in the manure. Snails eat the fluke eggs in manure, and the fluke hatches in the snail's gut. It escapes, covered in snail slime, a delicacy to ants. Once inside an ant, the fluke works its mojo by attacking the nervous system near the mandibles. It takes control of the brain, driving the ant to leave its colony as night falls. The ant climbs a single blade of grass, securing itself to the tip with its jaws. There it waits for a cow to eat the grass. Once devoured the fluke explodes forth. The circle of life begins again.

Night offers the lancet fluke the best chance for survival. If it remains in the midday heat, it will burn.

Another example: spores from a certain fungus infect a fly, sending tendrils deep into the insect's body. The fungus ravages the fly for several days, reproducing in the fly's stomach. It, too, takes over the brain, forcing the fly to attach itself to a high place at sunset. There it will die. At dusk when other flies are resting, the fungus erupts from the dead fly. Tendrils spout spores and shower the sleeping flies below. Sunset is the perfect time, the only time, for the fungus to infect other flies. The air is cool and moist just before nightfall, maximizing the likelihood of infecting other insects.

Wright scratches her head. The answer to "how?" begs the question "why?" Why create monsters that are largely nocturnal?

If forced to speculate, Heston would argue that nighttime conveys advantages to the parasite: under the cloak of night, victims are much more likely to be taken by surprise, thereby allowing further proliferation; also, the decay of the human body may be somewhat stayed by avoiding direct sunlight, humidity, and intense heat.

Fascinating, Wright thinks.

But for Heston, it is "quid pro quo" time, time to settle up accounts. Heston has a question in kind: just why is Wright so curious about all this?

The answer's not that simple, largely because Wright hasn't given it much thought. The answer might lie in her interests. She's always been inquisitive, she's always wanted to know just how things work. Her favorite class was high school biology. She excelled at it, as well as chemistry and physics. She planned on a science-based major in college—that is, until the curriculum was deemed sacrilegious and eviscerated by the church.

But a truer answer is this: there is a problem needing a solution. Something that needs to be worked out. Another mission she can perform. Another distraction.

If personal satisfaction could be measured metaphorically, if love, family, friends, and happiness could be represented by cathedrals, homes, parks, and monuments, Wright's heart would be a vacant lot.

Worse, construction is all but prohibited there because of a giant sink-hole that she is incapable of filling.

So she creates mission after mission for herself, hoping one day to fill the chasm.

If you can't fix yourself, fix the world.

She doesn't explain any of this to Heston.

There's a commotion. She hears Ian and Van shouting.

IT is a chilly and dark during the early hours of morning. Professor Tiehl walks the quad. He walks it every day on his way to Gregory Hall, to his class, Political Science 215: Arms Control and Security. But he has no real recollection of this course, his syllabus addressing nuclear non-proliferation and terrorism, or his role in academia. He doesn't even remember his students' names. He's just cognizant of their faces. He thinks about them . . . and he feels a voracious hunger swelling inside him. He hurries towards his classroom where he hopes they wait.

It's like that every day for Tiehl. He rambles to class before the sun rises and returns home after dusk. The sun is missing in his life. Gone, too, is the sing-song of the birds and the chirping of the quad squirrels. Those that survived left long ago.

Tiehl is virtually animatronic, his day pre-programmed like a pirate on the Caribbean Disney ride. His reality mimics the motions of a pendulum, swinging from work to home, always scanning for an elusive meal.

In life, Professor Tiehl was a creature of habit. Now he is more or less just a creature. One of the thousands that wander about oblivious to the campus crumbling around them and their own slow disintegration.

Gerome watches Professor Tiehl. He hides amid the rows of corn of the U of I's Morrow Plots, the oldest experimental agricultural field in the United States. Gerome doesn't wonder much about Tiehl, who lurches like a drunk past Foellinger Hall. He doesn't question who this man was. All he needs to know is what he *is*.

The telltale signs are all there. The shambling gate. The broken and sharp teeth. The dried and sunken skin. The shriveled ears, left pointed and bat-like as the cartilage gave way to time.

Gerome will return to his team's position in the Arboretum. They will come back when the sun is at its highest. First they will hit the Medical Center. There they will collect drugs of all types. After, they'll turn south to the Round Barns in hopes of finding animal steroids and med-ication.

Then, if time permits, they will visit Noyes Lab and the Chem Annex, the chemistry labs, to collect equipment, illegal tools like elec-tron microscopes, journals, and Bunsen burners, to their secret home.

When Gerome arrives at the Arboretum, he is greeted by his first in command. He has news. Maybe good news. One of the men has spotted smoke, plumes billowing from somewhere north, perhaps twenty or thirty miles from their position.

Gerome's heart leaps.

It always does when he finds survivors.

❖❖❖

IAN walks the dry creek bed, squinting against a low sun. It is an over-ripe orange, pulled low on the branch by frost, signaling the coming winter.

The foliage is turning. It becomes more and more perceptible as they move north. Ian gawks at what can only be called majesty: a clus-ter of dogwoods, leaves afire, fooled by unseasonably cool weather. But the fall colors, as beautiful as they are, herald loss. Ian is troubled by a suspicion. He is as entranced by the coming death as by the natural beauty laid bare before him.

Before him . . . a footprint.

Long, thin, and frozen in time by the baked sediment, at least until the next rain fills the stream, which will erase it like a natural Etch-n-Sketch.

Ian halts. He raises an arm, signaling those behind him. As trained, the trekkers drop to the ground scattering like a nest of bunnies into the wild. There they will stay until beckoned from their hiding places by Wright's all clear sign, the approximation of a sparrow call.

All of them, that is, except Van. Van is already jogging to Ian's po-sition. He wants to know what the fuss is about.

His partner, Anne, stands her ground twenty yards back caught in a state of indecision. She watches Van abandon her. Her head and torso point toward him, but her lower body turns as if to flee into a neigh-boring bush. She bites her lip anxiously, her eyes ping-ponging from Van to the safety of the leaves. Van. Bush. Van. Bush.

Ian's perturbed. He wonders aloud what Van is doing, why he has-n't taken cover. Ian's on point after all.

Van chuckles. Ian has got to be kidding. This is their first bit of action in days. Van cannot be dissuaded, despite Ian's pleas. "Come on, what did you see?" he asks.

Ian hushes him, angles his head from side to side. No monsters, but he does see Anne anchored in plain sight. "Van, you left that poor girl by herself?"

Van shuffles. It's not like she's his girlfriend. Anyway, she's fine.

Fine? Anne's stance is shaky, like a newborn deer finding its legs. She's scared shitless. She pees herself.

Van grunts. "Well, almost fine, unless you've seen something that will change all of that."

Ian gives up. "Okay. You win." He points at the footprint less than a yard away.

Van draws near, feigning a studiousness that got him through his coursework for years. "Feetprints," he says.

Ian sees the other prints now. Left after right, they careen drunkenly across the basin. Sometimes a print disappears where the earth had been too dry or too shallow to cast a relief, only to reappear like an apparition further away. He whispers, "Footprints."

"*Feet*prints," Van emphasizes. "If they were made by a single foot, like, hopping, they would be *foot*prints. But there are prints from two *feet*, so they are *feet*prints. There's a left one. Then a right one. And a left. Right. Left. Right—"

Enough, Ian gets it.

Van says, "Okay." Then he asks with the gravity of a surgeon asking for a colleague's concurrence, "So you agree that they're feetprints?"

"They are not feetprints. Each print is of a singular foot, thus, *foot*prints." Ian cannot believe he has allowed Van yet again to embroil him in a pointless and witless exercise.

Van says to trust him. He was, after all, a boy scout, trained to recognize and name various animal prints.

Ian looks at Van in amazement and comments on his friend's revisionist history. "You were not a boy scout. You were a cub scout, and a shitty one at that. You never made it past bobcat."

Van winces, the pain of one of his earliest failures visiting home.

There's more. "And you are anything but an expert on the English language and punctuation." Van used to read sentences aloud, imitating Christopher Walken's cadence, in an effort to correctly place commas.

Van defends "the Walken Method"—yes, he actually has a name for it—as being infallible.

"Really?" Ian asks. "Since when does a comma follow a preposition?"

"Since motherfucking *Deerhunter*," Van says.

❖ ❖ ❖

WRIGHT crosses the creek bed, a stalking tiger, nearing the bickering kids. She stops to help an immobile Anne. Anne's teeth are rigid and her legs, quaking. Wright coos, takes Anne's hand, and draws her to the shade of an oak. "Rest here," Wright says, to a staring and irresolute Anne. "I'll be right back. I promise."

Ian and Van argue raucously, their position exposed in the sun to anyone, or anything, within a hundred yards. Wright hears Ian say something, something about conjugating sentences and the *King of New York*.

"What the hell is going on?" Wright demands. Her eyes hint at fury.

Ian saw that look before, miles and days ago, back on the plane. He'd hoped he'd never see it again.

"Well?" she commands.

"Footprints," Ian blurts, pointing.

"Feetprints," Van mumbles.

She sees them and her rage begins to dissipate. She kneels in the dried clay and examines the prints. Her fingers probe the outline of foot—the right one—tracing the outline and the rise of the arch. One of them. Maybe a week or so ago, after the last storm, the storm that dumped them in the wilderness.

How does she know?

She can't know for sure, but there are good indications:

The path. It starts behind them, dropping from a high shoal. A person, a living person, would find the path of least resistance. A living person would walk ten feet to a shallower area. This thing just went over the edge. Then its tracks meander. Not aimlessly, so to speak, but without control.

"Like my aunt after the Kentucky Derby," Van jokes.

He's greeted by silence.

"She just likes her mint juleps."

Wright sighs heavily, but makes an attempt to bridge the divide. The condition may affect motor skills like alcohol, but loss of coordination could stem from deterioration, the rot of nerves and tissue.

Ian doesn't want to believe the monsters are here. Isn't another explanation possible? Maybe the prints are those of someone extremely weak? Or dehydrated? Maybe someone hurt himself or herself coming over the ridge?

"Not likely." Wright explains. Severe thirst might make someone delusional, perhaps even enough to walk around without shoes and make a jump from a small cliff. But there's more to it. Wright's hand hovers above the track, above the heel, making little circles. "That's an imprint of bone. There's no flesh on the heel of the foot."

Van is nervous. "The funny thing about mint juleps is . . . they taste horrible. The name implies refreshment, but they are anything but. Nothing more than bourbon with a garnish. It may as well be parsley—"

"Van, shut up," Wright interrupts. "I think it best that we keep this between us for now." And then she adds, "Boys."

Again with the "Boys?" It cuts Ian to the quick. Sure, he's not her equal, but a boy? Van, maybe. But Ian is more than a kid.

Wright sees Ian's consternation, mistakes it for fear. *Good*, she thinks. He should be fearful. Her satisfaction, though, is hollow. It is tempered by an urge, an ache, a compulsion to somehow reassure him. Maybe she'll relieve him of point tomorrow.

She orders Van to kick dust over the prints. "There's no need for anyone to worry about this now. Let's move."

Just footprints, Wright thinks, *probably a week old, heading on a diverging angle. Everything is fine.*

No. Certainty is a death sentence.

Wright decides to march them another dozen miles. She doesn't want to face Heston or the questions he will ask. So, she pairs with Burt. The Hestons can accompany each other, at least until Wright needs more answers.

❖ ❖ ❖

THIRTY minutes pass, Burt and Wright nary sharing a word. But Burt has theories of his own, and he can't help but cut the silence to disclose them.

"Have you ever seen a vampire movie?" Burt asks sheepishly, almost as if he's walking by himself.

Wright cleans the barrel of her pistol. She does this effortlessly while walking, while still scanning the tree line. She's done it a dozen times since the crash. You can never be prepared enough.

She reminisces about watching the Son of Svengoolie with her father Saturday afternoons. One scene sticks in her head: some actor fending off a vampire, maybe Christopher Lee, with a couple of candlesticks held to form a rudimentary cross.

"Sure," she says.

Burt steels himself for his next query. "Did you ever wonder," he gulps, "if there's any truth to the vampire mythos?"

The vampire mythos? Wright guffaws. "Like Dracula?"

"No," Burt replies, gruffly. Dracula, or Vlad Drakul, was as much a vampire as Princess Diana. Bram Stoker ruined a man and his Romanian heritage like some paparazzo. Imagine how all of England would have reacted if Stephen King had accused the Princess of lycanthropy.

"Like George Hamilton, then?" Wright jokes, eyes still on the landscape.

Burt thinks her question is a serious one. "True," he says, "George Hamilton played Dracula. But Dracula, again, was not a vampire. And vampires definitely aren't tan. There is something, though, in his portrayal, like Bela Lugosi's, like Gary Oldham's, even like the guy who played Blackula, loosely based on folklore."

Wright holds the barrel of her pistol to her eye, inspects it against the dying light. She is losing patience. "Your point?"

She's subtle, Burt muses wryly, like the Incredible Hulk at a tea party. Myths generally arise from a need, a need to explain something that can't be clarified, either through experience or science. "Maybe the vampire myth just served to explain something that people were witnessing."

Wright is clearly annoyed. "Do you think people witnessed some guy turn into a bat?"

"No, I'm not talking about bats. Vampire bats don't even come from Europe. That's just another myth created by—" But Burt digresses. "What I'm really talking about is the formation of a core belief of corpses returning to prey on the living . . . and consume them."

"Mythology, Burt," Wright shakes her head. "You just said it yourself: vampires are a myth. All myths can be explained away by good science. Example: the Cyclops, not a giant with a single eye, but an elephant skull discovered by the early Greeks mistaking the enlarged sinus cavity for an eye socket. Witness the creation of a fiction."

"Granted, but I'm talking about vampires."

He's right. Best to stick to one supernatural beast at a time. "Have you ever heard of rabies?" Wright asks.

"It's like distemper, right?"

"Kind of," Wright says, remembering her conversation with Dr. Heston. "But it presents . . . uniquely." Does Burt recognize the symptoms of those infected? The face and body contorting, animal-like; the violent behavior, especially the biting; the pain caused by intense sensations, like direct sunlight; the nausea induced by strong odors, like garlic. "Sound familiar?"

So she does know vampire mythology. "Yes," Burt allows. But can she explain away other bits, like escaping their graves to feed on their victims' blood?

"Poe," Wright says. Edgar Allan Poe, author of "The Raven," "The Telltale Heart," and "The Premature Burial." It is this last story that offers clues.

In it, a man suffers from catalepsy, a disorder that suspends animation, often mistaken for death. In the 19th century, embalming had yet to come into existence. So they would hold wakes, staying up, hoping death was temporary. Still, an occasional coma victim would wake, finding himself buried alive, tearing himself apart to escape the grave.

Burt offers another argument, "What about the bodies being disinterred? What about what they found?"

Wright doesn't question there's evidence, archaeological and historical, that people dug up suspected vampires. But their descriptions, horrifying enough to spark an epidemic, also accurately depict the natural process of decay.

Villagers exhumed a body, found fresh blood dribbling from the mouth and assumed the cadaver had recently feasted. But corpses liquefy, swelling as they decompose. Blood naturally bubbles, escaping from the mouth. The abdomen bloats, too, leading one to suspect the belly is full of flesh and blood. Couple all this with the homeless who took shelter in tombs, coming and going by night, Wrights says, " . . . and you have a legend."

Burt shrugs. "Still . . . "

"Still what?" Wright demands.

"Still," Burt continues, "it seems these monsters"—he fans an arm around his head, indicating the space surrounding them—" easily could have been mistaken for vampires by peasants in the 17th and 18th centuries."

Wright raises a brow. "Just what are you getting at?"

"What if this has happened before?" Burt posits. "You know, but on a limited scale?"

Wright scoffs. Is Burt actually suggesting a historical precedent for this plague? Ridiculous.

"Why?" Burt poses. He challenges Wright: Compare the similarities between these creatures and the vampires of folklore. Not the Hollywood Dracula crap, but the certified dead rising and killing, communicability through a bite, and their manner of destruction: fire and decapitation.

"But vampires are killed by wooden stakes," Wright states. "These are not."

Burt shakes his head. Vampires are only killed by stakes in "Buffy, the Vampire Slayer" and in other fictions. They were not killed that way in folklore. In European tradition, vampires were pierced, held fast to the ground by a wooden stake, sometimes of ash, pounded through their chests. The stake only prevented them from moving. They still had to be decapitated or burned. Either method sufficiently destroys, or at least inhibits communication, with the brain. "Maybe," Burt continues, nodding at Wright's handgun, "even better than that thing."

Wright can't believe they're having this discussion. The whole concept is insane. She says so. Then she tells Burt to shut up.

They walk the remaining miles in silence.

Then they set up camp.

❖❖❖

CITY Hall. The building houses both the city and county governments, although some dispute whether the latter qualifies. Usually the Hall is noisy with activity, the voices of aldermen, lobbyists, and protesters, stirring together into a blur. Nothing here is pure. Laws and policy are watered down, adulterated by anyone whose voice rises above the clamor.

But as Peter surfaces on the escalator, the Hall is quiet. *I need to get to the street*, he thinks.

As he exits a revolving glass door, the noise returns in a rush. Sirens, klaxons, alarms, all signaling emergencies, all competing for attention. But which is more important? The ambulance taking the secretary dying from a torn jugular—torn by the teeth of a bike messenger she greets every morning—to Rush's emergency ward? The black and white cruiser crawling through stacked traffic, unclear as to where to start to address the spreading chaos? The firefighters elbowing their way through the crowd, moving like salmon upstream, going who knows where?

This is not how emergency response is meant to work. This is not how Homeland Security, nor FEMA, nor the CDC intended it.

Peter has taken the courses, trained at the Center for Domestic Preparedness, readied to assume a supervisory role in an event or incident. But it doesn't take a mathematician to see things are out of hand and growing exponentially. There's no established incident command, no objectives, no plan.

Peter has a choice.

He chooses to go home to his family.

There is no shame in that. This is a free-for-all.

He grabs a bicycle, the one abandoned by the messenger, and makes his way north.

Chapter Fourteen:
Run for Your Life

FOUR hours into their morning push, and Van is not happy.

He does not like being alone, being on point. He'd rather be talking to Anne. Instead, she is talking to Ian twenty paces back.

Van hears her laugh lightly. Then he hears her ask Ian, "What's your sign?"

Ian doesn't know.

"When were you born?"

Ian answers.

"Oh, you're a Leo!" she says enthusiastically. "You're a natural born leader."

Van watches and listens, feeling the jealously building.

Twenty minutes later, it has all gone to shit.

They are fleeing, running for their lives.

"There's a house," Ian screams, and what's left of the group sprints hard.

Ian is first up the steps to the door. It's cracked open, and pops wide as Ian strikes it with his shoulder. He goes down, sliding across the floor, into the staircase opposite the entrance. He's up quickly, calling to others to move fast. "Don't look back!"

Anne follows, screaming.

Then Burt.

Jessica.

Van.

Last is Wright. She has to make up distance fast. She's in, and she shouts at Ian to shut the door. He slams it hard, lopping off the fingers of a trailing monster. They fly in all directions, and Anne cries out again.

Ian leans against the door, low and panting hard. Burt straddles him, his weight distributed high. A fingerless fist demands entry, pounding against the rotting wood.

"Where the hell did it come from?" Ian demands of a frozen Van, his eyes daggers.

Anne whimpers uncontrollably into Jessica's bosom.

Wright steps forward, allowing a slinking Van to find cover behind her. "Ian, we'll get to that later." What matters now is that he holds the door. She orders Van to assist.

Van hesitates. She grabs him by the shoulder and pushes him to Burt's side.

Wright mutters something about securing the place, then dashes deeper into the home.

The hammering continues, Van wincing with each thud against his shoulder. Ian leers at him, his eyes barely slits. Van sees the anger and responds, "I just . . . just didn't see them."

That's no excuse, Ian retorts. "Save it for the Hestons. They should be along shortly."

"My Lord," Burt exclaims, considering that the remains of the Hestons could already be slithering their way to the doorstep. The door bucks, and he leans harder into it. "Hold tight!"

"Man, fuck this!" Van exclaims. He starts to sob.

"Fuck you!" Ian lashes out. "Here's a suggestion—" Sometimes the difference between a suggestion and criticism is subtle. Sometimes it is not. "—Next time you're on point, try not to let any of us get eaten."

Van responds in kind to the criticism. "Fuck you, Ian."

Fuck me? Ian's engulfed in rage. He turns to Anne, back still pressed against the door. "You know," he says to the terrified girl, "I used to think Van could only muster 'fuck this' or 'fuck that' because he had too many thoughts to manage in his head. 'Fuck it' was just easier. But I was wrong, because the truth is that Van doesn't care about anything. He doesn't care about you, Anne. He doesn't care about you, me..." Ian laughs shrilly, a man losing control, " . . . God, he doesn't even care about himself."

Ian strikes a nerve. Van twitches, almost imperceptibly, but enough for Ian to take satisfaction.

Wright's return interrupts the bickering. Her return surprises the girls, and they squeal. "It's all right, girls," Wright soothes, petting their heads. "It's going to be fine." "That's how they initially got in," she says, pointing to the door. She eyes the men. The rest of this floor looks secure. She's going to look around for something to use to seal the door.

"Why don't you just shoot them!" Van cries, plaintively.

"Because she can't," Ian answers. "The gunshots will attract more of those things."

True, Wright thinks. Plus, she needs to conserve the ammunition.

"Girls, would you mind checking the drawers in the kitchen for knives, weapons . . . anything you think is valuable?" Jessica starts to protest, but Wright explains the kitchen is safe. "And, it is quieter." That convinces them. They move down the dark hallway before Wright mounts the staircase.

"Kari?" Ian starts.

She halts. "Yes?"

Ian's painfully aware of the eyes upon him. He stammers, "Be careful."

She permits a rare smile. "Don't worry. I will."

THE thing punches the door almost rhythmically, the metronome beats counting the seconds until Wright will return. It's just inches away, Ian thinks, just a rotten piece of wood between us. It is so close he almost confuses the beast's battering for the thumping of his own heart.

Minutes pass, each one moving with the speed of an epoch. Although Anne and Jessica have quieted, the monster persists, unabated. The door, fortunately, holds firm, but Ian cannot say the same for his resolve. He finds his courage quaking, the initial adrenaline rush receding.

He turns his thoughts to something else. His family. Song lyrics. Sex, or what he thinks sex might entail. But the noise outside forces such thoughts aside. It will be worse soon, worse when the Hestons join the visitor demanding entry. There will be more of them to come.

Only then does he realize the folly of Kari's search of the home. She should not be alone. His blood goes cold. More of them to come? What if they were already upstairs?

"Burt?" Ian calls between fist falls. "Can you manage without me for a moment?"

Burt stares at Ian, his eyes wide and questioning.

Ian nods his head in the direction of the stairs.

"Good idea," Burt agrees. He thinks the door has swollen in its frame some. That should help him and Van to hold it.

With that, Ian bounds up the stairs, three at a time. Toward the top, he stops. He lived most of his life in an old house, and he knows how to walk to minimize the creaking. Still, as he steps heel to toe, the last few steps groan under his weight.

He takes note of the blistering wallpaper. Sun-bleached, he can barely perceive the detail of birds flitting to and from bouquets of bluebonnets. "Kari," he squawks meekly, still hidden in the shadows of the staircase.

He peers left. A brightly lit room bathed in hues of baby blue greets him from the hallway's end. He opts, though, for the right, toward a darker burgundy room five paces past a full bathroom. A carpeted runner silences his tentative steps.

From the left, behind him now, something lurches forward from the blue room, a child's bedroom. It shuffles silently, shoulder to the wall. Its dead hands slide eagerly over the aging paper, convulsing like ancient spiders about to pounce.

Ian moves more quickly, unaware of the danger at his back. Once he passes the bathroom, he takes longer strides towards the end of the corridor. He whispers Kari's name again, hoping his appeal for an answer will elicit a response, before taking the final plunge through the dark threshold.

Hand to the frame, he swallows and steps through the entry.

The room is dark, save for two thin shafts of light cutting through the dust from a pair of southern windows. The beams barely escape the darkness of heavy drapes that imprison the room in blackness.

Ian's eyes slowly adjust to the gloom. He detects a great four-post bed standing solemnly before him. It anchors the far wall, dividing the room into two, presumably "his" and "hers," sides. Ian is stricken by the fastidiousness of the room, the made bed. Even in this family's final days, they bucked against the chaos, seeking refuge in order, things as simple as tucking in sheets and arranging pillows. For Ian, making the bed was always a chore. To these people, though, it must have brought them solace as their world caved in around them.

Wright steps away from a chest of drawers, into the struggling sunbeams. Dust dances about her illuminated face, glowing. *Like fairy dust*, he considers. Ian spies the hint of another smile.

He starts to grin in response, but checks himself. There's a sudden change in her expression.

Wright's face goes dim. Her full lips spasm.

She draws her pistol . . . and levels it . . . at Ian.

❖ ❖ ❖

IT doesn't happen in slow motion like in the pictures.

The gun is up and out in the beat of Ian's heart. The hammer connects with the percussion charge instantaneously. The muzzle flashes, and the bullet's away, long before the thundering report ever reaches Ian's ears.

It's faster than a synapse snap, too fast to elicit a reaction.

Too fast for Ian to voice, or even begin to formulate the question, "Why?"

The slug strikes with a sickening thud. Flesh and bone hit the wall behind where a falling Ian once stood.

Wright moves with surprising purpose and efficiency, a trained assassin unleashed. Before the body can even complete its descent to the floor, she's there. As the lifeless remains hit the carpet, she delivers the coup de gras: two additional bullets to the head.

Ian, eyes wide in disbelief, is balled up next to the shriveled corpse of a boy, perhaps his brother's age. The last of the residents of this old plantation-style house, the adolescent waited eighteen years in his bedroom, biding his time pacing from one blue wall to the other. His bedroom, a place of refuge for most teens, was an eternal cage. Or, it would have been if Wright had not mercifully released him.

"I'm sorry for that," Wrights says to Ian. She didn't have time to warn him. She extends a hand. "Are you okay?"

"I think so," Ian replies. "Thank you."

She is happy to see him, making her next statement all the more confusing. "You disobeyed instructions. You shouldn't be up here."

"I just—" Ian stops, aware that he, like Van mere minutes before, has made a mistake, one that could have been as fatal if he had made the decision to move left instead of right. He quickly apologizes and departs the room, Burt's demands for an explanation echoing up the stairway.

Burt's calls drown out Wright's barely audible whisper: Ian stay. It is okay.

No one, at least in Wright's recollection, ever had her back before. Every acquaintance-turned-friend-turned-lover-turned-distant memory had passed through her life with little more impact than a slight breeze. These men, mostly nameless and faceless apparitions, usually appeared to her in the dark hours of night. If she was lucky, one might leave an impression, even make his presence felt. Inexorably, they would retreat with the coming of the morning sun, their ghostly influence exorcised.

But Ian is different.

Her parents, too, are a distant memory. They are still alive, in fact, and eventually returned to her childhood home where they dwell. "Home"—that's what she calls it, because "house that I used to eat and sleep in" is too cumbersome, albeit more accurate. She has neither seen her mom and dad nor the house in seven years, and they live just twenty minutes away.

Home is a foreign concept to her. She packs and moves lightly, always a jacket and a scarf from her next stay.

It started when she was little. She ran away from home often. When she was eleven, she moved in with her fifth-grade teacher for a month. She was his big secret, and he promised that he would marry her and present her with a great gaudy bauble, a tag for her ring finger one day should she keep their relationship private. After a few weeks, she got sick of the abuse and moved out.

The pervert was hurt. He said she was afraid, calling her a "timid little girl scared of commitment, of being alone, of everything."

"You're right about one thing," she said, "I am a little girl. And you should be ashamed. But afraid?" She laughed. "Well, at least not of you!" She extended a finger—not her ring finger—and flew from his study like a caged bird released.

She never said anything to her parents or the principal. She continued to take his class, even participated in his Thursday study groups. During that school year, she never hinted at weakness. He would go on to give her straight As.

But in sixth grade, the world changed. And nothing really mattered after that. She volunteered for the military at thirteen, a mere child soldier.

Wright's move proved prescient, for a year later the military reinstituted the draft. Tours of duty were required of every man and woman. There, in the greater service of God and man, Wright came to recognize her aptitude: Survival.

"Survival Specialist?" her brother teased at their grandmother's wake a few years before.

They stood within feet of each other, but they couldn't have been more distant. They cautiously eyed each other over the tops of their coffee mugs, part of a collection aggressively pursued by their Nana. She had nearly a thousand mugs, purchased at garage sales and flea markets over fifty years.

"'Survival' hardly qualifies as skill set," he continued. "Aren't you really just a 'Living Specialist'? And, if so, maybe I should have a military career. After all, we're all just living."

"Really, Jim? All of us?" Wright motioned toward the casket in the next room.

"Shit," Jim sighed, eyeing the black lacquered box containing their grandmother's body and severed head. "You know what I mean."

"I guess so," she said, pausing to sip tea from a mug bequeathing her the title "World's Best Secretary." "Let's examine your definition of 'living.' If 'living' means losing a job, downing a fifth of moonshine every night, watching 70 plus hours of TV per week, and humping your wife twice a year—three times if she's having a particularly bad one—then I guess the military hasn't done much to prepare me for that."

"Hey!" Jim decried, holding his mug before him like a shield.

"Goodbye, Jim." Wright left the house, her last memory of her brother just his quaking mug putting the world on notice that his other car is a Cadillac.

❖❖❖

BUT Ian, this kid, shows her more just by looking at her, than, well, anyone.

If Richard had lived, he wouldn't have wasted a moment on her. No, he'd be too busy blubbering about his docile wife and their tow-headed baby to give a shit about some piece of ass he tapped between flights.

Not Ian, though.

Sure, he is stupid and careless, but only because he cares, cares for her. She feels an odd flutter in her bosom, but quickly dismisses once again the nagging suspicion that she may be falling in love with this boy.

❖❖❖

IAN slinks down the steps, rejoining Van and Burt at the entrance.

Anne and Jessica are in the living room. They whimper in the corner, shadowed by a great protruding fireplace.

"What the hell happened?" Burt asks.

Ian has problems finding words. They drift before coming to his lips. He struggles to fill the void. He almost says, "I fucked up."

"He helped me secure the floor," Wright exclaims from the staircase, bounding down them in twos. "We've got to fortify the rest of this place. We'll be staying for the night."

Chapter Fifteen:
Bathroom Break

THE hammer and nails are easy to locate. The home's owners left the tools on the kitchen island with a handsaw and crow bar. They make the front door fast by nailing the second floor's bathroom door across it. They move to assess the risks in other areas.

The house rests on a slope, meaning the primary means of ingress is the front porch. Unfortunately, it spans the width of the house, and the living and dining room windows require reinforcement.

The glass panes, save for the southern most window of the dining room, are broken and brown with blood. They are literally held in place by varying grades of scrap lumber.

As Ian fortifies the windows using portions of the dining room table, Wright pounds at the front door to hold the creature rapt.

If enough of them descend upon the house, the window casings themselves will not hold. Best, then, for the animals to focus on the traditional forms of entry.

Van finds a shotgun in the pantry. It is glued to the floor, its barrel caked, scabbed with blood. He comes upon it by following spent shell casings from the living room. Like a trail of breadcrumbs in a fairytale, the used cartridges evidence a tragic and violent end. One unused bullet remains in the chamber. He suspects the wielder saved it, purposely hoping for a few precious seconds to wrap his mouth around the barrel. Perhaps at the end, he just couldn't pull the trigger.

The owners had never gone far. When their attackers had roamed off in search of more prey, the family lingered, drawn by the familiarity. The husband is at the front door, his wife still feasting on the remains of the Hestons.

If faced with similar circumstances, Van promises himself he will choose the path of the bullet.

At any rate, the creatures will not gain access through the rear of the house. The windows are a good twelve feet, maybe more, above the lawn. Thankfully. The bathroom reeks horribly of mildew and mold. Burt throws open a window to air it out.

Though not enough to save them, the home's owners wisely demolished the back porch. They left its remnants to rot in a heap beneath the rear entry. Burt and Van stare down at the worm-infested fragments, sighing in relief. Burt smiles smugly, a flash from the wilds of his beard confessing his satisfaction that they are safe. Together they shut the door.

They should linger longer.

They should inspect the disintegrating mess with just a bit more scrutiny.

The do not realize the secret the debris hides. It is a secret that spells doom.

IT is decided. They will sleep together as a group. The dining room will accommodate them all.

Ian does not linger as he does most nights, waiting for an opportunity to share a furtive moment with Wright. Drained by his embarrassment and shame, tonight it is straight to bed. Within a quarter hour, he is fast asleep.

He doesn't wake when Wright, patrolling the floor, steps gingerly over him.

Locked in battle in another fever dream, Ian grimaces unconsciously.

Wright searches the room for prying eyes. Seeing none, she kneels to Ian's side and runs a finger across his cheek. She moves a piece of hair over his ear. She grins and then continues on.

Ian does not wake, but he is not oblivious to Wright's touch. When the closet in his mind opens to the thundering hands of his fiendish enemies, no infant lies there to greet them. Instead, Ian, The Man, stands before his attackers, and he launches at them with the fury of a cornered wolf.

For Jessica, sleep is elusive. The pounding on the door has yet to relent, and each punch is a hammer tapping her skull. She burrows under her pillow. She is growing madder by the hour, her brave veneer fading. Finally, sleep comes, but it does not last.

She awakes with a start to the sound of breaking glass; not the crash of a window, but something different. A sound akin to something distant, to a delicate Christmas ornament impacting the tree skirt . . . the soft twinkle of blown glass turning to powder.

She sits up and listens, her eyes gradually adjusting to the darkness. Slowly, the forms of sleeping bodies take shape in the early morning light, sprawled here and there like fallen soldiers.

The rapping at the front door continues, somewhat muffled. The creature's hand has been reduced to mush, deadening the sound of his weakening blows.

Jessica holds her face in her hands, her elbows resting on her knees. Please, God, make it stop.

Her small bladder once again aches, and for the first time in a long time she feels her spirits rise.

She has almost forgotten the hidden pleasure of sitting on a commode. She is sick of squatting in the brush, her rear a pin cushion for an assortment of sticks and bugs. Her lower left buttock itches incessantly. She suspects poison ivy.

Now, though, clean porcelain awaits her raw derriere. How nice it will be to use tissue paper instead of leaves! How nice it will be to do so in private!

Jessica tiptoes through the vestibule. She passes the stairway and mourns she cannot use the second floor bathroom. It is nicer than the bathroom near the kitchen (the former is pink and the latter smells of mildew), but it has no door. The boys used it to barricade the window.

She moves swiftly down the hallway, dancing as the pressure in her bladder builds. Into the darkness of the bathroom she goes, jigging like an Irish schoolgirl. Her hands search the back of the door frantically until they happen upon a deadbolt. She locks it, barely has time to drop her drawers before she sits hard on the seat. She sighs with relief, hissing echoing from the bowl beneath her.

Her enjoyment is relative. As much as she likes pissing like a human again, the putrid stench of rotting wood assaults her nose. A pipe bringing fresh water to the toilet has been steadily leaking for nearly twenty years, one of the few items left unattended on an ancient "honey do" list. A drip at first, the leak has become a steady trickle. It has permeated the drywall, the baseboards, the floorboards, and the load bearing joists beneath.

Dutifully, the beams have supported the weight of the toilet and its occupants for more than ten decades. But today, the boards rebel. The slight weight of Jessica is just too much to bear.

Creak.

Snap.

Jessica's eyes go wide. She shifts forward on her seat.

Pop.

She screams. The toilet bucks forward as the floorboards collapse.

The floor beneath Jessica falls away. She is tossed from her seat as it lurches forward, hitting her ribs hard against the splintering floor. She splays her arms wide for a hold as she plunges through the flooring. She grimaces, struggles to distribute her weight as evenly as possible. Her legs and hips dangle, she can only guess, into the basement below her. If she could just swing a leg over . . .

But the toilet pitches further, pinning her chest firmly against floor and hampering her escape. The contents of the bowl slosh, soaking Jessica's head and back. She gasps, the cold water startling her. "Oh, gross!"

With a low growl she claws to free herself. She stretches mightily, but her fingers cannot find a hold. "Shit," she sighs, then laughs out loud at the double entendre.

Between labored chuckles, Jessica half-heartedly calls for help. "Can anyone hear me? I'm having a problem in the bathroom."

A problem? In the bathroom? She snorts with laughter, then groans, her chest aching. She clears her throat. "Help, help, help, help, help," she mews like a starving kitten. "Help anyone?"

And then, from the cellar below her, comes the familiar sound of breaking glass.

What? Jessica labors to peer into the darkness that's swallowed her lower half. Blackness masks her legs. She stops straining and listens for further sounds.

She hears a soft shuffling and the sound of shattered glass scattering across a concrete floor. Almost rhythmic, it gets closer—and then silence.

Is someone down there? She wonders if Van is playing a practical joke.

Jessica feels pressure against her leg, something cold and wet. Her face goes blank . . . before white-hot pain shoots up her spine, so intense that she can do nothing but shriek uncontrollably.

THEY are up, clamoring about like blind clowns.

They hear the earsplitting screaming, but it takes them critical moments to discern whose it is.

Burt does the head count, assesses their situation before the others can even get their bearings. "Where's Jessica?"

Without responding, they are running, Wright, Burt, Ian, Anne, and

Van groggy and at the rear. Through the hallway they go, Jessica's bloodcurdling cries echoing throughout the old home's shell.

The screams bounce about in Van's head. Good God, she must be dying.

Someone in the lead realizes the screams are coming from the bathroom, and leads the circus to the door. Burt hits the oak door first, but to no avail. He retreats to ram it again, but instead bangs Ian immediately to his rear. Ian caroms into Wright, and Wright into Anne like some human billiards trick.

"We're coming, Jessica!"

"Hold tight!"

"We'll be right there!"

"Someone open the door!"

"It's locked!"

Jessica stops shrieking.

"Out of the way!" Van calls from their rear. They have barely enough time to scoot aside before he barrels through. He hits the door like a wrecking ball, his shoulder splintering the frame, popping the deadbolt. The door flies open, and he follows it, sprawling forward. His face and elbows plant next to Jessica's unconscious body.

"She's fallen through!"

"Grab her arms!"

"Get her out!"

Van's forced to the side, Burt and Ian each taking one of Jessica's arms. The toilet, though, holds her fast, pressing her against the dank floor. "She's stuck!"

"Van," Burt calls, "help us out here!" Van crawls to their side. "Lift the toilet when we lift," Burt instructs. Van seizes the commode with both hands, pushing its porcelain tank up and away from Jessica.

The floor beneath strains, moaning as the toilet's base levels out. "Is the floor safe?" Anne asks.

Still, Jessica is wedged tight. Burt urges Van to do more. Van pushes harder, Burt cries for Ian to pull, and they lift Jessica by her armpits.

She is clear of the toilet, she should free easily, yet somehow she remains trapped by something below.

What is she caught on? There's no time to formulate the question, let alone answer.

The floorboards rip from their moorings, Van's pressure just too great.

Crack.

Van and the toilet spill into the blackness of the cellar.

❖❖❖

VAN plummets, pirouetting. He stretches his arms before him, hoping to find a hold. Instead, his left arm hits cement, folding beneath him. Before the pain can register, he rolls, barely managing to avoid the falling toilet.

The porcelain hits with a heavy slap, bouncing, splintering, spinning half around and rolling once, before coming to a halt at the edge of a faint circle of light.

Van turns to the sky. He sees the dimly lit hole above him from whence he fell. Burt and Ian have drawn Jessica from the hole, and Anne starts crying.

Wright calls to Van, asks him if he's all right. Van rises and assesses his forearm. It doesn't look broken, but it hurts like hell.

Wright's silhouette calls back to him. "Hold on," she says. "Don't move. Stay exactly where you are." Her flashlight flickers alive, trains on him.

"Why?" Van questions, his eyes trying to adjust to probe the darkness. "I need someone to look at my—" Van's eyes fall on a pool of dark liquid, not four feet from where he stands. He freezes. What's going on here?

Something in the dark answers him. Glass breaks in the gloom. It reverberates against the dark walls, masking the location. Van senses it is close.

❖❖❖

JOLENE Heston was never curious in life. She never sought to enrich herself by opening a book, nor had she sought education. She went to college simply to earn her "MRS," and she did so when she married an M.D. Learning was a chore, and knowledge a bore. Independent thought held no joy.

She was content to drift, blown by the whims of her husband and peers. Truly a zombie in life . . . making it all the more surprising that she discovered the rotted cellar doors buried beneath the rubble of the back porch.

Miraculously, she had broken away from the attack. There were two creatures, drawn out of the woods, probably by the kids, their loud clothes and their loud conversation. She had told her husband that those kids would be the death of them.

They attacked from the right of the path. First the female, dark and wiry. She came from behind a tree, attacking Dr. Heston as he talked to his wife. Jolene saw it coming. She tried to warn him, but her words froze in her throat. He saw the panic in her face, turning just in time to present his throat to its gaping jaws. He squeezed his wife's hand for the last time.

The second creature followed the first closely. He was taller, somewhat less sinewy. The first's husband, Jolene thought. So much for "until death do we part."

She turned to run. It caught her by the hair, biting deep into her shoulder. She pulled free. She escaped . . . but not with her life. The bite was massive. She cried herself to her death, cradled in a bow of a tree watching her husband being savaged below. She "turned" with a jolt, her once tan body seizing, the throws of a grand mal. It shook her from her roost, and she soon began the short journey to the house.

Something in the recesses of Jolene Heston's mind drove her to the rear of the house, something less than primal instinct but more than just a buried memory. Something out of habit, something familiar, like the search for a soothing swim or a pina colada at the patio bar, may be even a quickie in the shed with their 20-year old gardener, Juan. But she found neither a poolside lounge nor a boy to shag, and instead she crawled beneath the fallen porch.

Her lithe body slipped easily between the timbers, and she chewed and clawed her way through the decayed cellar doors like an anxious grub.

Ms. Heston's hunger was insatiable.

The shelves were full of canned goods . . . apples, pears, and various preserves. These, though, were not to her liking. She wanted something more, something indescribable. Frustrated, she angrily attacked the jars. As she prepared to destroy a jar of beans, she heard footsteps from above. Cradling the preserves under her arm, she followed the footfalls until the heavens had revealed their bounty.

Chomping on Jessica's kicking legs was difficult, yet proved to be worth the challenge. Like a giant lamprey, she fervently filled her mouth with great chunks of flesh. Yet as quickly as the legs had appeared, they were gone.

But Jolene does not long despair. Manna has fallen from the sky yet again.

She lurks just ten feet from Van. She is ravenous.

❖❖❖

WRIGHT does not need to examine the wounds. She knows exactly what happened to Jessica. She orders Van to stay in the center of the circle of light.

Van reads between the lines. He knows he's not alone. "I don't want to be down here anymore!" he calls. He twists about in vain, attempting to find the would-be assailant.

There's shuffling, the tinkle of glass, to his right.

No, to his left.

Gurgling sounds bounce about, throwing Van into a panic. He edges closer to the darkness.

"Don't make me tell you again, Van," Wright demands from above. "Stay put!"

Too late.

What-Was-Jolene pounces on him from the shadows, driving her nails into his back and shoulders. She is draped on him, angling for a bite, angling for his precious jugular.

Van screams, whirling like a dervish. The centrifugal force catches the thing off guard, and Jolene loses her grasp, biting at air. Van stumbles, lumbering in a clumsy circle. The monster's grasp tightens again. It burbles into his ear. He punches upward with a flat hand, the heel connecting sharply with the creature's chin. Jolene's mouth hammers shut with an alligator snap. She struggles, but his hand holds her head in place just inches above his own. She rakes his cheeks with polished nails.

Van stares upwards, his frightened eyes making contact with Wright's. They plead for help as he holds the creature above him like a sacrifice.

Perfect.

Wright fires.

The bullet goes low and right, taking Jolene's pierced ear lobe. Shit.

She resets her aim, drawing a bead, and squeezes the trigger again.

This time she strikes home. Jolene's head pops backwards, her skull caving as the slug slams her frontal lobe. The bullet pancakes and shatters, bits of steel driving through the monster's cerebellum, its medulla. The shrapnel spreads and shreds the grey matter, liquefying axons, dendrites, and filling synapses with debris. The shards burst forth from the rear of her head, stirring brain matter in their wake. Chunks of skull and everything that allowed Jolene to ever love, reason, laugh, and, ultimately, cannibalize, sputter forth, raining with a heavy splat.

The talons that ripped at Van go limp. Jolene slips from his back with a thud. Van falls to his knees, looks over his shoulder at the carnage behind him.

Wright is worried about contagion. "Van," she implores, "don't touch that stuff!"

Blood and black rot cover the floor, the shelves, and, essentially, everything Van can see. He looks at her incredulously. "Are you fucking kidding me? What makes you think I'd want to?"

Burt watches everything unfold from his balcony-like seat. Despite Jessica's whimpering, Kari's barked orders, Van's calls below, and his own retching, he cannot drown out a voice in his head. It nags him, repeating a mantra, over and over.

Vampires,

Vampires,

Vampires . . .

Chapter Sixteen:
Everyday is Halloween

VAN is not badly hurt. Jessica is. Yet, by the way he carries on, and the manner in which she doesn't, one would assume the opposite to be true.

Jolene missed Jessica's artery. She will not bleed to death. That's the only good news. But she cannot walk. She already has a fever.

She will die.

And she will turn.

Wright thinks they have 48 hours, maybe more, maybe less. All they can do is comfort her.

Anne sits by Jessica's side in the bedroom upstairs reading Harry Potter to her, and wiping her brow. The others stew, waiting to hear Wright's plan.

But Wright does not have one. She sits alone, debating alternatives, shunning their attention, even Ian's.

A discouraged Burt stands at the open window of the master bedroom. He needs fresh air, but there is little of that. He watches the creatures below him. Twenty or so mill about now, their focus alternating between him and Ian, who stands at his side.

That is, except one.

Its eye sockets are vacant ragged holes, and it blindly bumps and claws at its peers. The smell of the living drives it mad, as it meanders about in circles.

"It's like Goddamn Halloween out there," Burt mutters.

They hear Burt's voice, and it agitates them. The blind one brushes against one of its brethren. It lunges. Its nails take hold of the other's shoulder and forehead, and its head cocks like a serpent ready to strike. Its thin lips pull back to expose a crater of broken teeth. Its empty eyes seem to stare at Ian for half a second before . . . it propels it skeletal head forward, slamming its jaws into the sunken flesh. Although sightless, it works quickly, tearing away at the nape of the neck.

Before its victim can register the attack, it strikes again. This time the blow is slower, less ferocious, but it still manages to sever the creature's dried jugular. The blind attacker quickly looses itself, sliding off its ancient victim's back.

"Son of a bitch," Burt murmurs, the blind demon spitting chunks of dead flesh. "Must not be to its liking."

Ian nods to the pasture outside the window. He's open to a conversation, so he bridges the divide. "How's this like Halloween?"

Burt raises an eyebrow. Slowly he pieces together the question's import. "Not like Halloween now. Now we give reverence to saints. It reminds me of Halloween *before*."

Before. Then. Used to. Previously. All temporal expressions describing another time, life before the dead walked. The terms no longer require context. Descriptions of antecedent events, almost universally, are assumed to have occurred before the New Order, unless further clarification is provided. Like "before lunch," "prior to church," etcetera. Ease-of-use may have driven the simplification, but Burt suspects something else. He suspects that fear played a significant role. It's as though the mere utterance of that period, of that time when things were right, might doom the speaker to fate worse than death . . .

A fate more than death.

Ian's eyes become saucers. "Do you mean that the dead walked then, too?"

"No," Burt replies. He decides to hide the conversation he'd had with Wright. "But long ago, people sure thought they did."

It was the Druids who first started celebrating something akin to Halloween. They celebrated with feasts to honor the dead. Samhain, they called it. It signified the end of summer, marked the beginning of the Celtic New Year. The Romans had a version themselves, called Feralia.

Pope Boniface IV supplanted the pagan holidays, creating a Christian alternative. All Hallows' Eve or Hallow E'en. Halloween was celebrated to honor the saints in heaven.

But the Christian holiday took hold in name only. Rather than burying Druidic traditions, components were cherry picked and incorporated. For instance: the Celts believed the dead returned to roam the streets at night during Samhain. Peasants dressed as ghouls to conceal their identities from these evil souls. Gifts and treats were left to pacify the spirits. Perhaps they would bless the givers with bountiful crops during the next harvest. Trick-or-treating evolved from there.

"On Halloween, we used to dress like that, like demons and devils and stuff," Burt says. "We didn't have monsters, none in the literal sense, anyway."

So, it was a continuation of tradition?

Burt nods. He recalls the Halloween of his youth. It was the only time of the year kids could embrace death and those dark things they didn't fully understand. "For some reason, it was a kick to be scared for just one day each year. We got a thrill out of it."

Ghost stories, haunted houses, monster and slasher films. A whole industry was born to feed, and capitalize on, the evolutionary need for a good scare. Human evolution was shaped by horror. Our ancestors lived in constant fear: predators, war, and disease. Civilization mitigated these horrors.

But the human body was still wired for fear, wired to be in a state of constant danger. When human beings first conceptualized themselves as something more than take-out for prehistoric cats, canines, and bears, a biological void was created. And mankind sought to fill that void artificially, the spectacle of Halloween being a method. In the 21st century, we still needed an adrenaline rush. We wanted to feel our spines tingle. We needed the hairs on our necks to stand at attention.

"But it was only fun, because it was pretend," Burt says. "It was temporary." Context is important; we only enjoy our fight or flight response if we know the trigger is fake. Horror movies were enjoyed in the company of others. Scary stories entertained in the safety of the home. And Halloween came, predictably, only once per year.

"Not like now," Burt sighs. He surveys the monsters below him. "Now every day's like Halloween."

Burt opens his mouth in the shape of an O and exhales. The window steams with his breath. He draws a smiley face with his index finger, first the long bow of the mouth, then two finger-point eyes. This does not cheer either of them.

Ian musters a nod, but he remains anchored to something Burt said about it being natural to be scared. He considers he's not a freak for being fearful. He's not a curiosity for secretly enjoying the thrill of fear. In the midst of all this death, he feels alive for the first time.

"Man, my arm hurts," Van says, entering the room. He sidles up to Burt and Ian. "What's up?"

"Nothing," Burt replies, matter-of-factly. He gives the interloper his back.

Van looks to Ian for a response.

"Just talking about Halloween," he permits.

"You mean costumes and candy and shit?" Van asks.

Ian nods.

Van leans over Burt's shoulder and asks, "Did you ever get dressed up for Halloween?"

Burt turns. He deliberates quickly. "I was Frankenstein once, but I'm not sure that was too terrifying."

"Frankenstein wouldn't be very terrifying," Van notes. "Frankenstein's monster, on the other hand . . . "

Burt takes a step towards Van. "Yes," he spits. "Frankenstein's monster. That's what I meant."

"What else?" Ian asks quickly, trying to diffuse the palpable tension. "What other costumes?"

Burt doesn't say anything. He and Van glare at each other, barely two feet of space between their faces.

"Burt, what else?" Ian asks again. "What else did you dress as?"

His eyes shift to Ian briefly before deciding to break off from his contest. "I was a vampire once. And a clown when I was ten or so."

"Clowns aren't scary," Van declares.

Ian begs to differ. "Clowns scare the shit out of me."

"Yeah," Burt adds, "think of all the serial killers that were clowns."

"Like who?" Van challenges.

"Like John Wayne Gacy."

"And who else?" Van argues.

Burt and Ian are quiet.

"Okay, so that's only one serial killer," Van says. "Anyway, clowns aren't proper costumes."

"What do you mean?" Burt asks defensively. He recalls his mother working on it, the ruffles alone taking hours.

"I mean it's not really a costume," Van replies eyeing the creatures below. "It's more of a uniform." He explains. He always explains.

There are few outfits one can wear and become the very thing the outfit represents. Putting on a surgeon's smock and a mask, for example, doesn't convey a medical license. But dress like a clown, and you automatically become one. Once you put on the make-up, don the green wig, and wear the size 27 shoes, for better or worse, you're a clown, at least until it all comes off.

Ian's confused. "Burt wasn't part of a circus. He didn't visit children in the medical ward. He didn't make monkeys out of balloons. And I'm pretty certain that he never rode around in a car chock full of thirty of his friends. He dressed like a clown on Halloween, Van."

"Intent and forum don't matter," Van sighs. "I'm talking about the activity itself. If you were to define a clown's key function, what would it be?"

"Make people laugh," Burt replies.

"Maybe a good clown makes people laugh. But let's take that idea a step further. Making people laugh just a product, a symptom, of entertainment."

"Okay, is there a point here?" Ian asks in exasperation.

Van continues to set the trap. "Clowns, by their nature, entertain people, right?"

"Sure," Burt allows.

"When you dressed as a clown," Van presses, "didn't you do it to entertain people?"

"Perhaps," Burt concedes with a scowl.

"So, in dressing as a clown, you, in essence, became a clown. It wasn't a costume. It was a uniform." They think Van has rested his case until his eyebrow arches. There's more.

There are other examples. Dress like a celebrity, and you're a celebrity impersonator. And it works in reverse, too. Take off your clothes, and you can be a stripper.

Ian concedes that this is funny, and he chuckles. "That's something to add to the resume, Burt." But with a glance to his side, Ian's good spirits are quickly dampened. "Holy shit."

Burt and Van step to the window on either side of Ian. All three peer from their perch, watching in stunned silence as a half-dozen more creatures burst through the forest and into the clearing below them.

❖ ❖ ❖

THESE latecomers move more quickly than the others, seemingly with deeper purpose. They are led by one, his dark hair matted and thick with flies. The Fat Man. He points an angry hand toward the window and lets forth a guttural growl full of rage and angst. His skin is pale blue—not dark and dry like those clambering before him—except for his hands, where there is none.

Autolysis, or self-digestion, is the first stage of decay. The body's own enzymes, no longer in check by the immune system, devour the membranes holding the cells together. The liquid seeps, depositing between the skin and the tissue beneath, the skin sloughing off. When it happens on the hands, coroners call it "gloving."

Sheets of skin fall away during autolysis, but here, now, it's limited to the monster's hands, maybe his feet. Ian recollects his conversation with Wright: mummification. Since the creatures remain upright, the liquid pours out of them like an upended bottle.

Unlike Burt's hero, Superman, Ian has no power of x-ray vision. Had he, he would see through the shroud of the being's stained sweat-shirt. He would see the creature's belly button, although slightly distended, is oddly devoid of maggots.

If Ian had Superman's superior hearing, he would perceive no "crackle" or "pop"—the sounds of wet rice krispies—of larvae gnawing and gobbling their way through the subcutaneous fat in the genitalia and throat. The fat had collapsed and leached from the corpses. Since there is no meal to be had, there are no guests over for dinner.

The ghouls' faces and bellies, although swollen, lack the severe bloat characteristic of putrefaction. Odd, as the dead generally cannot expel gas, for they have no working stomach muscles or sphincters. The small intestine collapses, sealing itself off and creating a "gut balloon." Perhaps, though, kinesis and vertical alignment are enough to allow the gas to vent. Perhaps it is the expulsion of the gas over the vocal chords of these things that gives them their monstrous voice.

Perhaps the bacterial colonies on the skin and in the intestines and lungs have nothing on which to dine. Perhaps the pathogen responsible for the transformation multiplied so quickly that its sheer numbers kept the competitors in check.

Perhaps.

Perhaps.

Perhaps . . .

Decay operates quickly. Three weeks after death, the body's organs turn to soup. The colon and lungs go first. Then bacteria chew through the palate to the brain. The liquid discharges from the ears, and a thick chocolate-like syrup purges from the mouth.

Without putrefaction, however, decay is slowed. In these creatures, the digestive organs and lungs remain, but now with as much purpose as an appendix. More importantly, the brain stays intact, well protected inside its bony fortress. And while the creatures cough bits of purge from time to time, the pace of overall decomposition is glacial.

"Who are they?" Van asks, although he already knows the answer.

They are the passengers that remained on Flight 183.

And they are famished.

❖ ❖ ❖

WRIGHT shakes her head as she looks out the window of the master bedroom.

Now there are forty of them, probably more. The new ones make a racket. More will come this evening. The windows on the first floor will not hold.

They need to act. And fast.

Wright knows they should leave, depart under the cover of night. But there will be casualties. And they need to set a course. And there's Jessica. . . .

Jessica's death warrant has been signed. They should leave her, Wright knows. Wright just can't bring herself to do so. Not just yet, anyway.

They need to buy time.

They move everything and everyone upstairs.

Then Ian, Van, and Burt go about the business of destroying the staircase. They pull up the stairs one by one, dropping them into the cellar below. They stop at the first landing, about eight feet up, the basement serving neatly as a moat.

JESSICA is getting worse. She's coughing and moaning. Anne no longer sits with her. Wright has sent her to the master bedroom. Instead, Wright reads to Jessica from an antique rocking chair, shotgun propped ominously against the wall.

It is hard for Ian to walk into her room. When he does, Jessica is sleeping fitfully. Wright sees him, puts her finger to her lip. Ian motions silently for Wright to join him.

In the hallway, they whisper and conspire, out of earshot of Jessica and the others.

"What's the plan?" Ian asks.

"The plan?" Wright takes offense. His tone seems to suggest she doesn't have one, or worse, he doesn't trust it.

Ian senses the defiance in her tone and ignores it. "I figure we need to leave here tonight, before dawn at the latest."

Wright sighs. And just how does he expect to do this? Jessica is in no state to travel.

"What?" Ian says. "Kari, she'll never be able to travel. Not with us, anyway. You know this. Why are you denying the inevitable?"

Because she is my responsibility, Wright wants to say. Because I failed her.

She doesn't need to say a thing. Ian knows what she's thinking. "This isn't your fault, you know."

Wright tries to be a good soldier, but a lone tear falls. She's shocked when it deflects off her cheek. Her shoulders start to bounce, her face cracking.

Ian draws her to him, buries her head in his chest. Her sobs are muffled in the fabric of his shirt, but not totally.

Burt leans out the master bedroom. He makes eye contact with Ian, sees Ian mouth, "It's okay," even though it is anything but. Burt nods, pulls the bedroom door behind him, affording them just a moment of privacy.

There in the darkness of the hall, Ian tells Wright what they will do, what they must do.

She nods, her hand on his shoulder.

Next he explains to her, over her objections, why he must leave them and strike out on his own.

Chapter Seventeen:
Bait and Switch

WRIGHT wakes Jessica. They need to talk. Jessica can guess why. Jessica knows she's changing. She can feel it.

Inside Jessica, a war is raging. The enemy has invaded, and her body mounts a response.

Jessica's complement molecules are first to attack the invader—something more complex than a virus, something less than a protozoa. The complement molecule's job is simple; latch onto the invader, punch holes in its membrane and break it down. Then call for help.

This is in accord with the invader's plan. The intruder lets the complement molecule do its work and prays for it to call for reinforcements.

Jessica's macrophages respond to the beacon. They probe with fine hairs, filopodia that wave about like fishing lines, increasing the area the warrior cells cover as they sweep for intruders. Filopodia snare trespassers and retract quickly, allowing the macrophages to swallow their enemies whole.

Just another step in the invader's plan. It allows itself to be consumed without a hint of fight.

As the macrophages lumber forth, they signal the immune system to act, loosening and widening blood vessel walls so more macrophages can attack. They dispatch molecules to drag other immune cells, like roaming T cells, to the battleground.

This is the third step of the invader's plan. It wants the roaming Ts on the frontline.

Later, they will become Jessica's own worst enemy.

In a perfect world, the macrophages make their way to the lymph nodes. There, B and T cells, with faces as distinctive as jigsaw pieces, look for bits of the invader, bits called antigens presented by the macrophage like trophies of war. When presented with the antigens, T cells bearing the right receptor multiply, forming three regiments.

1. Killer Ts, T cells that search for infected cells. They are the Special Forces. They identify the contaminated cells and force them onto their own swords.

2. The infantry, or inflammatory Ts. They rush to the site of the breach, spraying deadly poison. The inflammation they cause allows

other immune cells to enter the fray.

3. Helper Ts infiltrate and provide military intelligence. They work with B cells, binding to antigens. Once locked on, the T cells spy on the visitor, providing signals to the Bs to create antibodies. The antibodies attach to the invaders, rendering them harmless.

But Jessica's immune response fails to escalate. The regiments do not form. For the macrophages are nothing more than Trojan horses, the invaders hidden inside. Ensconced within the cells, the invaders go to work severing the macrophages molecular knives. It's a neat piece of mischief, for the macrophages can no longer present bits of the enemy to the audience of Bs and Ts in the lymph nodes. Since there are no antigens, the existing Ts lack reinforcements.

And there are precious few Ts ready to handle the crisis. Those that do respond get twitchy, adopting a slash and burn policy, assassinating friend and foe indiscriminately. The collateral damage mounts, and the war further spirals out of control.

Yet another phase of the invader's plan. Dead host cells and antigens pile up and start to rot. The macrophages cannot remove the dead and dying soldiers from the battlefield quickly enough. The body becomes over-stimulated, septic, and attacks itself.

The few trespassers who fail to find homes in macrophages have another trick up their sleeves. They change their coats, by manipulating the position of the DNA on their surface. They change their skin so often, the antibodies fortunate enough to survive the fire fight cannot match the pace.

With little in the way to stop it, the attacker makes its way forward. It knows where to go. The body is a closed system, full of bouncing chemical markers. The invader circulates through the body, sensitive to all the molecular "smells." As it nears the brain, it detects hormones released by the hypothalamus, a gland controlling critical bodily functions, like circadian rhythm, homeostasis, and . . .

Hunger.

The scent is a trigger, telling the invader to stop its caterpillar-like progression, and start burrowing.

The brain's blood vessel walls are tight knit and form a daunting barrier, the blood-brain barrier. The wall keeps large molecules from seeping in from the bloodstream into brain tissue.

Or, at least, that's the concept. Jessica's barrier is compromised. The invader presents a protein, not unlike the one resting on the surface of the rabies virus, that opens a passageway in the blood vessel walls and into the individual nerve cells. As if uttering the magic phrase, "Open Sesame," the invader enters the cavern of the upper spinal cord, following the nerve to the brain.

The invader moves fast, finding the hindbrain in less than thirty minutes time from entry. Technically, the body barely has time to mount an immune response. Yet the invader makes sure some of its troops linger throughout the Jessica's body, especially near her lymph nodes.

It wants to be discovered. It expects to be discovered. That's all part of the plan too. It wants to cause as much damage to the immune system as possible.

Why? Because it doesn't want to be like its cousin, the parasite responsible for the resurrection of cadavers.

Its cousin (one day the microbe will have a nice sanitary name like NAP Type 2) is the milder form. It shuns attention. It has been living in Jessica's brain since she was a child—just as it inhabits most people, hiding in their grey matter, cocooned in a cyst, like toxoplasma gondii, which infected billions of cat owners prior to the New Order. When Type 2 does break out, a rare occurrence in the living, it is immediately checked by the immune system. The infected might exhibit symptoms of the flu, or they may not show any signs at all. Only natural death unlocks its secrets, just as Heston hypothesized.

The version tearing Jessica apart, Type 1, has mutated to exploit the immune system. This evolutionary improvement increases both its virulence and the opportunity for contagion. It does not want to stay hidden in the brain like Type 2, kept in check by a jealous co-star. This invader is a media whore, and unlike its camera-shy relative, it is ready for its close-up. It will have its time on the stage, the director be damned.

And the stage? The brain.

This is where the invader takes up permanent residency, building its base in the brain stem, spreading throughout the cerebellum and along the top edges of the brain to the motor cortex, the area responsible for bilateral movement and locomotion.

The brain. This is where the invader will reign, driving the decedent's actions through chemical manipulation. It hijacks the hypothalamus, stimulating the ventromedial nucleus, mimicking the triggers for hunger. It spurs the need for food intake—although most of the devoured flesh spills from the monsters' torn cheeks or rots in their esophagus or stomach.

The brain. This is where the invader will reproduce, using the facial and glossopharyngeal nerves to carry it from the brainstem to the decedent's mouth, just a bite from finding a home in its next victim.

The brain. This is the organ that must be destroyed to halt the trespasser and its host in their tracks.

❖❖❖

JESSICA can feel her body being rampaged. She can feel it losing the war and her mind losing control. Her appetite is growing. "I don't want to become one of them," she says to Wright.

Wright hands her the shotgun. She reminds her that there's only one round. She's got just one shot, so to speak.

Jessica isn't worried. "It's a shotgun," she jokes. "There's some room for error." She agrees she will wait until they are clear. She smiles, tells Wright to tell Anne goodbye.

She's looking forward to heaven. She can't wait to find out how Harry Potter ends.

❖❖❖

WRIGHT awakens the others during the darkness of the morning hours. There are a number of questions. "Where's Jessica?" "Where's Ian?" Wright provides them the opening details of the plan.

Once the crying subsides, Wright carries on with the briefing.

When they jump from the bathroom window, they'll need to move quietly, and they'll need to move quickly. They should run flat out for half an hour. Wright will keep pace with the slowest. After that they can slow to a jog. Once at the highway, they will track north. She tells them to count mile markers. They will rendezvous ten miles north, near the closest overpass.

It is a hasty plan, and it has lots of holes. Van decides to point one of them out. "What if we get lost?" Van asks.

"Make sure you don't," Wright says.

Then they hear Ian's cries. It's time to go.

Van is out first. He drops silently, no sign of the monsters. He hears shouts in the distance. The howls have drawn them away. *Poor Ian*, he thinks.

Anne's bag almost hits him in the head. He grabs it, steadies Anne as she jumps. She grunts when she hits, but Van has her up and moving in a beat. Van thinks he hears Burt, then Wright, drop from the window. He doesn't wait to find out. They can handle themselves. Van will watch the sky as they run, keeping the coming light on the right side of his body.

They run, following the line of a deer path. Van's heart is beating hard in the cage of his chest. He opens his mouth wide, an effort to silence his panting. He keeps a hand out, ensuring Anne is at his side. Branches and brush whip their legs.

There's a gunshot. A shotgun blast.

Anne crumples, starts to sob. Van quickly puts a hand over her mouth, an arm around her waist. "Not here," he whispers. They have to keep moving. There will be time enough later to mourn Jessica's death.

❖❖❖

IT is funny that Ian would choose to play decoy, to lead the creatures away from his friends. Funny because of a similar choice eighteen years earlier. A choice that would save Ian's young life.

Once Peter is past the Loop, he progresses more swiftly. It takes him just under an hour to reach the front steps of his brownstone. He trips up the steps, spilling onto the porch below the bay window. He curses, holds his knee, goes for the keys.

The door opens before he can get to it. "Oh my God, are you hurt?" a young woman asks. She embraces a child and runs to greet him. Her hand goes to his face, cradling it to make sure it is indeed him.

They kiss hard, Peter trying not to crush Ian between them. He looks hastily about. "Let's go inside. Fast."

For the next several hours they watch the expanding coverage on CNN. The world, it would seem, is on fire.

Reports are coming in from several major cities: New York. Miami. Detroit. Minneapolis. And now, Chicago.

The Mayor declares martial law. The newscasters warn to stay inside, doors locked, curtains drawn, and lights down when possible. But there is a terror plain on their faces that belies this advice.

An internal voice tells Peter they are wrong. The voice tells Peter to get out of this city. Go south, it says. Fast.

She packs while Peter readies the car. She grabs a photo album, some of Peter's clothes. She grabs what he's thrown on the bed, what he wore today, a navy striped tie and dress shirt, and then jeans, socks, underwear, whatever. She can hardly think straight, she doesn't know how to prepare.

Peter decides to take Mr. Carr, their elderly and solitary neighbor, with them.

He helps his wife carry the suitcases down the stairs. Ian is crying. He wants his stuffed Curious George. The front room is darkened, and Peter can't find Ian's stuffed animal. His wife tries to help and makes the mistake of turning on the light.

"Turn it off," he says, with a hushed intensity.

She does so without delay, but has the damage been done?

Peter creeps to the bay window, peers through the curtains. On the street three men stand under the lit street lamp. One turns, meets his glance directly. He lurches towards their home. The others follow.

Shit. Peter turns, hurries his wife and son to the rear of the living room. She tries to grab the suitcases. He tells her to leave them.

There's pounding on the steps, next at the door.

She urges Ian to be quiet as the shadows cross the window. Three, four, now five of them. One slaps the window with an open hand, then slaps harder. It breaks. They come through.

These people care not for pain. They tear themselves apart coming over the broken glass. Peter cannot fight them. They are not people. They are wild animals. He rushes his wife and son into the closet.

"Don't wait for me. Get to your mother's!" he shouts. "I love you!" He slams the door and begins furiously screaming at these things, these intruders.

He has their attention. Shit. He runs.

They follow.

PETER returns to his home nearly twelve hours later.

He spent the night on the roof of the corner store. From that vantage point he spied them, dozens, if not hundreds, stumbling about like drunken Cubs fans, with one key difference: Cubs fans generally don't eat other fans. The crying peaked toward midnight. But both it, and the crowd, thin towards morning.

He uses alleys and gangways to get home, hiding in dumpsters and underneath cars.

Home. Not anymore. The living room is in shambles. There's no sign of his family, nothing but a hastily scribed note. The lettering is bleary with her tears, yet still legible. It says: "Peter, Mr. Carr found us. We are driving to mother's. We are fine. God, where are you? I love you. I'll love you forever. J"

Their bags are gone. The car is gone. They are off to Kentucky. Their flight from this place is confirmed, Peter sighs. Thank God. Time for him to leave, too.

He steps gingerly out the front door, picks up the messenger bike, and rides off.

❖❖❖

WRIGHT and Burt track the mile markers, counting ten on their journey north. There's no underpass, though, so they keep walking, keeping to the high weeds. Four miles further they find an overpass. But no Van. No Anne.

"Where do you think they are?" Burt asks. "You don't think they went the wrong way?"

Wright shrugs her shoulders. "Your guess is as good as mine." She can only hope they went the wrong way. She hopes it's not something worse. She turns 360 degrees for a sign, anything that might—

And then she sees it, a hint of Van's red, hooded sweatshirt deep in the meadow. She sighs in relief. Van's inside it.

The four sit quietly for the next several hours, waiting for Ian. His diversion worked, but he should have rejoined the group by now.

Finally Wright tells them they need to move. They need to return to the woods where they'll set up camp for the night.

❖❖❖

WRIGHT decrees no fire this night. It's still too dangerous. So, they chat low in the coming darkness, heads hung.

Anne talks about Jessica. She says she's the sister she never had. She catches herself: *was* the sister she never had. She was so sweet. The others agree. She already misses her, Anne sobs, more than she misses home.

Like I miss Ian, Wright thinks. She's only catching portions of the conversation. She's too consumed with pain. She can barely wrap her mind around Jessica and Ian's legacies, both barely adults, both sacrificing for the greater good. She should have sacrificed herself. She shouldn't have let Ian do it.

She tried to talk Ian out of it. She said it was too risky. She should be the one to play the role of the pied piper of the damned.

But Ian was resolute. He said no. The group needed her if they were going to survive. The stakes were too high for Wright to decide to risk all their lives. The risks were not too high, however, for Ian to gamble his own. He argued with fervor. While he might not be as strong, he's definitely faster and more agile than Wright. Plus he doesn't know how to use a pistol or a machete. He can't navigate like Wright. And he ultimately consumes much more food than her. Without him, there would be more rations for the others. He closed by saying, "The needs of the many outweigh the needs of the few. Or the one."

"Isn't that from *Star Trek*?" she asked, half laughing, half crying.

"Yeah. *Wrath of Khan*. I kind of stole it," Ian admitted with a smirk.

"You are such a nerd."

Then Ian touched her arm.

She leaned in.

And he went for it. He went for the first kiss.

It was a soft, long kiss. His lips were firm, and they silenced her escaping breath. For moments, they stood chest to chest, locked together in an iron embrace. Then Ian suddenly pulled away and squeezed her shoulders. He turned down the hall, leaving Wright with just the synchronized drumming of their hearts, a sound that still resonates inside her.

❖ ❖ ❖

SHE wants to say something about Ian now. She should say something about him, but the words don't come. She feels like she's going to puke. Her heart is breaking.

But Wright doesn't need to say anything yet. Van wants to talk.

"I've known Ian almost all my life," Van starts. "He's not perfect, although he'd like you to think that. He's too much of a straightedge. He's a pain in the ass. But he's always been my best friend. Whenever I needed an alibi, he was there, either to help me craft one or serve as one. Whenever I've faced trouble, he's been the one to bail me out. He's the only one to ever give me his ear, even when I'm talking smack.

"Ian's never once thought about himself. He's saved my ass over and over and over." Van's voice cracks, "And now he's saved us all."

They nod in unison, sighing heavily.

"*I'm* a pain in the ass?" says a voice somewhere behind Wright.

"Van, you should walk in my shoes."

"Ian!" they cry in harmony.

Wright spins, spotting his face in the moonlight, and draws him close. He is filthy, but she hugs him anyway. Her embrace is firm, but momentary. She realizes the others are approaching, and releases him. She wipes tears from her cheeks.

"Sorry I'm late," Ian apologizes.

❖ ❖ ❖

"WHAT happened?" Van begs.

Ian says there's not much of a story to tell. He made a racket and got the ghouls' attention. He headed south, monsters in tow. But the creatures spread wide as they tracked him, and Ian had to push farther before turning east and driving north.

Or at least that's the version Ian will leave them with. He's left out some parts. Actually, most parts. The scary parts.

As his friends escaped, Ian ran about the house, shouting at the demons in the yard, screaming at the monsters on the porch. They spun almost leisurely, gasping, ambling toward him, arms outstretched. There were yards, expanding yards, between him and the nearest creature. This is going to be a breeze, Ian thought. If he didn't watch out, he would lose them and defeat the entire purpose of this excursion.

So, he stayed close, mere feet from the dead, tempting them like a professional baller playing keep-away with a group of small kids. He led them to the front walk, down the deer path, and past the spot where the attack occurred on the Hestons . . .

The Hestons.

Fuck.

It dawned on Ian that he had not seen Dr. Heston since the attack. Not outside the windows, not on the porch, not on the lawn . . .

Then he felt an icy hand lock on his ankle.

Dr. Heston let loose a guttural growl as he pulled himself from the shrubs. He twisted to sink his teeth into Ian's calf.

Ian shrieked. He pulled loose, falling in the process and landing at the edge of the path. Heston snapped at air.

At that moment Ian grasped with equal parts horror and revulsion just why he hadn't seen the doctor earlier. It was because there wasn't much of Heston to be seen. was no Dr. Heston, just the remainder of what was once him, limited to a head, a torso, and a single working arm.

The rest of him no longer existed, chewed and devoured by ghouls whose digestive systems ceased to function decades before.

Heston loosed another piteous moan and inched toward Ian, his one arm dragging him forward through the dirt like a gondolier moving his vessel with a pole. His lone eye—the other was nothing more than a dark, empty socket—met Ian's own and locked. It accused Ian of failing him and his wife. It betrayed his empty needs. It conveyed the pain of a lost soul that will never be relieved.

Ian's face broke, tears streaming. *Shit, 's no time for this*, he thought. Wiping his face with his sleeve, he mustered a weak, "I'm so sorry." He wanted to put Heston out of his misery, but were no tools, not enough time. He was losing valuable seconds, the droves of creatures almost upon him. Goodbye, Dr. Heston.

He decided to lose them in the woods, off the path. With that, he took off with a sprint, moving deep into the foliage.

The branches and the roots grabbed at him, slowing him as they tried to lay claim to his body. He ran blind, unable to shake the things behind him. They only needed a hint of his scent to propel them unflaggingly.

Ian panted hard, his lungs straining to capture oxygen. He was lightheaded, losing his orientation. He was no longer sure he was heading south. In fact, he couldn't discount the possibility he might be running in circles, about to lap the very monsters hot on his tail. God, what if he's leading them back toward . . . he thought about slowing to gain his bearings, but then it was too late.

He bounced off the trunk of a thick cedar, its roots digging deeply into the soil of the forest. He spun for a glimpse of his pursuers and took three backwards steps. And then he disappeared.

Chapter Eighteen:
The Accidental Spelunker

FOR thousands of years, the native trees channeled rain through the earth and into the slightly soluble bedrock below. The runoff percolated through the limestone, forming veins in the rock. Over time, these veins expanded, interconnecting and creating fissures, and those fissures expanded further. A channel the size of a small stream flowed thirty feet below Ian. Washed out bit by bit, the rock could not support the substrate. The cave collapsed inward, forming a sinkhole thirty feet wide that swallowed the forest floor and dragged several cedars down to the depths. They jutted out of the cavern like crazy tusks from a boar's maw.

The sinkhole snatched Ian from the brink. The slope was steep, and Ian flipped end over end. As he bounced toward the cave's mouth, his ribs struck something sharp—a rock or a cedar limb? The blow forced a voluble groan. Ian sailed over the lip, and into the jaws of the grotto. Suddenly, Ian was tumbling through the air in silence. He prepared for the impact. A dozen feet later, he hit. The stream that awaited him was shallow, perhaps a yard deep. The splash was closer to a "splat," and it barely broke his fall.

The cold took his breath, and Ian sucked air. He shook and pulled his wet hair from his brow. He surveyed his predicament.

He was in a cave. He deduced this from subtle hints he gathered in the darkness. His breathing echoed against the cave walls. He thought he heard the flutter of bat wings flitting to and fro. Dampness hung in the air. A slow current dragged at his jeans.

As his eyes adjusted, further clues revealed themselves. The water reflected the stars of the night sky hanging above the cave's circular mouth. As Ian shifted his weight, the water rippled and hundreds of points of light danced before him. The mirror-like surface was framed by a number of large cedars that had come to rest on the floor of the cavern. The downed trees were stacked like a bunch of giant and haphazard tiddlywinks.

He palmed the limestone walls. They were wet and smooth, and the wall's angles too severe.

Then there was a stirring above him, at the edge of the sinkhole's entrance. A shadow fell and plunged into the water just six feet from Ian.

One of them!

Quickly, Ian dove deeper into the cave. He submersed himself completely, swimming like a frog under water. Ten feet later, he stopped and squatted, just his head above the waterline. He opened his mouth wide to take a silent breath, then he sank a few inches so just his eyes and the top of his head were exposed.

The creature exploded from the underground stream, gurgling and writhing from side to side. It was slighter than Ian, maybe a woman.

It's hunting me, Ian thought.

But fortune was on Ian's side. The monster could not find him. He was hidden in the darkness. The echoes of flapping wings of bats in flight disguised his breathing. The stream masked his scent. For now. It would be only temporary.

He needed to act.

He inched toward the creature on his hands and knees, careful not to stir the water. He stayed to the perimeter, well in the shadows. His left hand came across an oblong rock. *Better than a dirt clod*, he thought, grasping it. He would sneak up behind this thing. He would crush her skull.

But then another creature fell into the abyss with a splash and a sputter.

And then another.

And another.

And another.

His plans changed quickly, completely. He needed to get out.

Now.

Panicked, he started backing down the cavern passage. He might elude them by moving deeper into its labyrinth.

No. Despite the creatures popping up and bobbing about him, something gave him pause. Something that took form in a single whispered word on his lips. Deathtrap.

No. He would not find refuge in the cave. He needed to get out.

But how?

He looked up, down, right, left. Sky, water, a dozen or more monsters before him, slick rock walls, fallen trees.

Trees.

There was no time to deliberate. It would have to be the trees. He would climb their broken limbs like a trellis.

Ghouls plummeted into the hole like lemmings. He went forward into Hell.

A fiend surfaced near Ian, and he brought the rock down on its skull like a miner swinging a pick. Another burst forth, and he struck at it, too.

He swung the rock methodically. He swung it with precision and calm. He swung and swung and swung.

His body remembered this motion. "Muscle memory," they call it. His nerves, tissue, and even bone recalled similar blows. He let his mind go blank, and his body harkened back to a summer fair. He had only been fifteen, and he had just met a girl. He had had a crush on her. He had seen a giant stuffed bear held high by a carnie. He had set out to win it, and spent every day for a week at the arcade for a week trying to collect enough tickets. Every day from morning to dusk. Every day playing whack-a-mole.

He finally had won the teddy bear. Whether or not he had given it to the girl didn't really matter. At least not now. The female creature was about to pounce.

❖❖❖

IN spite of her wicked and torn face, Ian recognized her instantly. She was the mother from Flight 183. Ian dared not think of what had happened to her infant. He needed to focus on the task at hand. She pounced, and Ian did not hesitate.

He splintered her braincase. Then he was off, scaling the oldest of the felled trees.

They clamored after him.

The wood was soft, and it slid off in decaying chunks as he climbed. He could find no traction. Shit. This wasn't going to work.

He spied a cedar trunk dangling above him. It ran at a 15-degree angle to the cave floor, extending beyond the cave's mouth. He was going to have to go for it.

He threw his weapon with all of his might at the nearest ghoul. The rock struck the nearest of the things in the chest. It took a few steps back, then kept coming.

Ian leapt, grabbing hold of the decaying tree. It was slick, the top covered with a deep moss. He fought for a grip. His legs dangled before the creatures' mouths. Ian resolved he would not go the way of Jessica, God rest her soul. Quickly, he swung his feet upward, a lunging demon just missing him. He wrapped his thighs around the base, locking his ankles together. His weight now distributed, his hold improved.

He hung there like a three-toed sloth, a sloth acutely aware of the groping claws and open maws beneath him.

What now?

What now? Move your ass up! Get around to the top of this thing!

But that was much easier contemplated than accomplished. He loosened his legs' clutch, and pulled them forward. Then he tightened it again, and advanced his hands. Then he drew his legs inward again. He moved like this, inch by inch, like a caterpillar, for nearly twenty minutes until his head struck the limestone rim of the sinkhole. Once there, he was able to wriggle around to the top of the shaft, his shoulder buttressed by the soil.

Birds were singing. Daylight was approaching.

Ian crawled, digging into the soil with his heels, clutching at bits of root with his nails, literally clawing his way out of the pit. Hand over hand, he used his elbows and forehead to anchor him. His face was low, just inches from the ground, and his vision limited to the patch of dirt directly before him. He pulled, tugged, and pulled some more. He thought he could feel the pitch of the earth changing, little by little becoming less sheer.

He glanced up to see if he might be closing in on the rim.

Shoes.

Muddy and worn shoes. Less than twelve inches from his face.

Ian's eyes moved upward. Soiled pants legs. A bloated torso.

And then the smell.

And the rasping growl.

His eyes tracked upward still.

The remnants of hands stretched toward him, ready to steal his soul.

An eager, almost smiling skull gnashed its teeth. Its face, though disfigured, was unmistakable.

It was the Fat Man.

❖❖❖

THE showdown between a protagonist and his nemesis caps off an adventure, whether it be literature or cinema. Every moment, every movement, has been just a prelude designed to make the climax that much more powerful and visceral. It is classic good versus evil, and the scene promises to connect all the dots and tie together all the loose ends. It's what the fans have been waiting for. They expect to be blown away.

Unfortunately, Ian is not an author, screenplay writer, or director. He doesn't know the rules. If he had known, maybe this battle would have been a bit more elaborate. A bit more staged. Had Ian had foreknowledge, he would have fashioned a sword out of ash or ninja throwing stars from some old vinyl albums.

No. All Ian had was a passing knowledge of judo.

Defensive Tactics was a required course in the New Order, and judo, or the "soft method," was a key component of that curriculum. Students were taught to use an opponent's strength against him by applying force indirectly, to adapt to circumstances, and to use leverage and momentum to keep an attacker off-balance. Basically, use your opponent's weight against him.

This climax was as boring as a math equation, really. The monster was leaning over Ian. (A) His center of gravity was too high, and (B) his weight was displaced forward. (C) His footing was poor, his shoes having little traction on the incline and (D) atrophied muscles compromised his balance. The monster was (E) either not cognizant of his surroundings or unable to process that information and modify his pursuit of Ian.

What do you get when you add A+B+C+D+E?

Ian grabbed the Fat Man by the wrist with his right hand. Tightly. He ignored the fact that it was greasy to the touch, that he felt the skin sloughing off. He pulled the creature toward him, careful not to jerk him too fast (thus possibly dislocating—or, yuck, detaching the arm from—the shoulder) or too slow (thus allowing the creature to roll back on its heels and find traction). Ian drew the monster in evenly. As he slowly pulled, he rolled to the left onto his back and tucked his elbow, quickening the pace and shifting the thing's weight to a single foot.

The monster tumbled over Ian. He bounced, the earth punching his kidney with a grunt as gas belched forth. End over end he flipped. Ian watched him disappear into the chasm.

If this had been a Hollywood climax, Ian would have some swift witticism at the ready, like, "Enjoy your trip, see you next fall" or, "Thanks for the hand." But all he could muster was a muttered, "Fuck you."

Roger Moore would have been so disappointed.

The fans would have been disappointed, too. The climax is supposed to come at the end of the story. Yet there's more story to tell.

Ian caught his breath, then ran.

The monsters could not follow. They lacked his speed and his nimbleness, their fine motor skills a fraction of what they had once been.

❖❖❖

WRIGHT stares at Ian suspiciously. She knows there's more to his story, that he's hiding something. Maybe it's something traumatizing. Maybe it's something secreted to protect the group and their rising spirits. Whatever it is, Wright is sure it's for a reason.

Conversations are returning to the usual. The mundane. The comforting.

What do you miss most?

Food?

Your bed?

Your family?

This is good for them. Generally. But Ian is sick to death of talking about everything he misses. He's too hungry to talk about food, too tired to talk about his bed. He welcomes Wright's suggestion to check the perimeter with her.

Anne sulks as Ian and Wright leave. "How about a story, then? Anyone know any?"

"I've got one," Burt replies. "A little before your time, but still pretty good. 'A long time ago, in a galaxy far, far away—'"

Van interrupts. "Please tell me this isn't *Star Wars*."

And with that, all that was pleasant and previously enjoyed evaporated.

Burt's jaw drops. He asks, "What's so wrong with *Star Wars*?"

Van gives him two words: Frank Herbert. They guy who wrote a little novel called *Dune*. A novel so good, it was made into a movie . . . twice. And *Star Wars* is totally derivative of *Dune*. A copy. And copies are never as good as the original, especially when they're not authorized or credited.

Van turns to Anne, explaining the premise. Essentially, *Star Wars* and *Dune* are the same story, but *Dune* was written ten or more years earlier. "And," he says, "George Lucas totally stole it."

"That's okay," Anne says. "I haven't read either of them."

Van's brow wrinkles. "No, it is definitely not okay. You deserve to hear *Dune*, the original, the *novel*. *Star Wars* is just series of movies that recycled the same themes."

Burt leans in. "Just a series of movies that grossed billions of dollars. Anyway, science fiction, as a genre, regularly recycles themes. Like the orphan of humble beginnings, who struggles against evil and discovers his inner strength in the process; the prophecy of the 'one' who will ultimately bridge the gap between light and dark and bring peace; or—"

"No," Van interjects, "I know you *wish* it was that simple, but it's more than coincidence. They not only share characters, they share key plot points."

"Really, guys," Anne says, sensing the building tension, "I don't mind hearing either story."

They ignore her.

Burt doesn't believe him. "Give me an example," he begs.

Van chews his lip. "Well, it's been a little bit, so you'll have to forgive me if I've forgotten some names and places."

Burt smirks. "Duly noted."

"Okay," Van sighs. "Here goes." And with that, Van begins what can only be called an oral treatise, an exposition on setting, character, and theme. He stands up. "In column A, we have *Dune.*" He gestures with both hands, indicating a pillar on his left. "In column B, we have *Star Wars.*" He says *Star Wars* with disdain. "First, the setting. In column A . . ."

Dune . . . is set largely on Arrakis, a harsh desert planet prone to fierce sandstorms.

Star Wars . . . is set largely on Tatooine, a harsh desert planet prone to fierce sandstorms.

Dune: Arrakis is situated on the edge of the galaxy, but it carries significance because spice mining.

Star Wars: Tatooine is situated on the edge of the galaxy, but carries significance because of spice mining.

"Remember spice in *Star Wars*?" Van asks. "Remember that cheesy pod race in *The Phantom Menace*? Anakin raced through the spice mines."

Dune: Spice is an addictive drug that improves mediation, increases longevity, and grants the power of prophecy.

Star Wars: Spice is an addictive drug that improves meditation, increases longevity, and grants the power of prophecy.

Dune: Spice is so popular a commodity, it is smuggled on the black market and inspires battles for control (the Empire battles Paul Atreides).

Star Wars: Spice is so popular a commodity, it is smuggled on the black market and inspires battles for control (the Trade Federation blockade of Naboo).

"Han Solo was a spice smuggler for gangster Jabba the Hutt, right?" Van asks.

"Yes," Burt says. He clears his throat to say something else, but Van continues. He's on cruise control.

Dune: Arrakis was once covered by water, and great caches of water are stored underground.

Star Wars: Tatooine was once covered by water, and great caches of water are stored underground.

"In *Star Wars*, prospectors search for untapped subterranean water." Van pauses. "I doubt it's a coincidence that George Lucas named a topographical depression on Tatooine the 'Dune Sea.' Seems like a nod and a wink to Herbert, right?"

He's greeted by silence from Burt.

"And then there are the characters..."

Dune: Arrakis is under the jurisdiction of an Empire.

Star Wars: Tatooine is under the jurisdiction of an Empire.

Dune: Struggles among political dynasties are instigated and quelled by an emperor (the Emperor pits the House Harkonnen against Paul Atreides' father, the popular Duke Leto).

Star Wars: Struggles among political dynasties are instigated and quelled by an emperor (the Emperor Palpatine pits various planets and civilizations against each other).

Dune: an orphan undoes The Empire.

Star Wars: an orphan undoes The Empire.

Dune: The orphan's father is murdered (by the Baron Harkonnen).

Star Wars: The orphan's father is murdered (so to speak, by Darth Vader).

Dune: The murderer, in the end, turns out to be the orphan's . . . grandfather (gasp!).

Star Wars: The murderer, in the end, turns out to be the orphan's . . . father (gasp!).

Burt cuts in. "Darth Vader didn't really murder Anakin Skywalker."

"Really?" Van replies. "But isn't that exactly how Ben Kenobi put it?"

Burt nods reluctantly. "Okay, I get it."

"Wait," Van says, "I'm not done yet."

Dune: Mysticism is explored through the Weirding, or Bene Gesserit, Way.

Star Wars: Mysticism is explored through "the Force."

Dune: The orphan (Paul Atreides) receives mental and physical training allowing him to sense the future (called the 'Golden Path').

Star Wars: The orphan (Luke Skywalker) receives mental and physical training allowing him to sense the future (or "disturbances in the Force").

Dune: The orphan can alter others' perceptions or command them into action with his voice.

Star Wars: The orphan can alter others' perceptions or command them into action with his voice.

Dune: The orphan can communicate with dead ancestors (the deceased Harkonnen drives his sister insane).

Star Wars: The orphan can communicate with dead ancestors (Ben Kenobi mentors from the grave).

Dune: The orphan can defy the laws of physics (he realigns his own metabolism to neutralize a toxin).

Star Wars: The orphan can defy the laws of physics (he can move objects with his mind).

"And, also," Van continues . . .

Realizing there will be no story, Anne rolls over and tries to sleep.

❖❖❖

"DO you think it was a mistake," Wright asks, once they are out of earshot, "leaving those two alone together?"

"Nah," Ian replies. But he really isn't thinking about Van and Burt. He's thinking about the night. This night. A full moon illuminates the landscape before them—every tree, every fallen branch, every rock. Their surroundings are nearly luminescent. It's almost as though the terrain is glowing from the inside. It's magical.

But it could also expose them. They are easy targets in this light. Ian feels vulnerable.

He thinks about Kari's question again and corrects himself. "Maybe."

❖ ❖ ❖

"ARE you done, now?" Burt nearly spits.

"Almost. Let's talk about themes."

Genetics.
Dune: Paul Atreides' powers are based in genetics (the product of Bene Gesserit breeding programs).
Star Wars: Anakin Skywalker's powers are based in genetics (his blood contains 'midichloridians,' whatever the hell those are).

Prophecy.
Dune: Paul becomes the one of prophecy (the Kwisatz Haderach).
Star Wars: Anakin becomes the one of prophecy (the one to bring balance to the force).

Cloning.
Dune: a cloned soldier, Duncan Idaho, protects Paul.
Star Wars: cloned soldiers, stormtroopers, protect Anakin.

References to the Third Reich.
Dune: Imperial Sardaukar.
Star Wars: Imperial Stormtroopers.

Worms.
Dune: Arrakis is crawling with giant worms known for attacking ships involved in spice mining.
Star Wars: The asteroid belt is crawling with giant worms known

for attacking ships involved in spice smuggling (Millennium Falcon).

Assassination.

Dune: An attempt is made on Paul's life by an insect-like hunter-seeker that slipped into his bedroom at night.

Star Wars: An attempt is made on Queen Amidala's life by an insect-like creature that slipped into her bedroom at night.

"And then there are the Messianic references—"

"Enough!" Burt cries, loud enough to wake Anne. It is all too much for him.

Chapter Nineteen:
Van Wars – The Return of Brom Sybal

WHEN the world—Burt's world—went to hell, Burt was left with nothing to cling to. He lost everything on that fateful day, 18 years back.

He lost his girlfriend, Melissa.

He lost his unborn son.

He lost his family.

He lost his cat.

He lost his home.

He lost his job.

He lost his dreams.

He would have lost his mind, too, but Burt has largely repressed the events of that day. He has largely hidden the carnage beneath layers and layers of escapist fodder, comic books and movies that replaced his reality with that of Superman, of Luke Skywalker, of Neil Gaiman, and of J.R.R. Tolkien.

He remembers leaving the comic book store early. Something was wrong. There were too few customers. Even the regulars were missing. And they were never missing.

He had tried ringing Mel up. She hadn't answered. There shouldn't have been anything unusual about that. She was hanging with his sister. They were going to redecorate the second bedroom for the baby. Burt's sister, Heather, was particularly artsy. She was going to paint jungle scenes on the walls about the crib. But Burt felt there was something amiss.

Burt hardly recalls his fears being confirmed when he entered his home. It was an older place, but it was all he could afford. The door was ajar, and it groaned like a ghost as he pushed it slowly inward. He started to call for Mel, then saw the gallon of fresh paint turned over in the foyer. Moss green veins streamed across the floor and pooled in a corner. Green footprints, a woman's—maybe his sister's, by the size of them—gave chase down the hall.

Chasing what?

He followed them.

Past the dining room.

Past the bathroom.

Into the kitchen.

Burt barely remembers finding Mel and his sister there. He's repressed the image of them on the floor . . . tearing at Fido's carcass (God, they had thought themselves so clever in naming the calico after a dog) . . . blood and fur strewn about the room and . . . their mouths.

He doesn't recollect dispatching Heather. Or the weight of his grandma's heavy wooden rolling pin in his hand. Or the painful reverberations in his palm as Heather's head gave way.

He can't call to mind Mel's animal expression, her exposed canines, and her charge. Or her nails in his shoulder. Or his panicked grab for the butcher knife on the counter. Or the stabbing. Repeatedly in her chest and . . . belly. Or the cutting. Or Mel's head loosening from her shoulders.

He can't recall striking the match and burning the house, and the secrets it held, to the ground.

He spent the next three weeks holed up in his store's basement, reading every comic about the Man of Steel front to back. When he finished, he watched *Star Wars*. Then he watched it again. And again. Over and over and over. When the battery in his laptop died, he used his portable DVD player. When those batteries failed, he used the batteries from the store's gaming system. When those were spent, he pillaged the batteries from the fire alarm. And after those died, he was left to the machinations of his own mind.

But Burt did not like that place. No, he hated it. He wanted to be in another.

So he simply decided it would be so. It didn't take much more than that decision and time. Time to build a complex alternative reality. A new home he could immerse himself into completely. Convincingly.

In this world, he was a lone Jedi, traveling the outskirts of the galaxy, saving maidens from the Imperial scourge. It was a dangerous assignment, one that prevented him from embracing the trappings of friends and family. It was too risky, too dangerous, to let people get close, especially to someone like him, Brom Sybal.

Brom Sybal? Yes, he had even invented a *Star Wars* name for himself and a back-story that involved—wait for it—being orphaned. When he emerged from the basement, his beard long and hair tied in a Padawan knot, he was no longer plain old Burt.

Brom didn't survive long, however. It was one thing to pretend to be a Jedi in the darkness of a basement. It was another to pretend to be a Jedi in the light of day, without special powers, without a light saber or a starship. Brom couldn't exist in this new world. But neither could the old Burt.

So a new Burt was born, a Burt devoid of recent history. A Burt whose adult years would be bridged by the lessons of fantasy.

And now Van challenges this lie. Van seeks to turn the foundations of this current iteration of Burt into rubble. Van threatens Burt's very existence by exhuming the graves of . . .

No. Burt will not allow that to happen. He can't bear to lose Mel again.

"ENOUGH!" Burt screams again.

Van pays him no heed. "Take all of this, and couple it with Lucas' penchant to borrow from others—he admittedly appropriated from Akira Kurosawa—"

"Don't you ever shut up?!" Burt yells.

"—that proves," Van continues, sternly, "Lucas may have found his influences not so 'long ago,' and in a place not so 'far away.'"

Burt jumps up. He strides toward Van, fists clenched. "You obviously must not have had a daddy, because no one has taught you respect."

Burt finally strikes a nerve.

"Don't you dare talk about my father," Van growls. He's up, chest puffed out. His father is Roger Gerome. He's a hero. He risks his life every day so that insignificant people like Burt can live. Who does Burt think leads the way into the wilderness, locating medicines, supplies, technologies, fuel, and even survivors? Who does he think braved the bay sharks and discovered the colony on South Padre, as well as other islands, spared from the chaos on the mainland? "Fuck you! You should be reading comic books about *real* heroes. Like my dad!"

Anne calls for help.

Burt goes for Van. "You spoiled little—"

He doesn't finish his sentence. As he takes a stride towards Van, he feels an explosion in his stomach. He drops to his knees, gasping, to find Wright standing above him.

Van is emboldened by Wright's intervention. "Yeah, take that, you—"

Wright, still facing Burt, drops low and delivers a blow to Van with her elbow. He goes down hard, holding his groin with a groan reminiscent of a falling tree.

"You want a fight?" Wright hisses. "I'll give you psychos a fight. Don't you remember where we are?"

"He started it," Van groans, clutching his balls.

Burt says, "You little—"

"What was that?" Anne asks, her eyes wild.

They all heard it. A sound not so distant. A sound from the bluff above them. A sound just above the whisper of the wind.

Ian watches the horizon. It glimmers, backlit by the high and ample moon. Nothing but the profile of trees, their leafless branches groping like a witch's skeletal fingers across the night sky.

Ian exhales heavily, a freeing release. Nothing but the contours of trees. He thinks they are safe . . . until the creatures shamble out like apparitions from the shadow forest's columns.

They must flee again.

❖❖❖

"I thought you said you lost them!" Van yells at Ian as they dash off.

Ian thought he had, yet it is Wright who answers for him. "No," she defends. They arrived too quickly to have followed Ian. "They followed us."

She tells Van to move.

The horrible moans are lost within a few hours, but their echoes resonate in Wright's head.

She pushes on.

They find their way to the highway once more. The moon is low, and darkness once again masks their trail. Yet it hides their path forward, as well. Near daybreak, they slow to a walk. They are exhausted. As they lean on their knees, they discover they have stumbled into an immense clearing.

A giant cement structure stands before them, guarded by four turrets. Twenty-foot-high fencing and razor wire—and dozens of monsters—stand between them and the building.

It is a prison.

Wright sees someone on the ramparts, but she does not call for his attention. He already sees her, and he is already signaling to someone outside her view.

She knows they're exhausted, knows they're running on fumes. But they need to make their way to the gate, and they need to do it now.

Wright leads them single file. They start off at a brisk walk, but the creatures key on them promptly. The monsters leave the fence's perimeter, setting a beeline for them. The protagonists make a dash for the gate.

Wright draws her firearm. She waits for the monsters to get close. She shoots when the first gets too near their flank. The thing takes a scalping shot to the top of its head. Anne screams, pulling Van close, as the dead thing falls. Its legs go out from underneath it. It writhes, but not in agony. Its motor cortex has been destroyed, and it no longer has control of its limbs.

The second stands directly in her way. Wright comes straight at it and fast, almost too fast. As her heart rate increases, her mind starts limiting the range and amount of information it can process. Her senses narrow. Her world slows. The sound dies down around her. Her vision goes dark at the sides.

Everything becomes crystal clear.

It takes her three shots to bring this monstrosity down. She sees each discharge: the bullet to the shoulder, the second to the cheek, the third striking the spinal cord just below the skull. It falls forward, its mandibles working furiously. She catches it at the chest with a forearm, just avoiding its broken teeth—sharp like a vampire's—and shoves it away fiercely.

Another approaches from her right, and she puts two rounds into its chest. It slows, but the caliber is too small to drop it. It lunges at Burt, the last in line, and he avoids it with a shrill sob.

They are thirty feet from the gate when it opens. Four men in riot gear emerge, shotguns extended. *Police officers*, Wright thinks.

They signal them to enter and fan out. They fire at the creatures. Their weapons are devastating. Cartridges explode and go wide, spinning the things by the shoulder, mowing them down at the knees, tearing their heads from their torsos.

The group collapses in a pile in the courtyard, shaking and quivering, withered by starvation and fatigue. They hold each other, weeping as the gate closes behind them.

They are safe.

Chapter Twenty:
History Lesson

THEIR rescuers are not police officers. They are prisoners, and they feed Wright and her team from the bounty of their garden. There are tomatoes, carrots, beans, and corn. And there's more: chicken!

The survivors gorge themselves, or at least attempt to, each realizing in turn that their stomachs have shriveled, deprived of true sustenance for so long.

Afterward, they are shown to cells, rooms where they can sleep. And they do, long and hard.

When they awake, there is a fresh change of clothes for each, prisoner garb to wear while their clothes are washed. They are split up, the women shown one shower, the men another.

Once rested and bathed, they are asked to join the residents—they prefer to be called residents rather than inmates—in the gymnasium.

Wright notices there isn't a single person dressed in a guard's uniform. No police. Maybe they are wearing prison clothes too? Or maybe prisoners saved them?

Yes, the guards had indeed cut and run at the outset of the epidemic.

But the residents have many questions, too. There's nearly twenty years of history that has yet to be catalogued.

Wright takes it upon herself to detail a lost past.

The condition spread far and wide, touching every town in every county in every state in every nation of every continent with its dark and sickly finger.

"Chicago?" someone asks her.

"Gone," Wright replies. Places like Chicago witnessed the worst of the plague's ravages. Unlike southern towns, cities in the north had largely illegalized not just the mere possession but also the ownership of firearms. Only the police carried handguns. But Chicago's police force of 13,000 could do little more than witness the carnage. Within two weeks of the plague's emergence, the city was dead. Its great towers, its renowned museums, and its magnificent mile of shops were nothing more than catacombs for millions of ghouls.

The federal government, obviously, failed. It should not come as a surprise. After all, this is the same government that couldn't stop a plane from hitting a tower, let alone two; couldn't find a single terrorist in the middle east in an area no bigger than New Jersey; couldn't determine whether an impoverished country had weapons of mass destruction; couldn't prevent the financial collapse of the greatest economy in the world; and couldn't do anything, really, that governments are supposed to do.

That's what happens when leaders are chosen less for their intelligence and more for whether they'll have a couple of beers (and maybe a shot of whiskey or two) with some good ol' boys down at the local tap.

How odd then that these good ol' boys, the very people who ensured federal failure and the deaths of 250 million through the ignorance of their votes, ultimately became the salvation of humanity. How odd that their conviction in an inalienable right to hunt with AK-47s, in a definition of marriage limited to a single man and woman, and in a single absolute Christ would turn the tide and ensure the continuation of the human species.

The tide turned in the Bible belt. It only makes sense. The south had everything in its favor. The residents were able to defend themselves (it is a land where guns outnumber people); steadily repopulate (it is a land where children marry and beget more children); fortify and expand their boundaries by ten or more miles each year (it is a land that exists to export God's word); and begin a new civilization.

But Wright suspects they had something else, something she will keep to herself for now: an evolutionary advantage.

The human body has evolved a magnificent defensive array, an immune system built over millions of years. Natural selection—mutation, cellular diversification, and evolution—allowed the forebears to humanity to fight viruses, bacteria, and parasites in succession. Yet, as highly refined as the human body is, it cannot fight all infections. Some bugs are too fast. Others can go under cover. And sometimes the human immune system overreacts, using such force that it causes collateral damage, destroying the very cells it is assigned to protect. Avoidance, in the end, is the most effective method of controlling diseases.

Behavior plays a significant component in avoiding illness in all animals. Creatures big and small are driven by instinct to shun others who show signs of illness. Humans, though, can go it one better. Humans not only know to avoid others who are sick, but to steer clear of those who *might* be sick.

But here, too, the immuno-response can be excessive, triggered by a belief that people who are somehow different harbor diseases. The response can be so strong that it supplants all reason. Here, racism can wear the mask of patriotism. The Nazis linked the Jews to leprosy, typhus, cholera, and dysentery. Neo-Cons, the "new" breed of conservative, blamed the swine flu epidemic of 2009 on Mexican immigrants.

But this fear of others, Wright expects, helped the Bible belt. Their suspicions of outsiders served them well, limiting their exposure to strangers and the disease that might come with them. Xenophobia, strangely enough, may have helped save the human race.

As the United States fell away, in its vacuum rose a federation; not a federation of states, but a federation of churches. Christian leaders assumed the mantle of power, spreading the gospel that the plague was the harbinger of the final days of man. The holy compact grew to stretch across the middle south.

The church assumed authority of law enforcement and the judiciary. What was left of the city and state tribunals did not contest the move. How could they? So few of them remained intact at the beginning of the New Order. They needed the church.

Commerce—a barter system at first, but commerce still—grew steadily, subsidized by in part by scouting parties to the wild, scouting parties led by Roger Gerome. Employment comes easily to those who are citizens. The price for citizenship is conscription. Four years of border duty, or two years in Gerome's service, will buy someone a substitute for the American dream. Most opt for border duty.

Students are now taught a mixture of hard academics and fundamentalism, constantly reminded of God's ability to punish and destroy any modern day Sodom and Gomorra. The students are drilled, just like their elders serving in the armed forces, to combat and survive incursions. Although fewer and farther between, their tales still instill terror.

Wright stops. "Are there questions?" She expects a flood from this group of thirty, but there is only one hand raised. Wright nods. "Yes?"

"My name is Connor. I'm, I guess, what you might call the leader here."

"Hi, Connor. Thank you for your hospitality."

"Oh, yes. So, what can you tell us about it—I think you called it a *condition?*"

Funny, Wright thinks. *They want answers just as I do.* But she must tread carefully. She's aware that the chaplain and a group of prisoners near him are shifting in their seats uncomfortably. "We'll never know for sure," she says. "There is no government-sponsored work on this, although there is a rumor in certain circles that a group of scientists is holed up in a missile silo working on this. But it is only a rumor."

"Is it a virus, like the cold?" Connor asks.

There's grumbling, then someone near the chaplain calls, "Heresy!"

The more things change the more they stay the same, Wright reflects.

A man stands, pushing his chair aside. "What we are witnessing is a perversion of the transubstantiation—the symbolic act of eating the body of Christ, the bread, and drinking of his blood, the wine. It is God's revenge. Plain and simple." He is a balding, grey little creature. He is a murderer.

Ian regards him, thinking, *Gollum*. God's will? He's heard this all before.

"Mr. Ridge," Connor says, "that's enough." Then he says something that sends a chill up Ian's spine. "I want to remind everyone this party is under my protection. They are not to be harmed. Should any hurt come to them, I will personally see to it that you hang from the southeast turret. I'll push you from the gallows myself. Understood?"

He barely has control, if he has any at all, Ian thinks.

There is no response from the residents. A mountain of a man rises, and Ian thinks Connor is going to be challenged. Instead, the man says, "Connor asked you question. Do you understand?"

The room nods in unison, even Van. All nod, except Gollum.

Gollum stomps off, the chaplain and a handful of others following him from the room.

"Thank you, Mr. Creedy," Connor says, then to Wright, "My apologies for Ira's outburst. Please continue."

Wright decides she has nothing left to say. It's best that way.

They retreat to their cells.

❖❖❖

"ARE you awake?" It comes in a whisper, soft, but intense.

Wright opens her eyes, hand at her firearm. Creedy kneels at the side of her bunk. "Can I talk to you a moment?" he says.

"What is it?" Wright asks.

"Not here," Creedy replies, nodding toward Ian's cell across the corridor. "Alone."

She studies Creedy, then nods her assent.

"This way," Creedy says, exiting the cell. "Follow me."

The springs groan gently as Wright shifts her weight from the mattress. She regards Ian through the bars, then moves on. She pursues Creedy down C Block's narrow passage . . . completely unaware that Ian has overheard every word.

Creedy's hulking frame fills the width of the passage. Despite twenty years of squats, presses, lifts, and curls, Creedy still maintains a gazelle-like grace and fluidity. He moves quickly and silently through the labyrinth until he arrives at a pair of glass doors engraved "Library, Suite 107."

"We're here." He ushers Wright into the room with a giant hand.

She brushes by him into the darkness. She feels him follow, hears him flip switches on the wall. The fluorescents flicker, row upon row winking to life.

They stand before a cavernous room. Row after row of shelves, each brimming with books, span the expanse. Novels, nonfiction, magazines, treatises, journals and other tomes of varying size, color, and subject matter. Wright hasn't seen anything like this in a long time. She parts her lips to speak—

"Thirty-thousand, nine-hundred and three," Creedy says, anticipatorily.

Wright regards him, stunned.

He blushes. It goes without saying. He has had a lot of time on his hands.

"At least I know where our tax dollars were going," Wright muses.

"LOOK, I've brought you here for a reason." He's nervous. There's sweat on his lip. It must be good. "Connor and I don't necessarily agree with the others about the plague, but it's pretty dangerous for us to talk about it. I'm a big guy, a guy who can defend himself, but no amount of size or strength is going to protect you when someone puts a shiv in your ribs during your sleep, you know?"

Wright's eyes are wide.

"Okay," he chuckles, "maybe you don't know. Let me just say this: I'm not so sure we're facing Armageddon. I'm not agnostic, but I just don't think the epidemic is of, well, divine origin."

"So," Wright toys, "you think this is an epidemic?"

"Don't you?" he asks, offering a quick smile. "I'm no doctor, so I can't say this is a pathogen. But I'm pretty sure it is. But we have to view this in broader terms. We need to think more expansively."

Her earlier discussion with Burt tugs at Wright's subconscious again. Here, an opportunity is presented to clear the air a bit and brainstorm. "I'm glad you said that, because I'd like to ask you a question."

"Please do. Ask me anything." Creedy misses being able to have a dialog with someone, especially a woman.

Wright hesitates, studying Creedy a full second as an internal debate rages. "Okay," she resolves, "but you have to promise me you won't tell anyone else." What she is going to ask is heresy.

Creedy's never been one to bend to another's will, even when it's been in his best interest to do so. "That, in a nutshell, explains why I'm here. But it also explains why I can't just accept that this"—he indicates the space around him, beyond the confines of the prison, with up-turned palms—"as God's will. I mean, why would God spare inmates? We're a bunch of murderers, thieves, rapists, and drug dealers. We're the original monsters that society hid away and forgot. But God does-n't forget. And if God was concerned about heresy, I wouldn't be here right now. I'd be one of those things outside. So, yeah, I promise not to say a word. Fire away."

"Do you have any books about the occult?" she asks. "Specifically, vampires."

❖ ❖ ❖

AN hour later, Wright faces Creedy across a broad library table, dozens of books and loose papers spread between them. Creedy is silent, and Wright feels the need to fill the vacuum. "I know this seems crazy . . . "

"Crazy," Creedy repeats, nodding. "Sounds crazy, but let's be hon-est: crazy's not in short supply these days. Think of it like this: fifty years ago, any talk about zombies would have seemed crazy, too. But not now. So tell me why you want to know about vampires."

Ah, the "why." The "what" part was hard enough! The why is a lit-tle more complex. "Essentially," Wright stammers, "the assumption that the epidemic is novel—I mean a unique event—might be false." The skeptic in her begs her to stop, but Wright pushes ahead. "I'm having a problem accepting that recent events"—and she uses the term 're-cent' loosely in the context of human history—"represent earth's only experience with the plague."

Creedy cuts through the jargon. "You think this might have hap-pened before? And vampire lore might prove a window into that past?"

Wright feels stupid. "I don't know, perhaps—"

"Wait one second, there's a book I've forgotten." Creedy is off, marching into the stacks. Wright hears him mumbling, "Where is it?" then, "Bush, Bush—Ah, here it is!" He emerges from the stacks, a book open before him. He bumps the shelves hard with a shoulder, dislodging several treatises on U.S. foreign policy. He fumbles to catch them, but they clatter to the floor. Rather than gather them, he proceeds to the table. "I'll get those later," he huffs.

"What do you have there?" she asks.

"This," he announces, as if introducing guests at a royal dinner, "is Haim's *Ghosts, Goblins, and Things that Go Bump in the Night.*" He passes the book to Wright. "Although they pretty much leave me alone here— I don't make waves and it doesn't hurt that I am as big as an ox—I keep this hidden."

Why? The book would be considered profane. He has to hide lots of books, or else Ira Ridge, Ian's Gollum, and the others will burn them. Where does he hide them? Lots of places. This one he hid behind the memoirs of George Bush.

"Father or son?" she asks.

"W."

A memoir of his presidency? "You're right; no one will ever look there," Wright chuckles. Hard to believe they were actually better off then.

❖❖❖

WRIGHT flips through the pages, scanning images of ghosts, demons, witches . . . and then one particular picture catches her eye. She backtracks to page 86. There is an etching of a skeletal creature, its fingers and lips missing. It devours what looks to be a human hand. She reads the caption under the etching:

"Wendigo."

She hands the book over to Creedy.

He squints as he reads. "'The Wendigo: a vampiric monster in Algonquin mythology.' They're presumed to have once been human, preying on Native American hunters." He stares hard at Wright. "It kind of looks like one of those things out there!"

Wright nods. She takes the book back and turns several pages ahead. Again she stops. "Look at this one."

Creedy gawks at the picture of a humanoid eating the corpse of a woman by the light of the moon. "Loango," the caption under the illustration reads. "It says this vampire's from Africa."

Wright turns the page. "Bruxsa," she says, eyeing the drawing of another ghoul. She reads for a minute, then summarizes. "Apparently, also a vampire. This one was known to eat its own children. Many cultures believe that vampires prey first on family and loved ones. Their incarnation gives shape and face to taboo."

"No," Creedy enjoins, "they're wrong." The writer. The folklorists. They're wrong. "These things simply covet what they know."

WRIGHT is reading the book's table of contents. It contains a listing of vampire lore by nation.

Albania: Sampiro, Lingat;
Armenia: Dahkanavar;
Assyria: Ekimmu;
Australia: Yara-ma-yha-who;
Babylonia: Lilitu;
Bavaria: Nachtzeher;
Belarus: Mjertovjec;
Benin: Asiman/Obayifo . . .
"My God, this book is full of these things."
Bohemia and Moravia: Ogoljen, Mura, Vilkodlak;
Bosnia-Herzegovina: Blautsauger, Lampir;
Brazil: Lobishomen, Jaracaca;
Bulgaria: Krvoijac, Obur;
Burma: Thaye/Tasei;
China: P'O, Ch'ing Shih;
Crete: Kathakanko;
Croatia: Pijavica;
Czech Republic: Ogoljen;
Dalmatia: Kuzlak;
France: Melusine, Moribondo;
Germany: Alp, Mara, Nachtzehrer, Neuntoter;
Ghana: Asasabonsam;
Greece: Lamia, Empusa, Brukulako, Vrykolakas, Catacano, Callicantzaros;
Gypsy: Sara, Mullo, Dhampire;
Holland: Mara . . .
Wright reads aloud. "'Although the origin and details differ region-

ally, all cultures believe in the undead returning to life to devour the living.'"

Hungary: Liderc Nadaly, Pamgri, Vampyr;
India: Baitol, Bhuta, Kali, Churel, Punyaiama, Rakshasas, Chedipe;
Indonesia: Ponianak, Buo;
Ireland: Dearg-dul;
Italy: Vampiri, Strix, Strega;
Japan: Kappa;
Macedonia: Vryolakas;
Malaysia: Lansuyar, Penanggalan, Langsuit;
Mexico: Cihuateteo, Camazotz, Tlahuelpuchi;
Namibia: Otigiruru;
Peru: Pishtaco;
Philippines: Aswang;
Poland: Upier, Upierzyca;
Polynesia: Talamaur . . .

"In fact, in Christian society, the vampiric taboo can be traced all the way to Leviticus 17:14 . . . "

Portugal: Brusxa;
Prussia: Gierach, Stryz, Viesczy;
Romania: Strigoi, Muronul, Nosferatu, Vircolac;
Russia: Viexczy, Uppyr, Oupyr, Ereticy, Vampir, Myertovets, Vurdalak, Upierzhy;
Saxony: Neuntoter . . .

" . . . to paraphrase, 'Blood is life and whoever eats of the blood shall be cut off from God . . . '"

Scotland: Baobham Sith;
Serbia: Vlkoslak, Mulo, Dhampir;
Slovenia: Vukodlak;
Spain: Vampiro;
Sweden: Vampyr;
Thailand: Phii;
Tibet: Wrathful Dieties;
Uganda: Obayifo;
West Indies: Asema, Loogaroo, Sukuyan;
Yugoslavia: Vlkodlak, Mulo, Vukodlak . . .

" . . . Those unfortunate enough to die at the hands of these monsters are doomed to the very same fate: to walk the Earth in eternal damnation."

Vampire.

Creedy sits motionless, his mind racing. "It is an interesting premise," he allows. *Interesting?* Interesting is a term used by people to describe simple wonders. It shouldn't be used to summarize that which cannot be or dare not be comprehended. No, this hypothesis can only be deemed Scary As All Hell.

"Truth be known," Wright admits, "it's not really mine." She tells Creedy of her conversation with Burt.

Creedy has questions, though. "If these creatures are modern-day vampires, why didn't an outbreak decimate our ancestors? How is it that humanity survived for as long as it did in the face of something so virulent?"

Good questions. "Maybe the pathogen mutated." Then she thinks again. "Maybe it hasn't changed much at all." Wright wishes Dr. Heston was alive. He might have some answers.

Creedy scoffs. "I'm not one for conspiracy theories. And believe me, I've heard them all in this place."

Wright's not suggesting a government cover-up. God knows the government had enough trouble just getting the garbage collected. "All I'm saying is, there's a lot we don't know, and the government has never been particularly helpful in shedding light on dark ambiguities."

Like?

"Like mass disappearances," Wright offers. Like the Mayans. Like the colony of Roanoke. Or Hoer-Verde.

Six hundred people disappeared at the latter, the only clue some scribbling in a public school. It said, "There is no salvation."

"What if those societies were forced to migrate because of this or some similar epidemic?" *Worse*, she thinks, *what if they disappeared from the fossil record because they were consumed?*

That reminds Creedy of a story, a biography he read once about a guy named Sir John Franklin. He was an explorer out of England looking for the fabled Northwest Passage, a passage north from Europe to Asia. He left with two ships and 120 men. The ships and the crew disappeared . . . for the most part.

"What happened to them?" Wright asks.

"No one's really sure. It became the fixation of Britain, though, and forty plus ships went looking for him." They found nothing but a trail of death: first, the graves of three soldiers, members of Franklin's team who died in the first days of the expedition, much too early; then, a life boat containing two more corpses, one badly mutilated; and, finally, in a spot so barren the Inuit did not even name it, the remains of thirty sailors. They hadn't frozen to death. They had been cannibalized, their only remains piles of skulls, mutilated corpses, and broken long bones. Those deaths struck Creedy. "But it's a huge logical leap to link *that* to *this*. And if it is a plague, why didn't it wipe us all out back then?"

"Globalization," Wright considers out loud. "Those people who disappeared—colonies and outposts and the like—were all fairly isolated." Sometimes they were cut off by mountains, sometimes by oceans. But 21st century man, despite all of his advances in science and medicine, had one significant disadvantage: a global economy. The global economy finds its roots in international trade and travel. Instead of ships and horses and wagons, commerce moves at high speed via jetliners, passports, and bullet trains. "That, or a recent mutation has allowed it spread more quickly."

But that doesn't explain why incidents are documented so intermittently. Creedy offers an idea, something from Haim's tome. He flips through it hurriedly, stopping and thumping a page entitled, "Vampire Epidemics through the Ages."

Wright reads a series of dates and locations from a list:
Istria (1642)
East Prussia (1710 and 1721)
Hungary (1725-30)
Austrian Serbia (1731-2)
East Prussia (1750)
Silesia (1755)
Wallachia (1756)
Russia (1772)

It is a history of vampire attacks, four centuries' worth, assuming it's not just a chronicle of mass hysteria.

CLAP.

A sound. Somewhere in the library, somewhere from within the labyrinth.

"What was that?" Wright asks, rising from her seat. Her face crawls with worry.

Creedy doesn't twitch. "Don't worry," he says, not looking up from the book. "That happens a lot around here. Old periodicals tend to take on a life of their own."

Great, Wright thinks. *Zombies, mummies, vampires, and, now, ghosts.*

Creedy has a thought. Maybe they can determine what's what if they can connect the vampire epidemics to a historical cause.

Wright's game, but she has no idea what the periods have in common. But what better place than a library to start investigating? "Where are the almanacs?"

Chapter Twenty-One:
Ill-Starred Indeed

WRIGHT focuses on natural phenomena—drought, glaciers, earthquakes—while Creedy examines societal changes—colonization, war, population migration, plagues. They work for hours, mapping each event in tidy rows and columns. If the dates match or approximate a vampiric episode, an "X" is placed in the appropriate box of the matrix.

Unfortunately, those marks prove few and far between. Try as Wright and Creedy might, they can't establish a pattern.

Wright grows frustrated with this exercise. She tosses an almanac on the table. It lands face down, its spine nearly breaking. Wright immediately feels guilty. How could she callously damage something so precious, a book so . . . rare?

She picks the almanac up, running her fingers along the binding, inspecting it for damage. The book falls open to a page concerning cycles of the moon. There are illustrations of the moon's phases, a lunar calendar.

A voice whispers in her ear, a memory from the first days of their journey. The little voice is Anne's, and it says, "As above, so below."

As above, so below.

She and Creedy looked everywhere. Everywhere but toward the sky. Space, the final frontier. "We haven't looked at the stars or planets. What if there's an astrological link?"

So they search, digging into the card catalog, flipping through microfiche, churning through the periodicals. Then Creedy discovers an article printed in 2003 in the *National Geographic News*, "Way Out Theory Ties Comet to Origins of SARS." He hands it to Wright. "What do you think of this?"

It looks as promising as any other lead. But before she can answer, the doors of the library crash open.

A horde of prisoners charge in.

They are led by Ira Ridge. "Seize them!" the Gollum shrieks. "Seize them!"

❖❖❖

THE struggle with the prisoners is short.

Creedy's trial is even shorter.

The prisoners convict Creedy of heresy after less than five minutes of testimony. Chaplain Cadavori abstains, nervously washing his hands of it like a modern day Pilate.

Creedy calls for Connor's help. But Connor has outlived his usefulness.

His knowledge proved invaluable to the prison; he maintained the generator, knew when to rotate the crops, and managed the collection and filtration of water. Now the prisoners had learned of another world, a world outside these confines, a world they plan to escape to. And none of Connor's know-how matters there.

"I'm sorry, Creedy," Ridge says. "Connor can't hear you. He's outside the walls, making some new friends."

It's a coup, a power grab. Creedy's sentence is death. He will go to the gallows the next morning.

❖❖❖

WRIGHT, Van, Burt, and Anne are prodded from their individual cells into a larger pen. "Where's Ian?"

Wright gets her answer hours later. Ian is tossed into the cell unceremoniously. The prisoners found him in the mess hall. He takes a seat across from Wright and Burt and waits for their captors to clear the cell block before speaking. "What's SARS?" he asks.

Wright is puzzled. "Why?"

From the pocket of his jeans Ian pulls several folded pages. He casually tosses them towards Wright's feet.

She eyes Ian curiously before picking up the documents. She unfolds them. Her jaw drops. It's the article about SARS and space and her handwritten timeline of the vampire epidemics. "How did you get these?" she asks, holding the documents before Ian's face.

Then she remembers the noise of the falling book. "You were in the library? Why?"

Ian is shamefaced. "I thought you might need some help."

Wright feels her face go hot. "And what makes you think I would ever need *your* help?"

It's Ian's turn to get mad. "Let's just say I'm questioning your decision-making skills lately."

"What?"

He will not be intimidated. "You heard me," he seethes. Wright taught them to never wander from the party. She taught them to never go anywhere by themselves. "And I don't think departing with a convicted felon who (a) is bigger than a mountain gorilla and (b) hasn't seen a woman in two decades constitutes prudent judgment."

Touché.

They stare at each other, no further words passing between them.

Burt eventually breaks the stalemate. "SARS? What's going on here?"

WRIGHT passes the article around. They read in turn.

Severe acute respiratory syndrome, or SARS, inflicted thousands of people at the beginning of the millennium. It's source remained cloaked in mystery—some thought it evolved naturally, while others said it jumped from another species—until a group of British scientists determined its evolution was completely independent. It did not share an evolutionary history with other coronaviruses, leading the researchers to speculate SARS found its origins in space. It fell to Earth, along with the hundred tons of space debris that fall each year, landing in China. Carried in the debris trail of a comet, the virus entered the stratosphere as Earth passed through the particles. The fallout likely occurred east of the Himalayas where the stratosphere is the thinnest.

Extraterrestrial origins would explain why epidemics occur so randomly; why infection rates cannot be easily modeled, and why, bombarded by radiation, mutations occur so suddenly.

Wright doesn't remember much about SARS, just Jay Leno joking about it on the Tonight Show.

Burt rubs his beard. In the end, SARS infected tens of thousands of people. In the end, SARS didn't matter. Burt groans, "Geez, comets and meteors."

"Technically," Anne says, "comets and meteors are not the same. Meteors come from comets."

Anne notices Wright staring at her. Staring at her like she's daft, like she's grown a second head. Then Wright says, "Anne, what else do you know about comets?"

WHEN clouds of interstellar material collapse, heavy under their own gravity, suns are born. Rocks, dust, and gases swirl, eventually pooling together as planets and satellites. But, in the far outreaches of space, bits and pieces of the new solar system sit, discarded and forgotten like broken toys. In the blackness in the Oort Cloud and the Kuiper Belt at the fringes of the Milky Way, these outcasts are interned for eternity.

Usually.

The solar system is a "system" after all, and an order dictates the movement of its celestial members. But sometimes in a patent challenge to that stability, a rock breaks free of its inky confinement. Urged and whipped by gravity, the comet has one of two fates: it is either expelled from the solar system, doomed to roam interstellar space, or, it moves into the inner solar system. Comets that remain in the solar system are caught in the jealous pull of the sun and the planets, eventually settling into a predictable orbit.

"It's like a beautiful cosmic dance," Anne gushes. Some dances, it seems, are longer than others. If the orbital path takes less than two hundred years, the comet is classified as a short-period comet. More than 200 years, the comet is deemed to be long-term.

Away from the sun, a comet is generally just ice and rock (solidified carbon, organic material, nitrogen, oxygen, and water) several miles wide. The ice and rock forms a nucleus. As the comet approaches the sun, the surface ice starts to melt. Gases and dust are expelled, creating a large, glowing aura. This, the head or coma, can grow thousands of miles, surpassing the width of most of the solar system's planets. Solar winds rake the comet, dislodging gas and dust and forming two distinct tails. The longer of the two, the blue gas tail, can reach several million miles in length.

The material that is blown from the comet follows in its parent's orbit. The orbits of planets intersect with the comet's path. The rocks and dust, now called meteors, slam into the atmosphere, creating brilliant displays, meteor showers. The heat destroys most before they can reach the Earth's surface.

Those meteorites that survive are interstellar shuttles, carrying a whole suite of organic materials, amino acids, and even living cells safely to the Earth. Large meteors usually explode before impact, 600 to 15,000 miles above the surface, their precious cargo protected within the debris, within a cosmic rain.

Isaac Newton theorized comets played a role in creating life. Earth's early oceans were full of organic molecules carried by comets and primitive meteorites. These organisms would eventually evolve into multi-cellular creatures.

Wright considers this. The ability to give life, and then to take it away in increments, first the dinosaurs, now us.

"Anne," Wright asks, "do you want to tell us how you know all this?"

"My mom was an astrologist, before," she replies innocently. "She taught me a lot."

The admission strikes Wright. Anne is fearless. Astrology borders on heresy for two reasons: it is predictive and only God has that power, and it borders on hard science, on astronomy. Yet here this young woman sits, a testimony to the fact that the tighter the church clenches the more freedoms slip through its iron grip.

All of them are testimonials to this freedom in their own ways, really: Dr. Heston's stubborn reluctance to let go of science; Burt's escape into his banned comics; Van's bad-boy image and his love of illicit books and movies; and Ian's freedom of thought, his hunger for knowledge. She asks herself, just how much freedom has the church seized? Just how much freedom can they ever really seize?

"What's this other paper?" Burt asks, pointing to Wright's timeline.

"Just working on a theory," Wright says. "Technically, *your* theory."

❖ ❖ ❖

WRIGHT modifies her timeline. She crosses through drought, plague, and war, replacing each word with "Comet." She has more questions for Anne. "What is it called when a comet approaches the sun?"

It's called the perihelion.

"Do you know of any specific perihelions?"

Some. Which ones does Wright want?

"Any," Wright replies. "All."

Wright compiles a less-than-complete list. She writes "DNK" when Anne does not know the specific period.

Comet: Borrelly
Orbital P: couple years (short)
Known approach to the sun: DNK

Comet: Brorsen-Metcalf
Orbital P: 70 years

Known approach to the sun: 1989 or 1990

Comet: D'Arrest
Orbital P: less than 10 years
Known approach to the sun: 2008

Comet: Encke
Orbital P: 3.3 years
Known approach to the sun: 2007

Comet: Giacoboni-Zinner
Orbital P: DNK
Known approach to the sun: DNK

Comet: Hale-Bopp
Orbital P: 4000 years
Known approach to the sun: DNK

Comet: Halley
Orbital P: 76 years
Known approach to the sun: 1997

Comet: Hyakutake
Orbital P: 30,000 years
Known approach to the sun: DNK

Comet: Ikeya-Seki
Orbital P: 900 years
Known approach to the sun: DNK

Comet: Shoemaker
Orbital P: DNK
Known approach to the sun: DNK

Comet: Swift-Tuttle
Orbital P: 120 years
Known approach to the sun: 1980(?)

Comet: Tempel
Orbital P: 5 to 6 years

Known approach to the sun: 2005

Comet: Tempel-Tuttle
Orbital P: 33 years
Known approach to the sun: 1998

Wright focuses on those orbits between twenty and a hundred years, narrowing her list down to Brorsen-Metcalf, Halley, and Tempel-Tuttle. She then works backwards, documenting the orbital periods, noting those perihelions by year if they occurred within a dozen years or so of a vampiric incident or epidemic.

Coronado/Zuni Indian attacks, New Mexico, 1540
Brorsen-Metcalf perihelion: NA
Halley perihelion: 1529
Tempel-Tuttle perihelion: 1533

Tadhq O'Carroll, Ireland, 1552
Brorsen-Metcalf perihelion: 1566 (post)
Halley perihelion: NA
Tempel-Tuttle perihelion: 1567 (post)

Cormac McCarthy, Ireland, 1601
Brorsen-Metcalf perihelion: NA
Halley perihelion: 1605
Tempel-Tuttle perihelion: 1600

Istria vampire epidemic, 1642
Brorsen-Metcalf perihelion: 1636
Halley perihelion: NA
Tempel-Tuttle perihelion: 1633

Croatia (Giure Grando), 1672
Brorsen-Metcalf perihelion: NA
Halley perihelion: 1681 (post)
Tempel-Tuttle perihelion: 1666

Rohr accounts ("De Maticatione Mortnorum," or "On the Chewing Dead"),
1679
Brorsen-Metcalf perihelion: NA

Halley perihelion: 1681 (post)
Tempel-Tuttle perihelion: 1666

Hungary vampire epidemic, 1692-1699
Brorsen-Metcalf perihelion: NA
Halley perihelion: 1681
Tempel-Tuttle perihelion: 1698

East Prussia (a.k.a. Northern Poland) vampire hysteria, 1710
Brorsen-Metcalf perihelion: 1707
Halley perihelion: NA
Tempel-Tuttle perihelion: 1698

Haidamack, Hungary (Count of Cabreras), 1715
Brorsen-Metcalf perihelion: 1707
Halley perihelion: NA
Tempel-Tuttle perihelion: NA

East Prussia II, 1721
Brorsen-Metcalf perihelion: NA
Halley perihelion: NA
Tempel-Tuttle perihelion: 1733 (post)

Hungary II, 1725-1734
Brorsen-Metcalf perihelion: NA
Halley perihelion: NA
Tempel-Tuttle perihelion: 1733

Austria Serbia, 1730-1734
Brorsen-Metcalf perihelion: NA
Halley perihelion: NA
Tempel-Tuttle perihelion: 1733

East Prussia III, 1750
Brorsen-Metcalf perihelion: NA
Halley perihelion: NA
Tempel-Tuttle perihelion: NA

Silesia/Olmutz incident, 1755
Brorsen-Metcalf perihelion: NA

Halley perihelion: 1757 (post)
Tempel-Tuttle perihelion: 1767 (post)

Wallachia, 1756
Brorsen-Metcalf perihelion: NA
Halley perihelion: 1757 (post)
Tempel-Tuttle perihelion: 1767 (post)

Russia, 1772
Brorsen-Metcalf perihelion: 1777 (post)
Halley perihelion: 1757
Tempel-Tuttle perihelion: 1767

Cologne, Germany, 1790
Brorsen-Metcalf perihelion: 1777
Halley perihelion: NA
Tempel-Tuttle perihelion: 1799 (post)

Tillinghast, 1796
Brorsen-Metcalf perihelion: NA
Halley perihelion: NA
Tempel-Tuttle perihelion: 1799 (close)

Rose family, Rhode Island, 1874
Brorsen-Metcalf perihelion: NA
Halley perihelion: NA
Tempel-Tuttle perihelion: 1866

New England (Mercy Brown), 1892
Brorsen-Metcalf perihelion: NA
Halley perihelion: NA
Tempel-Tuttle perihelion: 1899 (post)

Manchester, England (Hillgate sighting), 1969
Brorsen-Metcalf perihelion: NA
Halley perihelion: NA
Tempel-Tuttle perihelion: 1965

Malawi (Governor Eric Chawaya), 2002-2003
Brorsen-Metcalf perihelion: 1989

Halley perihelion: NA
Tempel-Tuttle perihelion: 1998

Romania (Toma Petre), 2004
Brorsen-Metcalf perihelion: 1989
Halley perihelion: NA
Tempel-Tuttle perihelion: 1998

Tempel-Tuttle seems a prime candidate. Almost. Unfortunately, five of the epidemics occurred just prior to its perihelion. More importantly, three of the most significant outbreaks—Hungary 1692-1699, Hungary 1725-1734, and Austrian Serbia 1730-1734—although ending post-perihelion, began three to seven years prior.

"Shit," Wright whispers. Perhaps it isn't Tempel-Tuttle at all. Perhaps it's not even a comet.

"But that doesn't matter," Anne explains, confronted by Wright's concerns. Meteor storms follow a comet's pass near the sun because the gases, dust, and ice are superheated. But they also can occur as the comet approaches the sun. Comets start expelling vapor and rock years before reaching perihelion.

"Years?" Wrights asks, almost begs, for confirmation.

"Sure," Anne says. There are dozens of accounts of the Leonid meteors—those meteors created by Tempel-Tuttle—preceding perihelion by ten or more years. "Think of a comet like an ice cream cone. What's your favorite?"

"I don't know," Wright says. "Vanilla."

"No, vanilla can't be your favorite," Anne states.

Wright is growing frustrated. "Why not?"

"No one likes vanilla," Anne says, "unless, of course, they're covering it in chocolate or putting it in a float or something."

"Of course," Wright says, mockingly. "Fine. Mint chocolate chip."

"Oh my gosh," Anne gushes, "That's my favorite, too! I think I love mint chocolate chip milkshakes the best—"

"Anne, please," Wright interrupts sternly. "Please tell me about comets."

Anne frowns a bit. "Right, comets. Imagine you have a cone of mint chocolate chip—do you like cones or would you rather have it in a cup?"

"Anne," Wright growls.

"Cone it is," Anne declares. "Mint chocolate chip ice cream in a sugar cone. Well, as soon as you buy that ice cream, it starts to melt, right? It melts down the side of the cone. You can lick most of it before it drips, but some always does. That always happens a little before you go out into the sun. But, if it's a summer day, and you walk outside with it, suddenly, the ice cream melts even faster. It's going to run down your fingers and drip on the ground and make a big mess, right?" She smiles.

Ice cream. An odd but effective metaphor that all but seals Wright's conclusion. Tempel-Tuttle has been killing, in drips, for years. As meteors melted and slid from the comet like trickles from a scoop on a cone, they fell, millions slamming the Earth at speeds more than 150,000 miles per hour. They carried with them the seeds of epidemics past and present, becoming more virulent each pass as the sun's rays deconstructed and rearranged the invader's genetic material.

Perhaps the church was right in one regard.

Perhaps it truly is the end.

Chapter Twenty-Two:
Head Off (or a Dog's Tale)

THE next morning, the residents pull Wright from the cage. They offered Creedy the traditional last request. He asked to see Wright one last time.

They lead her to him, past a swarm of inmates busily making plans, busily readying themselves for their departure. They are packing and fueling a bus. Wright sniggers. It is a diesel. With all that noise, they'll bring every ghoul in the county to them. They may as well ring a dinner bell. A gong. They won't make it twenty miles.

"You know," Creedy says as they slip the noose around his neck. "I never told you what Franklin's ships were called."

"Sir John Franklin?" Wright asks, tearing.

Creedy nods, and smiles lightly as they tighten the knot. "One was the *Terror*. The other was the *Erebus*."

The inmates spin him round. He faces the sky and miles of land.

"The *Erebus*?" Wright poses.

"Yes," he says over his shoulder. "Erebus. It's the name of the mouth to Hell." The mutineers prepare to push him from the tower.

"It's a comet," Wright calls quickly. "The comet is Tempel-Tuttle."

"Tempel-Tuttle," he says to himself. She cannot see his wide grin.

He steps from the ledge before he can be shoved, before Wright can thank him. The rope whirs as it un-spools. She watches it slipping away, uncoiling like some massive frightened snake. She watches it disappear, yard by yard, until it snaps taut.

And then she allows herself a release like never before. The tears fall in torrents.

❖❖❖

"IRA?" Chaplain Cadavori asks, anxiously.

It is always a bad idea to interrupt Ridge when he's working out, especially when he's trying to blow off steam. And lately, Ridge is always blowing off steam.

Ridge is bench-pressing his weight, plus nearly half more.

The weight room is Spartan, just like the cells, devoid of any posters or photos or anything else conveying individuality or revealing a sense of self to another.

Ridge ignores the chaplain. He grunts through another set, finishing with a climactic yawp, and rests the bar on the rack. He huffs once, twice, then sits. He is, despite his diminutive size, a brick, thick across the chest and arms. "What do you want?" he finally demands.

The chaplain can't make eye contact. He stares at Ridge's knotted hands, the very hands that strangled Connor in his sleep. "Can I talk to you about the prisoners?"

It is a funny question, one that could invite a query: *Which, them or us?* But it invokes no such response from Ridge. He knows exactly who his prisoners are. "They will be executed."

Ridge cannot bring them along, not even the women. They know the truth, and he must return to society something other than an inmate. He has concocted an elaborate back story to ingratiate them into their new society. They are missionaries, helping the indigent and the homeless and the lost by spreading the word of God in post-Katrina New Orleans. The story goes: they fended for themselves with other survivors until another hurricane struck. They are all that's left, and they were forced to move north per God's will.

They will rehearse this story over and over and over. Those who can't learn and stick to it will find their trip cut severely short.

Cadavori is uncomfortable with Ridge's answer. "But they haven't done anything wrong, per se. How can we execute women and children and expect to stay in the good graces of God?"

"Easy," Ridge says. "We just need more rope. Then we can push them all from the turret."

"Yes," the chaplain reasons, "we could do that. But measure the risks."

Like?

Like some search party finding their twisting, writhing bodies hanging from the parapet. Wouldn't it be better to simply imprison Wright and her companions for eternity, thus resolving two issues? First, they avoid killing innocents and slandering Christianity. They would surely curry favor with their Lord and Savior for their blessed trip by showing such mercy.

Second, they would ensure their bodies are never found should a search party find its way to their remote neck of the woods. "Rescuers aren't going to investigate a prison for survivors. They will be entombed in their cells forever."

Ridge considers this for a moment. He likes the second part. "I've made a decision," he says. "We let them live and rot to death and back in the prison."

"Very good," Cadavori nods. He beats a hasty retreat. He doesn't wait for Ridge to change his mind.

❖❖❖

WRIGLEY.

They used the word often.

Wrigley.

They would repeat it, like a mantra.

Wrigley. Wrigley. Wrigley.

They would say it especially when they seemed unhappy, displeased. Wrigley.

It was an ugly word, a word they would yell. A word they would shout like an accusation whenever she wet the carpet or chewed on a shoe.

Wrigley!

But it wasn't her fault. Usually they would sleep very late into the day. When they did eventually wake, they wore pained expressions and grumbled at each other. They would ignore her, stepping around and over her, the male sometimes giving her a slight kick and sending her scurrying. Then they would debate about whose turn it was to walk her.

Oh, how her small bladder would ache!

And then they would leave again, only to return as the birds started singing, just before the break of dawn. They would smell acrid, like yeast. Then they would inevitably fight, the human female's shrill voice baiting the male, telling him to "get a job," calling him "worthless." When she was really angry, she would say worse, insulting the size of his manhood.

During these moments, the female would call the larger male "Lennie." His name was Phil, and he would ask why. The woman without a name would say, "Because you're a big, dumb fucker who has never read a book." He would ask why again. And she would say, "Because you ask questions like that, you obtuse asshole, that's why."

So the puppy called Wrigley would have the occasional accident. She knew it was wrong—they would put her nose in her own urine and smack her about the face with a rolled newspaper—but the pain in her belly was excruciating. She could not help herself but go. She would seek relief behind the couch or a chair, areas she hoped they wouldn't find.

Besides, the rug smelled of cigarettes and beer and things more foul than a bit of puppy pee. They might not even notice.

Or maybe they would. Maybe they'd show her a bit of attention. Maybe hearing that word wasn't so bad.

Wrigley.

Because she was often left to her own devices. She would explore and tug and pull and chew. Her brain was developing, and she needed sensory input. Everything was new to her. Everything foreign. Without human hands to pet her coat, to rub her belly and scratch her chin, she was left with her mouth as her primary means of tactile stimulation. She had one toy, a stuffed bunny, but she had grown bored with it. So she would chew, gathering information on an object's density, its elasticity, and, unfortunately, its sturdiness.

This hadn't been a problem when she was still suckling from her mother and wrestling with her brothers and sisters. They had only taken her from her home and family two weeks before, after she had turned two months old, but it felt like an eternity.

She wondered how long she would have to continue like this.

She didn't have to wait long for an answer.

❖❖❖

ONE night Phil/Lennie and the female came home early (at least early for them). They were quarreling . . . again. But this fight was unusual. It was the male who was the aggressor.

"I can't believe you, you fucking bitch!" He slammed the front door after they entered. It hit with such force that it bounced from of the frame, remaining wide a few inches. Phil left it like that. Part of him wanted to close it again, but it would be like replacing an exclamation point with a question mark.

"Phil, look at me. That guy bit me!"

Phil walked over to her, pulled her hand away from her neck. He roughly tugged her towards him, then spun her under the hallway light. He pushed her chin to the side so he could get a better look.

"Looks like a hickey to me."

"Phil, he drew blood!" she exclaimed.

"Fine. Looks like a bad hickey."

Their argument moved into the bathroom. The puppy called

Wrigley inched toward the door, watching them from the safety of the hallway. In the back of her maturing mind she wondered if someone was going to feed her.

The female looked into the mirror, craning her head up and to the side for a better view at the purple welt on her throat. Phil started to brush his teeth.

"Motherfucker," she spat, with a pained sneer.

Phil wanted to ignore her, but couldn't. He'd never been the one on top, the one with control in their relationship. Heck, any relationship. But now, his chance was here. No more taking his frustration out on the dog.

"Well, I guess you shouldn't have been making out with that douche bag, huh? Let that be a lesson."

"Fuck you, Phil, I wasn't making out with him," she lied.

"No, fuck you. He had his hand on your tit! He was all over you like some kind of animal!"

He spat toothpaste, and she raised a hand to his shoulder. He brushed it off and stormed towards the bedroom.

"Phil . . . " She couldn't muster anything else. She stared at herself in the mirror, and a stranger stared back. She was sweating. She felt weak and sick to her stomach.

She couldn't believe this was really troubling her so. She had made out with boys behind Phil's back before. There was the bartender, the cop, and that guy and his buddies in the club. Oh, and Phil's best friend, Ryan. Hell, she had blown Ryan. Twice.

No, she couldn't be sick with guilt over this.

It must be the alcohol.

She looked at the mark on her neck again. A bite. A love bite. No, she corrected, a *lust* bite.

But it was more than that. The puppy called Wrigley knew it. She could smell the infection. She could smell the poison in the female's bloodstream.

The puppy heard a voice. It was a voice from inside her.

When the humans had taken her from her mother and siblings, she had rushed to her mother's side and tried to burrow beneath her. Her mother nudged her forth and kissed her, telling her not to be afraid. She told her of a voice that would always be with her, a voice called Instinct.

"Instinct?" she had asked.

Yes. "When I was your age, I was taken from my mother. I was scared, too. But my mother told me that she would always be with me. 'Although you will be far away,' she said, 'I will never leave you. You will hear a voice called Instinct, and when you do, you will know that I am speaking to you, too.'"

The puppy had looked confused, and her mother smiled and continued. "You will hear the voice of Instinct even when there is no body to project it. Instinct is like a ghost in that way, walking with you wherever you go. But don't fear. Instinct is collective, and when you hear its voice, know that your ancestors—every dog who has come before you, me, my mother, her mother, and so on—are guiding you. My voice will be added to theirs, and I will never leave you."

Instinct spoke to her now. It said, "Hide, Little One. Hide and wait. I will speak to you again soon." So the puppy called Wrigley lowered her head and tucked her tail between her legs. She scampered to the safety of the kitchen and laid down next to her stuffed rabbit. She licked the toy, lapping at an area where the stuffing was starting to show.

She hoped the female would continue to forget about her.

But the female didn't.

The puppy was woken hours later by the deep coppery smell of blood. Somewhere in the apartment a butchering was underway, somewhere down the hallway.

The bedroom.

The scent penetrated the little dog to her core, grabbing her and shaking her senses awake, just as she would shake her bunny toy. It rattled her, told her to whine and stay put. Fear told her to expose her belly.

But Instinct said otherwise. "Do not listen to Fear," Instinct whispered. "Go forth and investigate. Go forth and do not be scared. You are a Dog. You are the embodiment of Loyalty, true, but you are more. So much more. You are the very form of Cunning and Intelligence. You were designed by the Gods to survive and add your voice to Ours. You will pass Our voice forward. Do not listen to Fear. You can assume the shape of Rage. You are lightening fast. Your hide is thick. You are Bark and Bite, Claws and Fang. You can be the stuff of nightmares."

The little dog known as Wrigley stood up. Her head high, she trotted across the linoleum, her little nails clicking. She stopped at the end of the hall and listened.

Slurping. From the master bedroom.

The odor of blood was intense. It made her head reel. It set fire to her senses.

Go forth and investigate.

She moved deliberately down the darkening hallway, toward the bedroom door. It was cracked, and she tried to peer in.

All she could see was the foot of the bed, Phil's leg dangling over the edge. And the blood. The tan comforter had turned a dark burgundy.

She needed to see more, but the angle wasn't sufficient. She pressed forward, her little head wedging the door open.

The room was dark, the sounds of gulping growing louder. The rug before her was wet and soiled. The female was on top of Phil. She was naked and hunched over him, her face tucked into his neck. The boxer pushed ahead.

The door creaked.

The female spun, gasping, her eyes like saucers. She looked right, left . . . then down. She grinned, her teeth full of rot. She purred with satisfaction and stretched her scabbing hands towards the dog.

The female had never tried to pet her before. Yet this was not the clue that made the hair on the puppy's back stand on end and her muscles tense.

It was the smell. A stink that her forebears had come to know. A stench they learned from failed births, from the carnage of the hunt, from the trenches of war.

Death.

The female leaned toward her, her wet hands getting closer.

The puppy let loose a guttural growl. She foamed and snapped, her back arched.

Then something strange happened. The female paused. Something inside of the ghoul made her hesitate if just for a moment.

But a moment was all the little dog needed. She turned tail and was down the hallway and out the front door before the monster could grasp what was happening . . . or her.

Monster.

Finally the female had a name.

And the dog called Wrigley shed hers.

❖ ❖ ❖

PETER Sumner watches the creature. It paces outside the McDonald's in Alsip at dusk. Most of them retreat from the light of the day.

This one is out early.

This one doesn't see him yet. Peter wonders what the hell it's thinking.

Are the creatures conscious? Peter doesn't know. He's not sure he can even define the concept. He's not sure what consciousness even is.

Is Peter conscious? He thinks so. But he wonders how much of his definition of who he is may be just a by-product of his individual experience.

After all, humans are not aware of most brain activity: heart rate, digestion, breathing, even posture. The brain processes an extreme amount of information, but people only remember those things that receive their full attention (and sometimes they don't even remember that much). Somehow, humans are able to accomplish a number of tasks without ever being aware. Maybe what humans perceive as consciousness is nothing more than a movie review published after the film's been seen. And if that's the case, it may not matter whether or not there's a "ghost in the machine."

But Peter feels he has free will. He believes he acts through intent.

Prime example: when he sees a puppy at the base of a dumpster along the side of the golden arches, just 30 feet from the monster, he picks up his bike and rides straight toward it. He speeds down the middle of the street, no effort spent to escape the eyes of the ghoul.

Peter's anterior cingulate cortex activates. This is the part of the brain associated with free will. This is the portion that fires when someone does something selfless, something stupid. The anterior cingulate cortex is a key difference between Peter and the horror that has stopped pacing the sidewalk and now pursues him.

The invader inside the revenant's brain has cut off the frontal lobe, essentially lobotomizing the brain front to back. The creature moves with purpose, the desire to feed, but not with free will. In essence, it can do nothing but obey the chemical signals of the invader within. It must chase Peter, it must capture him, it must consume him, just as it dined on its friends and neighbors. It has no choice.

Peter is at the dumpster, but he has scared the puppy. Drawn underneath the container by the promise of old burgers and fries, the brindle boxer shudders, hidden in the shadows.

Peter coos, "Hey, buddy. Here, girl." The puppy inches forward, crawling army style, still unsure.

The ghoul turns the corner. It looses a guttural growl, gases in its bloated belly gurgling forth passing over its vocal chords.

There's no time. It will be on him in a moment. Peter looks for a weapon, finds a fifth of vodka left by a wino that finally made the decision his life was more important than the bottle. He picks it up and scampers to his feet.

The thing is almost upon him.

He rushes it.

He takes the bottle, spout first, and slams it into the creature's blue face, breaking its aquiline nose. It rakes at him with rotting hands, and Peter pulls it by the collar, closer so he can further drive the flask into its demonic mouth. He is so near, he smells the decay, the methane venting forth.

Methane.

He reaches into his pocket, searches frantically. Yes, there!

Out comes the lighter. In a stroke, the flame flickers forth. He brings it to the monster's face, and shoves himself free, landing on his back as the vodka burns above him.

The revenant is ablaze, yet it feels no pain. It continues to look for him—even though its eyes have boiled and its skin blisters—driven by the invader inside, arms outstretched, groping. It takes a single step forward.

Then, *boom.*

The methane ignites. The ghoul's head is blown from his shoulders just before the flames flow further down the thing's gullet into its chest. A chain reaction, the stomach ignites, detonating and spreading the foul monster across the parking lot.

Peter shields himself. *Just like a vampire in the movies,* he thinks.

The puppy, terrified, shoots out from the dumpster and into Peter's lap. It whines and whimpers, and Peter strokes it. "It's okay, little one. It's okay."

He puts the puppy inside his coat, letting it snuggle close. Moments later it is asleep in his warmth.

He strokes her neck. She has no tags. "What am I going to call you, girl? How about Addison? Do you like that? Addison? If not, we can always come up with something better later."

She licks his hand. Addison it is.

Then he's on the bike again, the two of them heading south.

❖ ❖ ❖

THE prisoners are close to departing. They have packed everything, but will leave their witnesses behind.

"We should beg them to take us with them," Van says.

"No, we shouldn't," Wright corrects.

Even Ian has to ask, "Why?"

"Because they are going to die out there." She wants to know the direction they are heading, because when they escape—and they will escape—they are going to go in the opposite direction.

They sit quietly for hours, listening to the prisoners below, fearing that they've been abandoned forever.

"The good news," Van says, "is that we won't have to serve on the front, now."

"I suppose," Ian replies, "but I was really looking forward to the future."

Wright's ears perk up.

"The future?" Van asks. "Like what?"

"Like getting married, for one." Ian looks at Wright, then shies away. "I was looking forward to getting married, and starting a family."

Van scoffs. "What type of dreams are those?"

Anne interjects, "I think they're nice dreams. Don't you, Ms. Wright?"

"Anne," Wright says smiling, "call me Kari from now on, okay? And, yes, I do think they are nice dreams." She sits back, pondering Ian and his disclosure.

As evening approaches, the chaplain arrives. He has brought meals for them—last suppers, Wright thinks—and asks them if they'd like to pray with him and share their last requests.

Wright might not make it home, might not even make it out of this cell. She has a notion. It is crazy, reflexive, and totally out of character. But she decides to act on it anyway. She wants to be assigned to a new mission.

Her heart beats heavily in her bosom. "Ian," she asks, "will you marry me?"

Ian freezes. His face gives Wright second thoughts about this course. "You know, it's okay if you don't. I know I'm a little older and—"

"Yes," Ian nods, a grin stretching across his face. "That sounds great."

"Holy shit!" Van yells. "Can I be your best man?"

❖❖❖

THE chaplain agrees. He never imagined such a final request, but he is obliged to honor it. He asks them to come forward now. They don't have much time.

"Wait," Van says, "wait one second." He runs to the corner, starts rummaging through his bag. "Aha!" he exclaims. He tugs at something out, beige and navy, and strides to Ian to present it.

It is Ian's father's necktie. Van rescued it from the pile of belongings left behind in a tree bow.

Wright takes it, wraps it around Ian's neck, quickly tying it. She murmurs a rhyme about a rabbit as she does it, going around the tree, through a hole. The tie hangs evenly, ending at the belt buckle at his waist. Perfect on the first try.

The "I do's" are exchanged quickly. The chaplain does not need to tell Ian he can kiss the bride. They are kissing before he can even pronounce them husband and wife. Van, Anne, and Burt, still stunned, clap enthusiastically.

"Enjoy your meals," the chaplain says. "The pies are homemade, special. I think you'll be surprised by them."

And with that, the prison's former residents were gone.

❖ ❖ ❖

WRIGHT and Ian forego their meals. They sit in the corner, holding hands.

I'm giggling, Kari thinks. *I'm actually giggling!*

"Are you going to eat your desserts?" Van asks.

Neither of them answers.

"Okay, then I'm going to help myself." He digs in. It's pumpkin pie, and he is loving it.

In the midst of shoveling in his third piece, Van feels a pain in his jaw. "Fuck!" he exclaims. He spits, the bits of pie landing on the floor. But there's no splat.

There's a clink.

It's a key. No, *the* key. The key to the cell.

The chaplain may have been a man of God after all.

Chapter Twenty-Three:
The End . . . Well, Almost

THEY could wait until daylight, but it is best they go now.

The diesel engine drew the revenants from the prison, like witless children following the sounds of an ice cream truck.

In fact, the bus should attract monsters from every home, hotel, church, school, field, pitch, baseball diamond, food court, strip mall, Starbuck's, Target, tavern, bar, museum, zoo, pet store, hospital, gas station, dealership, fire department and police station—anywhere where people used to live their lives—right up the interstate.

So they need a different plan. Wright decides to cut east, forgoing the highway as a guide.

She watches the tree line as they exit. She won't look at the wall. She doesn't dare. She doesn't want to see Creedy, or what he's become, hanging from a tether.

But, Ian can't help but look. Creedy's no longer living. Still, he's not quite dead, either. He has turned, and he jerks spastically, bouncing off of the prison wall. Ian can't help but stare.

In a couple of years, the rope will rot, and Creedy will plummet to the ground. He'll get up again, even though his limbs will be shattered, and his crooked body will limp about, searching in vain to quench a craving that can never be satiated no matter how he tries.

Ian has a notion as he watches Creedy. Maybe the belief that vampires can fly took flight itself when someone mistook a ghoul's terrible fall from some lofty precipice for actual flight? Conceivably, but Ian doesn't want to stick around and recreate history.

❖❖❖

WHEN the bus breaks down, grinding to a stop less than two hours away, Ira Ridge goes insane. He screams at the driver to fix it. The chaplain says a prayer.

The driver ventures out, returning with a dire conclusion. He thinks the front axel is broken.

Ridge, in a rage, tells him again, "Fix it." And don't come back until it's done.

The driver hesitates. He has doubts: doubts about his diagnosis, doubts about his ability to make the necessary repairs, doubts about this excursion. But he has no doubt that Ridge will kill him if he doesn't try. Or at least look busy.

So he goes back to something approximating work, whistling to keep himself company and banging away on the undercarriage. So he does not hear the creatures when they crawl under the bus. His screams are muffled by the weight of them as they clamor over him looking for a piece.

Minutes later, there's a knock on the bus door. Ridge opens it, yelling, "I thought I told you not to come back until—"

Ridge screams as the demons claw their way in. The gunfire only assures that more will come . . .

. . . and that this bus will become a coffin.

❖❖❖

EXHAUSTED, twelve hours of ground beneath and behind them, the party collapses in a heap in the thick grass. They fall like dark dominoes upon each other in the twilight.

Wright uses Ian's chest as a pillow. He strokes her hair, and she wraps an arm around his waist. But as tired as Ian is, sleep eludes him. He stares into the sky, the constellations above reminding him of the twinkling lights of a Christmas tree.

Suddenly a pinpoint streaks through the sky, drawing a reddish line east to west.

"A shooting star," says Ian. Not the type of star you wish upon. It's a "grazer," a meteor that grazes the atmosphere instead of entering it. He remembers what Anne said about comets and the discord they bring.

In spite of what astrologists believed, scientists tried to quell the mass terror associated with comets and meteors. They tried to dissuade the belief in a death zone, a zone of poisonous gas in the comet's tail suffocating all planets passing through its wake. If the tail did indeed contain cyanogens, they would be too diluted to hurt Earth's creatures. But science did not stop farmers from letting their lands go fallow or cultists from taking their own lives. Even popular culture bucked science. Sir Arthur Conan Doyle wrote of deadly zones in space, and Hollywood made films about people turning to zombies upon breathing gas from the comet's train...

If they only knew how wrong, yet how right, they all were.

Wright feels Ian tense beneath her. "It's probably just another satellite," she says, reading his thoughts, "or space junk." Before the New Order, NORAD tracked nearly 900 satellites and 13,000 other items, mostly defunct satellites, booster rocket parts, and fragments of both. Without NASA, a military, or news stations to operate, maintain, or track them, satellites changed orbit or collided with junk, begetting more junk exponentially (a phenomenon known as the Kessler Syndrome) and falling from the sky. This happens all the time.

This brings Ian some comfort. He tries to sleep.

They listen to their own breathing for an hour or more, too tired and too scared to drift into REM sleep. They waver between alertness and slumber, hovering in a semi-consciousness. Their breathing is rhythmic, almost like a song, like row-row-row-your-boat in round, a trance-like incantation.

But Burt stirs. He breaks the rhythmic progression, blurting something utterly odd. "A transvestite," he says.

Van chuckles groggily, nearly delirious with exhaustion. So that's how it is with Burt . . .

"Van, a transvestite!" Burt repeats.

Van rolls over, staring at Burt the face. "Dreaming again?"

Burt meets his gaze straight on. "You said that clowns were the only thing you can become simply by putting on the costume. I've got another. Transvestites."

Van reasons for a moment. If you dress like a transvestite, meaning, if you cross-dress, you become, in essence, a transvestite, at least for the duration you're dressed like one. Burt's actually right. Van nods his approval. "Good one, Burt. Now, go back to sleep."

Burt smiles and drifts off to a world where deceased cannibals don't exist and heroes, like Brom Sybal, always win.

IT is two months since the crash.

Van regularly shares point with Ian. He's getting adept at it. His eyes are always moving, always inspecting his surroundings. He vows never to be surprised again.

Still, Ian thinks, Van can't seem to keep his mouth shut. Today he's decided to critique some of the finer points of the English language.

"Do you think," he asks, "there are Chinese people anymore? I mean, actual living, breathing, Chinese people?"

"I don't know," Ian responds flatly. "There were a lot of them, I hear."

"If there are, I hope we don't ever meet them."

And why is that, Van?

"Because English would be too difficult to learn."

More difficult than Chinese?

"Probably." Van rationalizes. "We don't spell words phonetically. If I'm Chinese, I'm thinking a word like 'ghoul,' G-H-O-U-L is spelled G-O-O-L, may be even G-U-L. I mean, it's bullshit that so many combinations of letters can make the same sounds."

GH can sound like a G or an F.

X can sound like a Z or a CKS.

C can sound like an S or a K.

T can sound like an ED, etcetera.

"We even have silent letters, for crying out loud! Ks, Gs, Ps, Hs, even Ts. Why? Letters don't want to be quiet!" There are too many letters, too many blends. "I bet we could cut the alphabet down to twenty letters or fewer if we tried. I bet the people who invented our alphabet made it so hard just to keep foreigners out. You know, making certain words secrets, like a password."

Ian grunts. He's not really listening, but that's not going to stop Van. It never has. It never will.

"And what about the plural form of some words? Why can't we just add an S to everything? But you've got things like deer and fish that don't get an S. Mostly, wildfowl, some hoofed mammals. Why not 'gooses' instead of 'geese,' 'mouses' instead of 'mice?' Or, if we're going to have special rules, let's apply them uniformly. If the plural of goose is geese, shouldn't multiple moose be called meese? And if the plural of mouse is mice, and louse is lice, shouldn't house be hice? So many rules, so many exceptions. It must drive non-English speakers crazy."

Ian just grunts. He wishes he was in the back, holding Kari's hand.

Then he hears something. He puts a hand on Van's shoulder, halting him. He shushes. "Listen."

There's a noise, the sound of fuzz, akin to breaking waves.

Radio static.

And then the undeniable sound of a voice.

There's someone ahead.

❖❖❖

VAN and Ian look at each other, their faces mirroring expressions of surprise. But then one of the reflections disappears as Van breaks Ian's hold and runs ahead.

"Van, no!"

"Hey!" Van shouts. "Hey, we're here!"

Van gets thirty feet before he feels the thud to his chest. Only then does he hear the gunshot. He touches his heart, raises his fingers to his face.

There's blood, lots of blood. It stains the fabric of the red polo.

He frowns and looks up, searching for the shooter.

The second bullet hits him in the forehead.

Everything goes black for Van.

Forever.

Ian is first there, Kari a moment behind.

There's nothing they can do but cry in anguish.

From his roost in a deer stand, just two dozen feet from the protected area, the soldier sees the rush of people to their fallen comrade and realizes his mistake. Ghouls don't cry.

There are four of them now. The youngest, a woman, strokes the dead man's face. She buries her head in his chest.j

He radios in, both the good and bad news, as a ginger-bearded man starts to berate him from below.

EIGHTEEN years after it all started, Peter is a hermit.

The weather turned bitterly cold that November eighteen years back, too cold to continue his trek. Peter needed to find shelter. He needed to hole up.

He blamed global warming for the early freeze. He cursed the government for not taking Al Gore seriously, then he cursed them for the plague.

Peter had studied the Gaia hypothesis in college and believed the Earth to be a complex system, almost like giant watch. When the watch's gears spin in synchronization, when all elements are in harmony, the time it keeps is precise and would make the Swiss proud. But when a gear spins too fast or too slowly, it can wreak havoc on the system, no matter its size.

Humans were a cog out of time, propelling the Earth to a cataclysm predestined by their decades of misuse of natural resources, pollution, overpopulation, and deforestation. A good watchmaker simply removes the defective gear and replaces it with one that works. And that, Peter assumed, is what Mother Earth had done.

He often wonders about how "they" got here. Global warming could have been the culprit. As the Earth heated, the glaciers thawed. Perhaps they unleashed bacteria encased in ice for millions of years and previously unknown to man. Peter read an article twenty years back or more about a core sampling taken from the Beacon Valley of Antarctica. It had contained dozens of bacteria. When defrosted, the bacteria sprung back to life, creating proteins and reproducing. While they constitute the oldest known life forms to mankind, they also constitute the life forms man knows least about. Scientists sequenced their various genomes, finding that 46% of the strand was unique, unlike anything they had ever seen.

Bacteria transfer genes, a significant factor in evolution. But, maybe, with the melting of the ice caps, genes were transferred across *time*, visiting a prehistoric pestilence on man.

Peter has lots of time to think about this and other things here in this cabin hidden deep in the woods.

He found this cottage near I-57. Unfortunately, he found the inhabitants, too, and he finished off what the plague had started. He barely survived the winter there, his canine companion his only anchor to sanity. In those short, dark days, days filled alternatively with hunger and the destruction of dozens of demons, Peter resolved that he was alone, likely the last of his kind.

So he spent the next winter there, and the winter after that, and every winter since. Finder's keepers.

This afternoon, as Peter stokes a warm fire, he is alarmed by the sounds of his dogs barking. "Jack, Molly," he calls to the descendents of his rescued boxer as he stokes embers in his fireplace. "Take it easy."

There hasn't been an incident in almost a year. They grow fewer and farther between, convincing Peter that his isolation is nearly absolute.

It's probably a raccoon outside the cabin again. Maybe a possum. Still, you can never be too sure.

The barking continues. They scratch at the door trying to get out. "Back," Peter says to them, and they quiet and clear the door for him.

They are an odd mix, something between a boxer and a wolf, the result of one of Addison's escapes—yes, the name of his old train station stuck—while in the throes of heat. These dogs are much too precious to be risked. They are the last of Addison's litter, the ones that chose to stay.

Most of the others ran off with the wolf pack.

They must have liked their chances better in the wild.

He occasionally sees them tracking him as he hunts, making sure he's still safe. He leaves them a bit of every kill.

But the risk of losing Jack or Molly to the pack is nothing. There's a bigger risk.

The dead things don't care what they eat.

So he goes alone. With a baseball bat. A baseball bat is about all it takes nowadays. Sure it requires a lot more patience, but that's okay. What else has he got but time?

He steps out cautiously, bat cocked. He takes a few strides forward.

He has cleared the trees for forty feet on all sides, and he watches the perimeter for movement.

Well, he thinks, *at least I might get some exercise.*

There's a rustling directly in front of him. He readies himself, but then there's movement to the left. Then from another position, even farther to the left, and then from the right.

Oh my God, he thinks. *They're everywhere.*

One directly before him steps into the clearing.

Peter readies his bat. He's not ready to die. Or worse. Not just yet. "Bring it," he mutters.

PETER is puzzled. This one wears protective gear, almost like a padded HAZMAT suit. It must be hideous under that body armor and facemask.

Peter looks at his bat.

This is going to take a lot longer than he thought.

Then the others step out.

They are dressed in similar camouflaged gear, each with a rifle drawn. Just what is going on here?

The one in front flips up his mask. He's human still, probably around Peter's age. He offers his hands, palms up, a symbolic gesture that says they mean no harm. He tells the others to lower their weapons.

They immediately comply.

Then he addresses Peter. "Easy, easy."

"Who are you?"

"My name is Roger Gerome," the man says. "What's yours?"

❖ ❖ ❖

ROGER Gerome's arrival is always trumpeted as an "event." Statten and the elders just can't wait to don their golden robes and glittering crowns.

Gerome's audience with them goes well, as well as these excuses for formality can go. They are pleased with Roger's most important discovery: antibiotics, both human antibiotics recovered from Swift Labs and animal antibiotics found at the University of Illinois. They are less pleased about this man Gerome has found.

Peter Sumner is married to a woman, and this woman has married another. They do not like the implications.

Roger tunes them out. He always does. He is anxious to get home and see his son.

It is not until his return home that Roger learns his son is missing. The elders never mention it.

It is a page from the church that waits for him on horseback. His youngish face is bruised, the result of another one of Statten's explosive outbursts. The page tells Gerome of Van's death. He even apologizes for it, asks for Gerome's forgiveness. He says he should have defied Statten's order.

What order?

Statten's order. The order to keep the crash of Flight 183 secret. The order to not send word to anyone, even Gerome.

Then the page leaves Gerome alone with his rage.

Epilogue

IAN stands before a grave, a headstone, in the cemetery near the church. Sons of heroes are granted such an honor.

Ian wears a suit, no tie. He clutches something red against his chest. Shoes.

He touches the tombstone, says a few words in his head. He smiles to himself. He's praying. Van would have teased him mercilessly for being such a hypocrite.

He examines the trainers. They are clean, like new. He spent hours scrubbing them, scouring until there was nary a trace of dirt or grass or . . .

A violent memory grabs him and tries to hold him firm. Ian shakes his head for release.

He grips all four laces and pulls them away from his body. He twists them back over themselves, then under and through, tying the shoes together.

Ian bends slightly at the waist. He hangs the red Converse All-Stars gingerly over the granite marker. He balances them, strokes the name etched there. V. A. N.

He is aware that Kari is watching him, tenderly, from the sidewalk.

Goodbye, old friend.

Ian joins her side and enters the church.

PASTOR Statten's lecture is winding down.

The church is full again this Sunday, but today Ian did not have to worry about finding a pew. He and Kari stand near a small fountain just to the left of Statten's pulpit. Kari holds a baby, and today he will be baptized.

Ian and Kari made a pact. They are going to keep Tempel-Tuttle's secret. At least for now.

For now, it's finally time for Wright to stop surviving and to start living.

As Statten drips water on the child's head, he says the baby's name. "Welcome to the family of Christ, Vincent "Van" Peter Sumner." He almost chokes mid-way through.

They worshippers clap thunderously.

Ian looks into the crowd, and beams at a man in the first row. The man who sits between Josh on one-side and Anne and Burt on the other.

Peter smiles back, a tear streaming from his eye. For once he thanks God, thanking him for these gifts of his son . . . and grandson. He shifts to Anne, places his hand on hers and squeezes.

She giggles and grins.

She is happy for Ian and Kari. She's happy for Peter. Mostly, though, she's happy for another reason.

Bits of Temple-Tuttel fell last night—the Leonids, red traces falling from the sky like the streamers that signal a new year. They danced outside the window, the window of a study housing an incredible collection of antiquities, reminders of a time before the New Order, and a tattered American flag.

The flag silhouetted Van's father from behind his desk as he spoke to her and a small band of people, his warriors, about a revolution.

Anne knows the truth. She knows the comet heralds a paradigm shift, the death of a regime, and the birth of a new one. The messenger's secrets will no longer be whispered. The whisperers will no longer cower. People will listen. People will follow. Or people will die.

Freedom comes with a price.

❖ ❖ ❖

TONIGHT it starts.

Tonight Roger Gerome will assassinate Statten while his team hunts down the elders.

This is the night this house of cards comes tumbling down.

Tomorrow holds a promise.

The promise of a new life . . . in the world of the dead.

About the Author

Matt Darst was born in Louisville, Kentucky. His early years were spent there and in Downers Grove, Illinois. As a youth, he was fed a steady diet of *Star Wars*, Svengoolie, and dog-eared Stephen King novels. His father and mother, now accomplished artists, encouraged Matt's creative side early on, especially writing.

Matt studied political science at the University of Illinois and received his law degree from DePaul in Chicago. For a time, writing took a backseat to school and work. That is, until he began carving out time to write a novel . . . a zombie novel.

Dead Things is Matt's first book.

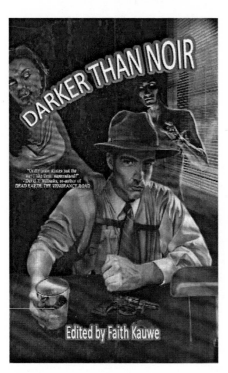

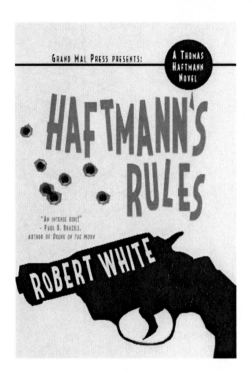

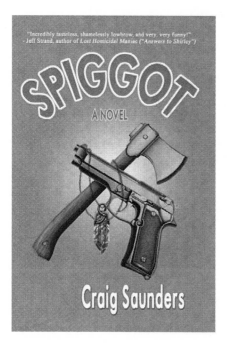

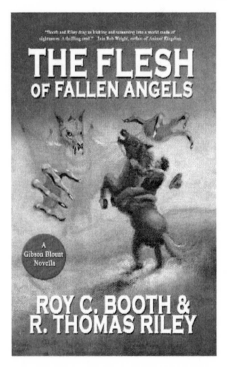

VISIT US ONLINE AT WWW.GRANDMALPRESS.COM

CPSIA information can be obtained at www.ICGtesting.com
Printed in the USA
LVOW041017020512

279994LV00003B/35/P